PRAISE FOR JACQUELINE WHEELOCK

Jacqueline Wheelock's novel, *A Most Precious Gift*, lives up to its name. It's a gift to every reader. Reminiscent of the downstairs lives in *Upstairs, Downstairs,* it brings fresh perspective to the lives of slaves in a pre-Civil War southern town mansion. A love story written with rare perception, it reveals the plight of a beautiful slave girl, Dinah, who struggles to live free, love, and marry the man of her choice. With energy and a fierce devotion to her Christian faith, she fights for the right of self-determination. And like many of us, she does so amidst her own negative thoughts constantly shouting, "You're not good enough."

—Judy H. Tucker, Editor/writer, *Coming Home to Mississippi*, University Press of Mississippi, 2013

If you love Downton Abbey, you must read A Most Precious Gift by Jacqueline Wheelock. Her novel carries you along on a current as swift as the Mississippi River. Lyrical, dignified and uplifting, Mrs. Wheelock's book is an unflinching glimpse of slavery in the Old South from the slaves' points of view.

— Diane Ashley, Best-selling author of nine novels and two novellas and winner of Carol Award, 2012

Jacqueline Wheelock will draw you into *A Most Precious Gift* with her wonderful characterization, her attention to detail and her historical setting. You'll feel as though you are right there in Natchez with Dinah and Jonathan as they fight their own personal battles to realize what the Lord has in store for them. This is a story you won't want to put down—and one you will always remember.

— JANET LEE BARTON, AUTHOR,
CBA AND *EPCA* BESTSELLER AND A *ROMANTIC TIMES* TOP-PICK AUTHOR FOR *LOVE INSPIRED HISTORICAL, 2014*

Author Jacqueline Freeman Wheelock has penned an engaging story in *A Most Precious Gift*, giving the reader an authentic look at the "downstairs" life in a Natchez plantation of the antebellum South. While the romance of Jonathan and Dinah captures the heart, the worth of this exceptional prose is in the deftly interwoven message of what true freedom really is. The title of this debut refers to this freedom, but the most precious gift is this amazing novel and what it leaves lingering in the heart of anyone fortunate enough to read its words.

— AARON MCCARVER *CBA* AND *ECPA* BEST-SELLING AUTHOR AND CAROL AWARD WINNING AUTHOR

A MOST *Precious* GIFT

JACQUELINE FREEMAN WHEELOCK

Scrivenings
PRESS
Quench your thirst for story.

2021© Jacqueline Wheelock

Published by Scrivenings Press LLC
15 Lucky Lane
Morrilton, Arkansas 72110
https://ScriveningsPress.com

Printed in the United States of America

Second Edition
Paperback ISBN 978-1-64917-133-7
eBook ISBN 978-1-64917-134-4

Cover by Rosanna White.

(Note: This book was previously published in 2014 by Mantle Rock Publishing LLC and was re-published when Scrivenings Press acquired the publishing rights in 2021.)

Published in association with Joyce Hart of Hartline Literary Agency, Pittsburgh, Penn.

To Frank and Clara Bell Freeman, my deceased parents, who consistently trusted my judgment enough to want for me whatever I wanted for myself.

ACKNOWLEDGMENTS

With all I have, I offer thanks to the Lord Jesus Christ whose grace ever astounds me. I also offer deepest thanks to my husband and children who believed in me from day one and never looked back; my agent, Joyce Hart, without whose unwavering confidence I might have given up; and the members of my critique group, the Bards of Faith, who have lent boundless support throughout this journey toward publication of my first novel.

1

December, 1860
Riverwood Plantation
Natchez, Mississippi

D inah Devereaux had a solid plan. All she needed to do was show her new master and mistress what an accomplished seamstress she was. Then she could make enough money to buy the freedom she so longed for, maybe even with the help of the Lord become a successful entrepreneur.

Glancing over at the pile of sickly-pink chicken parts, Dinah blew out a shaky sigh. Before she showed her owners anything about her other skills, she must learn her way around this infernal kitchen she'd been so unceremoniously shoved into seventeen days ago. She reached for a thigh part and flour-coated it for frying.

"Stop right there!"

Violette McMillan's shrill command rattled the windows of the tiny kitchen space as Dinah clutched the piece of floured chicken intended for the pot of bubbling grease. Barely managing to stop herself from pitching into the open flames, she braced for another of her kitchen mate's blistering tirades.

"Don't you know *nothin'*, girl? That ain't the way Mama Tavie taught us to fry them birds."

Dinah eased the piece of chicken back onto the worktable next to her. Not quite ready to face the gathering of tiny wrinkles that always appeared above the bridge of Violette's nose when something displeased her, she released another disheartened breath and spoke into the sweltering fireplace.

"All right, Violette. What am I doing wrong this time?"

"What you doing wrong? I'll tell you what you doing wrong. The same thing you been doing wrong ever since you come to work in this here kitchen. Everything."

Dinah lowered her head in agreement. When it came to preparing meals, Violette—three years her junior—was by far Dinah's superior. Or at least that's what Violette would have her believe. At any rate, Dinah had bent over backwards to treat this girl with the deference due her. But after only a few weeks at Riverwood Plantation, Dinah had somehow managed to make a mortal enemy of Violette McMillan, having not an inkling as to why.

"Sure as my name's Violette, every piece of that chicken you 'bout to fry is gonna end up with a bloody middle. That grease way too hot, wa-a-ay too hot."

Feeling like a two-headed monster with Violette craning over her shoulder, Dinah flicked back a loose braid hoping to create for herself a little space. Shocking new instincts prodded her. She wanted to turn around and light into this girl like an angry yellow jacket.

But no. Not today. Not when the chief of Riverwood's kitchen, a pert little woman known as Mama Tavie, had believed in Dinah—taken pains to show her what to do, explicitly stating she was depending on *her* to get supper started.

Sounding her signature snort of triumph, Violette finally eased back a bit. "You almost spoiled yesterday's supper and near 'bout to do the same today. Good thing Mama Tavie left me in charge 'cause you 'bout the clumsiest cook I ever saw."

"You in charge? Why, I distinctly heard her say . . ."

Dinah clamped her mouth shut. What did it matter who was in charge? Truth was she was quite possibly the worst cook in Mississippi, perhaps even in all the world. She slumped under the weight of Violette's truth about yesterday. Not only had Dinah managed to leave at least one dirty misshapen eye on each of the potatoes she'd peeled, she'd spilled a whole skillet of hot gravy onto Mama Tavie's spotless brick floor. And if that wasn't enough, when Violette tasted a mouthful of the collard greens Dinah had prepared, she promptly spat them out the door, pronouncing them boiled leather before dumping the rest of the pot into the slop bucket.

Eyes puffy from nights of crying and hands trembling from days of being terrorized by this crusty young dictator, Dinah glanced back and forth between the pile of floured chicken pieces and the pot of rapidly heating lard. Finally she resolved to face her foe.

"Violette? I thought Mama Tavie said the oil should always be crackling hot before I begin frying anything."

Something akin to uncertainty flickered in Violette's tea-colored eyes. She looked toward the window and lifted her double chin in an all-knowing smugness. "You supposed to catch that drumstick by the bony part and then lay it in the grease—easy like—not just plop it in there like you was fixing to do."

"But that wasn't a drumstick I was holding. It was a thigh. And what does how I lay it in the oil have to do with the chicken's ending up raw inside?" Dinah picked up a dishcloth to remove the pot of rapidly-increasing hot waves of grease. "I thought you said the problem was with the overheated grease."

"Leave that pot be!" Violette stomped her foot on the immaculate floor causing Dinah to drop the cloth and quickly settle her hands to her sides. Thank God she'd not lifted the pot of roiling oil yet.

"That's what's the matter with the likes of your kind. You think you so smart—knows all there is to know on God's green

3

earth 'bout everything. Truth is, Mama Tavie and me, we ain't really needing no kitchen help no how. I even heard Jethro say he could make much more use of you in Massa McMillan's fields than in here all the time stuck up under poor Mama Tavie." Violette touched her plump earlobes. "Heard him say it with these here two ears."

Dinah wanted to roll her eyes so far toward the ceiling that nothing showed except the whites. Instead her insides curdled at the mention of the man called Jethro. She'd heard about the black slave driver at one of the McMillan cotton plantations. From forcing his attention on the female field hands to beating his wife with his driver's whip, what she'd heard of the man held no promise of pleasantries. Everything she'd worked so hard to learn these last few weeks about kitchen work—since that awful fire in New Orleans left her homeless—was purposed toward staying here on Theodore McMillan's town estate called Riverwood and away from the fields of the infamous Jethro. She simply would not survive in the fields.

"Face it. You're your mother all over again, you know. And someday some planter will use you up in one of his fields before he sells you off to a place exactly like—"

No. Dinah pushed back the sordid memory of a place known to her only as The Gentleman's Caller. If it required the last breath she took, she would find a way to keep out of those blistering, unforgiving fields that could so easily lead to a place like that. Ultimately she would escape from her mother's destiny through her God-given skill of a seamstress-designer put to use in New Orleans for years. But for the sake of present survival, Dinah had to learn to cook.

Casting about among her thoughts for some semblance of self-defense against Violette's searing words, Dinah felt her pulse speed up a notch. Could the girl be right? Could Master McMillan be secretly contemplating a place in the fields for her? Had she missed something that first day when Mama Tavie was explaining what his plan was for her? It wouldn't be the first time

Dinah's annoying habit of running away with only part of someone's words had gotten her into trouble.

If only you'd waited for full instructions that terrible morning of your eleventh birthday, perhaps you could have saved your innocence.

"What-whatever d-do you mean by that, Violette?" Dinah's breath came in raspy spurts. "Weren't you standing there when Mama Tavie said the master's specific instructions were to bring me into the kitchen as a sort of . . . well . . . apprentice?"

"Humph. How was Massa supposed to know you can't make sweetened water? I reckon Massa must've had the notion that a slave woman old as you ought to know something 'bout cooking already."

Ouch. Dinah hadn't thought herself quite so old as all that. Though she'd heard Mama Tavie say Violette was little more than a girl, Dinah herself was only twenty. She ignored the urge to massage her bruised feelings with sympathetic self-talk. Didn't have time for such. Still, she found herself smarting at the sound of Violette's snickering.

"But from the taste of them greens yesterday, looks like Massa was way off in his figuring that time." Violette sashayed over toward the window. "Besides, the way I'm hearing it, if Massa hadn't been such close friends with that Master Devereaux man what owned you in New Orleans, he wouldn't've brought you here in the first place. As it is, you just here in the kitchen in the way 'til he can think what to do with you."

"Enough with the hearsay, Violette!" Dinah surprised herself by pointing a finger toward the upper floor of the dependency that contained both the kitchen and the sleeping quarters for the female house slaves. "Isn't it about time one of us checks on little Emerald?"

Her seething ire against Dinah suddenly boiling over, Violette wheeled around from the window.

"Oh, no you ain't gonna try to tell me when to check on my little sister. I reckon I ain't needing to find out from the likes of you how long Emerald should nap."

Flurries of cold stinging memories from a conversation she'd overheard years ago between Cook and her husband pelted Dinah. *"That kind of thing happens all the time to the likes of her. And why not? The poor little thing's the spawn of a field hand, a breeder. A prostitute."* There it was. The word she'd fought all her life to keep from flaring to the surface. Dinah's skin prickled. Wouldn't Violette's fangs be sharpened to a knife's edge if she knew who Dinah really was?

Wondering how long the bubbling pot would tolerate this fruitless interchange, Dinah swung her arm through the air in an upside down arc, motioning toward the chicken.

"It's all yours Violette. Fry it. Obviously, I'm not quite ready."

"That ain't no excuse." Rapidly shaking her head, Violette sidled up next to the window. "Mama Tavie be back in here in a little while, and she depending on *you* to have dinner well on its way. Whilst you so worried 'bout Emerald's rest, I expect you better make haste and get that chicken fried."

This time, Dinah allowed her eyes to freely search the ceiling. Lord. This girl could change horses quicker than a tardy dispatcher. As desperately as Dinah wanted to please Mama Tavie, she was beginning to wonder just how much more of this little rotund tyrant she could take. Sighing heavily, she turned back toward the fireplace where the pot hanging from the trammel had begun swaying to the will of the growing flames. Hungry tongues of fire licked their way up the insides of the greasy pot. Dinah froze, arrested by the memory of the fire weeks ago that had permanently separated her from the only home she'd ever known.

Mercy, Lord.

A nightmare revisited. Riverwood's kitchen transformed itself into Dinah's sewing room in the attic of the Devereaux's Garden District mansion. Paralyzed, she watched as the flames reached for the ceiling while the sound of her own calm words floated back to her.

"Violette, what must we do?"

Violette's voice shrank toward the far wall. "We? I ain't the one cooking that chicken. Only thing Mama Tavie told me to do was cook some greens that somebody be able to eat this time."

The untimely reminder of yesterday's ruined collard greens slid off Dinah like warm butter. All she could think of was, for the second time in the space of a month, fire was about to change her life. Along with the rooms upstairs that she and Mama Tavie, Violette and . . . *Emerald!*

"Emerald!" Violette's desperate cry collided with Dinah's thought.

Oh God no. Not sweet Emerald. Merciful Father, please show me what to do.

Instinctively, she grabbed a dipper of water from a nearby pail and flung it into the flaming pot. Several lobs of grease hit the wooden worktable, their crowns of fire quickly spreading across its surface.

Lord. She'd made it worse.

A blanket of doom wrapped itself around Dinah so tightly she could scarcely breathe. Violette screamed Emerald's name again as she beat out a hasty exit. Still, Dinah couldn't move. Her feet were bolted to the floor like the intricate grillwork on the terraces in the District. The kitchen at Riverwood—perhaps the big house, too—was about to burn to the ground.

And it's all my fault.

Water stung Dinah's eyes. Whether from the fire inside the kitchen or the icy fear inside herself, she couldn't tell. All she knew was for the first time since she'd left her solitary life in one of the richest neighborhoods in New Orleans, fear of working in the fields of Theodore McMillan's plantations had been instantly replaced with a hope to stay alive.

But her feet remained firmly planted in what was fast becoming another kind of field. The strangling killing field of Riverwood's kitchen.

JONATHAN MAYFIELD FIDGETED with his starched, neatly-tied cravat, his thoughts churning like the paddlewheels of a myriad of steamboats he saw each day.

This just wasn't done, going into a white man's palatial study, sitting down in some comfortably stuffed chair in anticipation of closing a deal like a real businessman. It just was not done.

Taking several measured breaths, he willed his long legs to a casual stroll before slipping his hand behind the left lapel of his frockcoat. Over the years, he'd become weary of the habit of checking for the precious piece of paper resting over his heart that declared him a free man.

The bogus piece of paper, he fleetingly reminded himself.

But halting the practice of checking often for the papers that named him a free man would be like plucking the green from a summer leaf. And today the habit was heightened to full throttle.

Jonathan picked up his pace again. Five more minutes and he'd be on the grounds of Theodore McMillan's sprawling town estate called Riverwood, ready to sit down with the man's accountant to name his price for the furniture Jonathan had labored over for a year. And he was counting on everything being in perfect order when he did so—from his shaved and scrubbed countenance, to his new clothing, to that ever-present yellowed piece of paper pressed against his scarred chest. His head jerked upwards as he conducted a quick scan of his surroundings. He thought he'd sensed a menacing presence among the trees looming above the sunken road, but . . .

Nothing.

Enough of this foolishness. He had to free himself from this unfamiliar tangle of nerves before he arrived at Riverwood, or he'd prove himself to be the bowl of jelly he felt inside. Shrugging around in his uncomfortable new frockcoat, he decided it was time to have a talk with himself, out loud.

"Now listen here, man." He slapped his hands against his

thigh as he paced out circles in the hardened dirt road. "Why are you acting like a scared little girl? You've already completed the furniture. Benjamin and Henry are just waiting for the word to haul the rest of it over here to the estate. It's only a matter of agreeing now on a final figure." He halted in mid-step.

Only a matter of agreeing on a final figure? Who was he trying to fool? Instead of the usual fare where he stood around knee-deep in sawdust waiting for a smug plantation accountant to give him a take-it-or-leave-it offer for work he'd poured his very heart into, Ted McMillan had given him carte blanche to design an entire suite and promised him the freedom to sit down and negotiate its worth.

"Like any other man seeking to make a profit."

The words caught in Jonathan's throat. Ted McMillan was treating him like a real man. Not like the quaking boy Master Ethan Mayfield had reduced him to just before he handed him his freedom nine years gone, but a whole and capable man.

I thank you, Jesus.

Jonathan was already more than a little thankful that he'd designed and built some of the finest furniture in the South since he'd returned from North Carolina as a trained cabinet maker six years ago. Doubtless, as a black man, he'd increased his coffers beyond his wildest dreams—even bought himself a two-story house similar to the one that the Negro barber, William Johnson, lived in near the river. But if he were truthful with himself, the money and acclaim he'd worked so hard to garner never seemed quite enough. If he could just feel like any other red-blooded American entrepreneur . . .

"What you need is a good wife to help move your mind over to a place o' peace."

He chortled to himself at Mama Tavie's unwavering solution for all his ills. A good wife. Nice to think about now and again. But the idea of handing over his emotions to a woman, the way Papa did to Mama, went past the case of nerves he was experiencing today to panic. Full and pure.

9

Boisterous laughter arrested his steps just outside the entrance to Riverwood. From the other side of the gate, a cacophony of men's banter assailed what little quiet he'd resumed. Jonathan stepped across a ditch and waited among a stand of oaks. He popped open the Tissot pocket watch he received last week as payment for a set of parlor furniture.

Maybe they would finish what they were doing before he had to go through the gates.

"Oh, yes suh," said a high-pitched voice bloated with swagger. "That filly called Dinah, she somethin' to BEE-hold, all right. The finest thing I seen around here in a mighty long time. Built like some kind of long-legged storybook princess, only with skin smooth and dark as molasses."

Punctuated by several fake-sounding coughs, a gaping silence sizzled with expectation of the man's next words.

"Why, she *almost* as good looking as I am."

Guffawing louder than a camp meeting service erupted from behind the shrubbery causing Jonathan to risk a better view. Must be that Eli Duggan fellow.

Jonathan scowled. According to Mama Tavie, Duggan had recently been promoted from one of the McMillan plantation fields to head gardener at Riverwood and given one of the well-kept cabins that housed Riverwood's outside workers.

And he'd left behind a harem that would rival King Solomon's.

Jonathan didn't recognize this "Dinah" Duggan was referring to. But just hearing him talk about the poor woman like that could cause the coils of Jonathan's naturally curly hair to alter their courses.

A short wiry light-skinned man stood with his back turned toward Jonathan. "You better watch that boasting, Eli. Somebody liable to show you a looking glass one of these days. Then you gonna get your feelings hurt, for certain and for sure."

More howling and backslapping. "Tell him, Jethro."

The one called Jethro turned slightly toward Jonathan, a

whip wrapped around one of his massive hands—grotesque hands attached to arms no bigger than fishing poles. Like Eli, something about the man raised Jonathan's hackles. Deep loathing quickened inside him. The despised loops of leather, their effectiveness enhanced with pieces of glinting metal and God-only-knew-what-else, spoke of the job of a slave driver. Jonathan took a bit of relief in the man's folly, for only a pompous fool would have a makeshift whip in his hand in the midst of a town estate where he had no say-so whatsoever.

Jonathan continued to shield himself behind the oaks while Eli pierced Jethro with a stare.

"Man, I ain't joking. I'm telling y'all. That girl took one look at me, and I could see her knees start to jellify."

The slave driver's profile lit up with new interest. "Aw, come on, Eli. Ain't no woman in the world gonna be that weak for somebody as ugly as you. The way I figure it, ain't no woman in the world that fine-looking for that matter."

"Yeah, you say that now," said Eli. "But you the only one of us out here what ain't seen her yet. Just wait 'til you get a look at her. You gonna be yowling like a slave catcher's hound dog." Eli jutted his chin in the air and offered his version of a canine expression. "A-rooo, roooo. Anyhow, you might want to look after your own business. Word is that you whip that wife of yours one more time and you gonna owe Massa money for destroying a piece of his property."

Jethro bristled so fiercely Jonathan felt at the moment he could be used to brush down horses. "Careful how you talk to me, Eli. Don't get biggity 'cause you done left the fields. There's always a way to get you back."

"Now, just a minute, Mr. Slave Driver—"

Clearing his throat, Jonathan stepped back across the ditch startling the small group of men. Perhaps he could stay a pointless altercation among these brothers. He passed through the gate and nodded curtly. "Evening, gentlemen."

Instantly, Eli sobered. Without a grunt of acknowledgement,

he bent his back to one of the hedges, the other members of the group quickly following suit. All except Jethro who scowled at Jonathan like he was a Cyclops with two ears flapping from his forehead. Jonathan inhaled deeply. Once again, his reputation for arrogance had preceded him. Though he had never met either of these men, he knew why Eli and Jethro despised him. Which was just fine since he had no interest in neither of these pieces of scum—nor their lackeys.

At least, that's what he told himself on a daily basis.

But once past the cypress pond near the gate and onto the long winding driveway edged with all sorts of graceful trees, Jonathan fought to keep his emotions in check. If they only knew how it grated him to see them labor for no pay, no hope to better themselves or their families. Though he had nothing for the likes of Eli and Jethro, deep in his heart, he recognized the perpetual joking back there for what it was, a way for a slave to get through another thankless, endless day. A familiar slice of guilt cut into his excitement about the upcoming negotiations. Why was he free while so many of his people remained enslaved? Biting back a rare urge toward a swear word, he glanced at his watch again. Only twenty minutes past two.

He was more than a half hour early for his appointment at three o'clock. What was he to do with the rest of the time? Pulling up the collar of his jacket, he hastened across the lovely expanse of lawn which he couldn't help comparing with the idyllic English parks he'd read about. He rounded the corner of one of the twin dependencies that contained the kitchen. Imagining the smell of baked sweets wafting through the December chill, he felt his usually deliberately-closed countenance volunteering a wide grin.

Hmmm-um. Nothing like a few of Mama Tavie's teacakes to take the edge off.

And since it was getting near on to Christmas, there'd probably be a batch on the kitchen sideboard, just waiting for the taking. Jonathan's mouth watered as he stole a moment to rub his hands together. Just seconds before a scream coming from the kitchen shattered his blissful anticipation.

"Emerald! Oh, Lord, my baby!"

Mama Tavie? Didn't sound like her. He exchanged a brisk pace for an all-out sprint, nearly running over the precious little wisp of a girl named Emerald standing in front of the door crying, a bedraggled ragdoll suspended by the leg from her tiny hand. Jonathan swooped her up and pushed open the door almost colliding with Mama Tavie's perpetually sullen kitchen aide named Violette. Handing off the frightened child, he made his way through a curtain of thickening smoke.

And then a vision. The back of a woman—her long, dark, velvety-smooth neck slightly listing to the side as though she were waiting for the unveiling of a rare painting. Even cloaked in the stifling haze, he thought her tall wispy form the most beautiful and perfectly aligned he'd ever seen.

2

Emerald's thin voice squeaked its way through the fog of Dinah's mind.

"Violette, me and Lucy, we scared. We seen the bogey man in my dreams. Miss Dinah, where you at?"

Sweet Emerald.

Dinah's heart melted. Somewhere in her muddled thinking pieces of unspoken sentences shouted at her, telling her she and Violette had woken up the little darling. Still, Dinah couldn't draw her eyes away from the fire, couldn't take control of her feet as the same rabid blaze that nearly took her life less than a month ago leapt out at her again, choking off her ability to act.

So then this was it. This was how it felt when one was about to stand before her Creator. God wouldn't show her a way out this time as He had back in New Orleans when she was caught between a wall of flames and a perilous three-story drop. And all these weeks after, the only way she'd thanked Him was by allowing the other slaves to think her something she was not and never could be, a lady.

Oh, God. I didn't plan this pitiful deception. It just happened.

And now His wrath was upon her.

She closed her eyes and entreated the Lord to assure her of

the one blessing she'd been asking for all her life: to be finally caught up into the embrace of the mother she'd never laid eyes upon. A mother she was both ashamed of and longed for. A mother completely cleansed of Dinah's detested father and all the Johns before him.

Lord, I know I've grieved you these past few weeks by not telling Mama Tavie about my mama. And for the shame I've brought upon myself and You, I do so humbly ask forgiveness. But I also know you as a God of grace and mercy, a God who has washed my mother clean up there in heaven. So I beg of you, when I get there, please let me feel my mama's hug for a moment. A moment or two is all I ask. This is my prayer . . .

A muscled forearm closed around her waist, sweeping her away from the hearth and the table covered in dancing flames as though she were a piece of airy lace. Had she died that quickly and gone to heaven? She looked around and up into the magnificent gray eyes of a man she'd never seen before. An angel, perhaps? Dinah redoubled her assessment.

No-o-o, ma'am. No baby wings here. Just smooth skin the shade of golden apples, with a neatly-trimmed moustache set between downward-curved full lips and flaring nostrils beneath a bridge beaded with tiny drops of perspiration. Augmenting the deep scowl of his brow was a scar on one side of his forehead, hinting of intrigue and adventure. Michael the archangel, maybe. Or possibly Gabriel. Most assuredly not an angel of the cherubim or seraphim order.

His build was powerful, his movements sure. With a steady hand, he set her against the opposite wall next to a clearly besotted Violette. He smelled of scented soap.

Definitely not an angel.

Holding Emerald close to her chest, Violette gazed up at the handsome stranger. "W-what can we do to help, Mr. Mayfield?"

"Keep out of the way." He secured Dinah with a stare. "All of you."

He grabbed an iron skillet hanging from a nail and covered the pot of raging grease then carefully moved it from the flames to the hearth. Slipping from a fine frockcoat that resembled nothing Dinah had ever seen on the backs of slaves, he set about using it to swat away the small combustions on the worktable, the sideboard, even the brick floor.

Definitely a man, a commanding man, at that. But a slave? Not likely. Not speaking like that or dressed in those clothes.

Emerald started to cough. "Violette, my throat hurts." The sweet little girl thrust her ragdoll toward her sister. "And Lucy hurt her finger, see?"

Violette bolted for the door. "Come on, baby. Me and you and Lucy, we gettin' outta here."

"Stay!" The man barked at Violette before quickly moving back toward the wall. He turned a softened request toward Emerald. "Please, sweetheart, just a few minutes longer? For Mr. Jonathan and Mama Tavie? I promise I'll make it better soon. For you and Lucy, too."

Dinah tried to press her back further into the bricks as "Mr. Jonathan" spotted a dampened rag and threw it toward Violette. Without thinking Dinah reached out and caught it. She pressed it to Emerald's mouth and nose as fresh air floated through the windows just opened by the stranger. Dinah startled as Mama Tavie herself swept into the cloudy room. She inched back the edge of the blue-checkered rag she always wore on her head.

"Goodness. What's done happened up in my kitchen?"

Emerald in arms, Violette rushed the petite woman, nearly toppling her over. Sputtering accusations, she pointed toward Dinah. "It's that new girl over yonder. Ain't got no business in no kitchen no how. Think she so cute. Now look at what she done did. Didn't even try to put the fire out. Just stood there like she was deaf and dumb. I tried to tell her she was frying that chicken all wrong, but she so busy primping, pinning up her hair and stuff 'til—"

"Hush up." Mama Tavie waved through the thinning smoke. "That's enough talk. Looks like the fire's on its way out, and I thank y'all for staying inside and fighting it long as you didn't hurt yourselves. I wouldn't want the missus to find out 'bout this unless she had to. I might've lost y'all as helpers if she'd found out."

Understanding sprouted in Dinah. So that was why the take-charge mystery man wouldn't let them leave. Protecting the interests of Mama Tavie, and ultimately of her and Violette, too. Admirable.

Mama Tavie pried Emerald loose from Violette's clutch and spun around to notice the agile, yet exquisitely muscled man who was on his knees snuffing a spark that was trying to ignite a leg of the worktable. Nothing short of luminous could describe Octavia McMillan's tiny butter-colored face, most of which was lost behind a huge grin. Smoothing Emerald's brow with one hand, she waved off smoke with the other.

"Have mercy! What you doing in my kitchen on your knees in the middle of the afternoon, boy? I ain't in the habit of leaving teacakes on the floor waiting for hungry rascals like you, you know."

Violette fluttered her eyelids, her voice taking on a syrupy seductive turn Dinah hadn't heard before. "That there girl right there. She didn't try to help poor Mr. Mayfield either."

Mama Tavie ignored her while the dashing gentleman who looked to be perhaps mid-twenties stood to a towering height. He straightened his cravat and slipped into his ruined frockcoat before clasping his hands behind his back and taking up a position in a corner near the open window.

"How's my favorite chef?"

"And you might as well take that coat right on back off, mister." Mama Tavie's hands assumed a shooing motion." I don't know where you headed today all dressed up, but you ain't going nowhere with all them grease spots on that nice coat shining like a heap of poor man's diamonds."

The man's golden skin turned the color of a mayhaw. Dinah could have easily missed his glance in her direction had her eyes not been glued to his every expression.

"But Mama Tavie. Surely you don't mean me to stand here in front of these ladies in only my vest."

"Surely I do."

With a resigned groan the big man peeled off the perfectly tailored coat and placed it on the charred table.

My, my. But he is fine looking.

For the first time in her life, Dinah thought she might be about to swoon. Affirmed by the adventurous looking scar over his right brow, the man's bearing was positively warrior-like. In seconds, she'd gone so far as to surmise he might have some of that royalty in his blood she'd overheard African slaves whispering about on the streets of New Orleans. Or—or maybe he was a descendant of the prince named Ibrahima who'd been captured from his home in Africa and once resided right here in Natchez!

Dinah gave herself a mental slap. Had she gone daft? With all the trouble she was in right now, the last thing she needed on her mind was an African prince.

"That's better," said Mama Tavie. "Now don't be pestering me 'bout that coat for a day or two if you ever intend to eat another morsel from this kitchen, Joe-Nathan Mayfield."

Suddenly the leonine prince Dinah had just decided she didn't need on her mind shook his mane of thick curls from side to side. He rocked back on his heels and roared, sending his earlier grave demeanor scurrying into oblivion. "Mama Tavie, you're the only person on this earth who can still call me Joe-Nathan and live to say it again."

"Just calling you what your mama and papa called you." Mama Tavie's gaze darted from Dinah to Mr. Mayfield. "Anyhow, what's so funny about me calling you 'Joe-Nathan' today? It's what I always call you, ain't it?"

Obviously deciding against answering that loaded question, the man fixed his eyes on a stack of covered teacakes taking shape through the fast-clearing smoke. "Well, it seems I got here none too early because . . ."

Violette pounced. "See, that's what I been trying to tell you Mama Tavie. That girl just about killed us. If it hadn't been for Mr. Mayfield—"

"Hush, Violette. You ain't doing nothin' but making things worse. Here, you take Emerald and go sit down over there somewhere 'til you cool off. I'll get to the bottom of this in my own way and time." Mama Tavie turned toward Dinah, her face radiating a hint of mischief. "Oh, Lord, where's my manners? Get away from that wall and come here, baby."

Me?

Still quailing against the bricks, Dinah looked around to make sure Mama Tavie was speaking to her. Seeing the lady nod, it dawned on Dinah how close she'd just come to singlehandedly ruining this kind woman's life. True, Mama Tavie was smiling, but she smiled at everybody all the time. Was she about to send Dinah packing to the fields? She undid herself from the wall and moved to obey the only person she'd come to trust at Riverwood. Swiping at the sudden treacherous tears undermining the dignity and poise her former mistress had instilled in her, she crept across the room.

"I'm so very sorry about your kitchen, Mama Tavie. I—"

"Shush, now." Mama Tavie wrapped small but strong arms around Dinah. "The Lord giveth and the Lord taketh away. This time He ain't took away nothin' much a'tall."

"Ma'am?"

"You heard me right. We'll have this place looking like new 'fore supper time." She shot a look at Violette. "And like I said, what's happened in here is going to stay twixt us here in the kitchen. I ain't wanting to hear nothin' about it from them others what work in the big house." She released her embrace and placed her hands on Dinah's shoulders. Gently, she turned her in the direction of the African prince who remained by the window, feet spread apart, hands still clasped behind his back.

"Now, honey, I want you to meet one o' the mens we folks

'round Natchez, black and white, is most proud of. This here Mr. Joe-Nathan Mayfield and he be free, don'tcha know."

Free. So Dinah had guessed right. Jonathan Mayfield wasn't a slave. She wiped her eyes with her sleeves, mortified at how she must appear. By now, her brain must surely be glowing visibly with nervous curiosity. Though she'd heard there were free people of color who owned property in the Garden District, she couldn't recall ever knowingly being this close to someone of her race who made daily decisions about the direction in which his life would go. Odd that she could actually share the same space with a free black person—breathe the same air even—yet he was able to do as he pleased all day every day while she remained a crimeless prisoner with little hope of early release.

Obviously discomfited by the introduction, the man nodded his head before bowing at the waist. When he straightened again, Dinah noticed the scar over his brow change colors, enhancing his rugged yet impeccable good looks.

"My pleasure, Miss . . ."

"D-devereaux." Dinah's voice had turned into a barely audible croak.

"She name Dinah. Dinah Devereaux." Mama Tavie patted Dinah's hand. "She just overcome by the fire, is all."

An awkward silence set in. Dinah knew she was gawking, but she was powerless to stop. She'd never met a black man who radiated such raw confidence and determination. Tugging at his vest, he took a step toward her.

"Devereaux? I had the opportunity to craft and install a bed for a Mr. Horace Devereaux down in New Orleans last year, at Mr. McMillan's recommendation as a matter of fact. A very likable gentlemen. Would you happen to know of him?"

Master Horace? This man knew Master Horace? What if he'd seen her and had already begun figuring out she had no business in anybody's kitchen?

"Miss Devereaux?"

"I . . . well, yes. I've heard of him."

Mr. Mayfield stepped back as though he'd spotted a rattler. Could it be that he'd overheard other things too about her blotched past, perhaps from one of Cook's gossiping sprees? "I beg your pardon, miss. It was presumptuous of me to probe in such a way. I assure you there was no intention to offend."

Behaving like an aristocrat in a novel who'd taken a major social misstep, the man steered the brief interchange to a clean halt. Not only was he free, he didn't sound like he'd ever been a slave. But then Dinah had been constantly reminded since coming to Riverwood that neither did she.

Silence struck again. Mama Tavie rushed in to fill the gap. "Free and making a real good living for himself. Got more orders for that fancy furniture he makes than he can keep up with."

"Uh, Mama Tavie, I don't imagine Miss Devereaux is interested in—"

"Hush up, boy, whilst grown folks talkin. Anyhow, this man's had to hire two other men to help him out." Mama Tavie turned back to the prince. "Joe-Nathan, your mama and papa sure would be proud."

Jonathan Mayfield squirmed like a schoolboy in the dunce corner, before his visage collapsed into something akin to pain. Was he still grieving for the parents Mama Tavie had mentioned? Or was he just plain uncomfortable in Dinah's presence? And if so, why? Whatever his reasons for sudden withdrawal, clearly he was here to see Mama Tavie and her alone. Dinah, however, was captivated past denial. Struggling to regain some semblance of poise, she dipped her head and offered her best curtsey.

"Please forgive my rudeness, Mr. Mayfield. In no respect have you offended me. On the contrary, I'm happy to make your acquaintance and thank you most sincerely for your unselfish rescue."

The cabinetmaker's imposing frame went rigid. He frowned, doffed an imaginary hat, and was out the door before Mama Tavie could even think of an objection. What had Dinah said wrong? She glanced over at Violette who speared her with a look of disapproval.

"Now see what you done? Suppose he decide to tell Massa about the fire? Then we all be in big trouble." Violette appeared hotter than the now-subdued pot of oil, signaling she was nowhere near finished haranguing Dinah about this latest gaffe. In truth, it did seem Dinah had made another enemy.

"But why? What did I say?" she whispered.

"Don't worry, honey," said Mama Tavie. "Long as there's teacakes 'round here, Joe-Nathan Mayfield'll be back." She patted her head and pinched her lips signifying an idea had caught fire. "You girls get that mop and broom and some scrubbing water and start cleaning up this mess whilst I step out for a bit. That boy always comes back 'ventually. But just to make sure he don't forget to show good manners and do the right thing, I'm going after him."

But Dinah knew he wouldn't be coming back, not to do the "right thing" by her. After all, it was only fitting that a gentleman like Jonathan Mayfield would keep his distance from a clumsy slave. And a woman with a heritage as tainted as hers.

"WHEW!"

Smelling of acrid smoke, hog fat, and female hysteria, Jonathan paused on the other side of the dependency to collect himself. What had just happened in there? He felt like he'd been about to smother beneath the charms of a hundred-pound, blackberry-colored, curtseying woman he'd known all of fifteen minutes.

Such grace and poise. Just like . . .

Mama.

Out of nowhere, childhood memories of the Mayfield plantation grabbed hold of Jonathan, misting his eyes with emotion. A time which usually he flatly refused to think of charged him like a runaway locomotive, a time unmatched in the last twenty years: listening to Mama at Christmastime sing about baby Jesus after a day's work in the big house as a lady's maid, though she was never titled as such; admiring the few bows and baubles from prior Christmases that the mistress had passed off to Mama; watching Papa as he watched Mama bake their annual treat of syrup bread chock-full of preserved watermelon rinds, love shining in Papa's eyes brighter than a cluster of stars. Finally, the three of them praying together before Papa gave him and Mama their yearly gifts of delicately carved pieces of woodwork to add to their collections.

That was before the yellow fever took Mama within a fortnight, and Papa, without a single thought for how much seven-year-old Jonathan needed him, vowed to follow her. Declaring he couldn't live without his one true love, Papa made good on his promise in six months. And as the years wore on and the pain of losing his parents kept digging a hole in his heart until he almost drowned in it, Jonathan swore he'd never marry. Marriage was just a trap for undeserved trials and in the end, unbearable sorrow.

But now that he'd made twenty-seven years, sometimes he wondered what it was like to return to the comfort of a kitchen like Mama Tavie's at the end of the day. To hold a woman close and promise to always protect her.

The way he'd wanted to do in there with Miss Dev—

Jonathan shook his head with vigor, checking his watch and forcing his mind back to the reason he was here in the first place. To negotiate his own price for his own work—the thing that had driven him to build the best cabinetry he'd ever built. Weeks before he ever put tool to wood for this commission, he'd debated with himself over design. There'd been the bedstead to decide upon. Would he build classic smooth bedposts or follow the twisted pattern? Neither. His choice for bedposts had been fluted—a nicely understated elegance worthy of Riverwood.

Pineapple finials or rosettes? Rosettes. Half tester or full canopy? Half tester. Then there was the molding design to pick: dentil, egg and dart, or a molding of his own creation? He'd finally decided to create his own. The armoire and dresser would, of course, complement the design of the bed. He'd ordered the best mahogany the tropics had to offer. Then for the last twelve months, after he finished working his regular orders during the day, he'd labored in his shop into the night over each piece, never allowing his workers to get past simple sawing or planing for this project, painstakingly carving with numerous gouges, chisels, and other instruments of the trade.

And now, in just minutes, for the first time since he'd left Thomas Day's shop in North Carolina as an officially approved cabinetmaker, he would sit down in what was perhaps the finest mansion in Natchez and state what he, Jonathan Mayfield, thought his furniture was worth. He flexed his fingers, conjuring up a dismissive laugh about what had happened minutes ago back there in that kitchen.

An aberrant transfer of Mama and Papa's love for him and each other. That's all it had been. Nothing to do with that Miss, what was her name? Develin? Devereaux? No matter. He wouldn't be needing to remember it because he was going to make doubly sure he would never be ambushed by her bewitching charms again.

3

Dinah fought to stave off the embarrassment plaguing her after the near-disaster of the fire. What must the fascinating Mr. Jonathan Mayfield think of her?

Nothing. He thinks nothing of you. Why would he? You're just another slave girl, after all. And he's a free man who can have his pick of free women—that is, if he isn't already taken.

She pushed the worktable, still holding Jonathan's fat-splattered frockcoat, closer to the smoldering fireplace and plunged Mama Tavie's custom-made rag mop into the bucket of soapy water in front of her. Why, oh why couldn't she do one thing right at Riverwood? She wanted to curl up on the greasy bricks underneath her feet and cry every tear she possessed onto the floor. Instead, she pinched in her lips and pushed the mop in tiny circles, trying to rid the surface, and her mind, of the horrible mess she'd made.

If only she could get back to the thing she loved—coming up with designs in her head and sewing them into reality. But how would she ever be able to present herself as an accomplished seamstress and make enough money to buy herself from Master McMillan if she couldn't learn to prepare a simple meal?

Thoughts flitting like a pollinating bee, she glanced over her shoulder at the worktable. Given the right fabric, Dinah could create for Mr. Mayfield a frockcoat that would make the one lying on that table look positively woebegone. If only she could convince the McMillans of the one thing she was good at. At least then she'd have secured a place at Riverwood until she could buy her freedom and start her own business.

If Jonathan Mayfield did it, so could she.

The metallic sound of Violette's cackle nearly punctured her eardrums.

"Crying 'bout making a fool of yourself in front of Mr. Mayfield, is you?"

Lord, I don't know what I've done to this girl, but whatever it is, please reveal it to me so I can try to fix it. Or I just might not be responsible for the next thing I say.

Placing the mop back into the bucket, Dinah leaned on its handle.

"If I were crying, Violette, which I'm not, it wouldn't be over some rude carpenter I barely know. It would be over the way I've failed to repay Mama Tavie's kindness."

"Oh, yeah, 'course it would. That's why you was looking like a love struck ninny a while ago when Jonathan Mayfield was here. I seen it in your eyes, you know, when he placed you against that wall next to me and Emerald. And I seen it again when you tried to curtsey like you some rich white lady. But you may as well know it now. Jonathan Mayfield is uppity and stand-offish, and he don't like slaves. You ain't got the chance of a fattened-up hog at killing time with that man."

A fat hog called up images of present company. But Dinah would not say that. No, no, no.

"And I suppose you do have a chance with him? Would that be your reason for that outrageous eye-flirting before he left?"

Violette hefted herself from the groaning chair she sat in. She placed Emerald on the floor with Lucy and started toward Dinah.

"Did you jes call me a flirt? I'll have you know if I wanted Mr. Mayfield's 'tention, I wouldn't have to shame myself trying to act like uppity society ladies like some others I won't name."

"Violette, please. Don't raise your voice like that in front of the child."

"I done warned you 'bout Emerald. She ain't no concern of yours." Violette moved in closer. "So you calling me trash, huh, to my face. Usually I teach people a lesson for even thinking such a thing, so I reckon you know what you got coming."

Just thinking about a physical fight with Violette caused Dinah's insides to implode with fear, but she never once blinked. Instead, she swirled the mop around in the pail of water before lifting it dripping into the air.

"Touch me and your flirting days just might be over."

What? Was that Dinah Devereaux who'd just leveled that threat? Dinah's knees tried to disintegrate. *Oh, Lord. This girl is going to pulverize me.* Having never fought a day in her life, Dinah thrust the mop handle behind her as though building up momentum before propelling it forward. She was inches away from flinging mop water in Violette's face when she heard the fireplace *whoosh* with fresh energy. Violette's eyes stretched to the size of mud pies. What now?

She turned around to Jonathan Mayfield's costly coat going up in flames. Could there be a worse day anywhere on earth?

ONCE MORE, Jonathan checked his vest for his pocket watch. Exactly a quarter of an hour left before he was to meet with Mr. McMillan's representative inside this Greek Revival temple called Riverwood. And, contrary to the gentlemanly image he so longed to project, he didn't even have a decent coat to wear.

He paced the short distance between the detached kitchen and Riverwood's back verandah. No way could he get back to his house in town, change clothes, and return in time for the appointment.

Suddenly Dinah Devereaux, plastered against the wall wringing her hands and biting the side of the most beautiful bottom lip he'd ever seen, seized his thoughts.

No way could he risk going back into that kitchen for his frockcoat.

A vein underneath the scar above his eye pulsed out his inner turmoil. The most important meeting of his life was approaching with every stroke of the clock, and here he was strung out between two rotten choices, lateness or unkemptness, all because he'd been waylaid by a curtseying damsel in distress. For the second time within the span of as many minutes, the past reached out and halted his frenetic steps. Suddenly, Jonathan was a young man again of eighteen years, head bowed, feeling six kinds of fools—years of hard-won self-confidence rapidly flowing from his breached soul to the feet of his master.

"Start your own business?" Master Mayfield smirked as he patronizingly clapped Jonathan on his shoulder. "You're a hardworking gifted boy. No doubt about that. And you may someday assist another man as a fine cabinetmaker. But understand me well, you'll never be considered a real businessman—never be able to make important decisions for yourself when it comes down to capital. It's just not in the makeup of your people."

Jonathan clenched his teeth, slitting the lining of his jaw and tasting blood.

"Blast!"

That day nine years ago, which had defined him with the sharpness of Mama Tavie's tin cookie cutters, rolled over him as though it had happened this morning. He swabbed his tongue against the inside of his stinging jaw and blinked away the doubt swirling in his head.

How was he going to get out of this present fix of having to meet Mr. McMillan's assistant looking like a slovenly carpenter? For certain, he'd crafted lots of fine furniture before. But this was not just about building furniture. It was about being a man who could stand shoulder to shoulder with any other man and negotiate a deal for what he'd created. One thing for sure, for nearly a third of his life he'd waited on this opportunity to sit down at a desk and actually negotiate his own price for his sweat, blood and God-given creativity. And no amount of misplaced chivalry toward a bunch of frantic women was going to derail him of a chance to prove his skills as a businessman.

He reminded himself that he kept good books. That should count for something. The furniture he'd sold in New Orleans had been called "unmatched." That ought to help. Brushing off his waistcoat and adjusting his cravat, he started toward the steps of the verandah. There was nothing for it but to meet with the accountant just as he was. In his shirtsleeves, smelling like . . .

A scorched kitchen?

Absolutely not. He had to have a fresh change. Praying McMillan's man would understand his lateness, he struck out across the yard toward the front entrance. Just before his name rang out with the force, if not the beauty, of a set of church bells.

"Joe-Nathan!"

Mama Tavie. He would've recognized that commanding little shout even if he'd been across the Mississippi River on the Louisiana side. Shoulders slumped, head thrown back, he halted, groaned inwardly, and waited.

"Just where you think you going, boy? You come back here."

It was she, all right. Coming to straighten out his manners, no doubt. If she hadn't been like a mother to him all these years, he might've acted as though he hadn't heard her just this once and run like a startled deer. As it was, he turned around to face her. The tiny turned-over boots she wore plowed the yard toward him.

"I want to talk to you."

Jonathan feigned a look of innocent concern. "Yes, ma'am. What's the matter?"

31

Placing her hands on her knees in a most indelicate fashion, Mama Tavie heaved a few breaths. "What's wrong with you, boy? Your mama taught you better than that."

"I'm sorry, Mama Tavie, but I—"

"Don't you come bringing me no excuses, neither. Your mama put her life on the line by begging Missy Mayfield to teach you how to read and write and act a gentleman. Wonder old Missy didn't have your mama whipped for even asking such a thing. But the Good Lord softened her heart and spread His grace 'round you, even after he seen fit to take both your mama and your papa."

He didn't take my papa. Papa chose to leave—

"And what do you do to show Him your 'preciation? You turn tail away from that poor girl in there, who needs all the friends she can get right now, like she just let loose a load of skunk juice. You don't know what that child's been through. What possessed you anyhow?"

Ordinarily, Jonathan would be amused at one of Mama Tavie's colorful lectures. But not today. He opened his mouth before quickly shutting it again. How could he explain to her the crazy effect that girl was having on him in there? Why, when she'd started to cry, he felt like he wanted to hit somebody when there really was nobody to blame—he, Jonathan Mayfield, who'd vowed to himself, and a few others, to forever avoid feminine entanglement like the yellow jack that killed his mother. Besides, he had much weightier things on his mind like the fact that he, an ex-slave, was about to transform a room at the esteemed Riverwood Plantation into a Mayfield original. No imported pieces, no mixing and matching with other furniture dealers. A lasting advertisement for the craft of an ex-slave. At his own price.

"Well? I'm waiting."

"It's just that I have other things on my mind."

A barb of conscience snagged him. *I know, I know, Lord. I had only one thing on my mind back there, Miss Dinah Devereaux, but—*

"Still waitin'."

Jonathan cleared his already-clear throat. Though Mama Tavie's English was sometimes questionable, she was far from being a fool. He had to think of something plausible and be quick about it.

"All right. You remember I mentioned to you that I've been designing and building furniture for a room here at Riverwood for more than a year." Mama Tavie nodded. "Well, I came out here today to talk to the man in charge and to get started installing the pieces. And never having been past that back verandah there . . . well . . . as an ex-slave it's got me a little r-rattled—"

Blast! He'd just hit a wall. She wasn't buying it. Knowing he'd worked in a number of the plantations in the area, she glared at him.

He groped around in his mind for another excuse, praying for something more believable to absolve his recent behavior toward Miss Dinah Devereaux.

"And uh furthermore, even though Mr. McMillan is out of town, I learned from a letter I received yesterday that he has offered me a room in the dependency, across from the one where you live, for a few days while I install the trim to accent the bedroom furniture I've already built. And like a dull-wit I said yes."

A flash of hurt streaked across Mama Tavie's brow. "So what's wrong with that? Don't you want to be near your old friend?"

Jonathan cringed. That wasn't the problem at all. He'd been too hasty with his half-truth. As a matter of fact, he loved the idea of being near the closest person he had to a relative for a while, and in truth, the arrangement had been just fine some twenty minutes ago. But now . . . now he didn't want to have to subject himself to those tantalizing eyes of Miss Devereaux's ever again. Dragging his palms from forehead to chin, Jonathan bit back a short reply.

"Mama Tavie, you know how dear you are to me, but I don't

want to spend my nights out here. It's as simple as that." He placed a hand on her small shoulder. "You know how it has always grieved me to see others working from sunrise to sunset for no wages while I get paid for what I do. I mean, what have I done to deserve such kindness?"

At least, that much was true.

"Nothin'. You ain't done nothin' to deserve it."

Thank you, Lord. Finally, something that resonated with her and diverted her thinking from the real issue.

"It's just His grace and timing." Mama Tavie looked up at him, faith and hope saturating her every utterance. "Just like with the Hebrews in Egypt, God's got his timing, and He gonna fix it for all of us by and by. Meantime, your job is to keep on praying, keep on believing, keep on being grateful. And keep on hiring as many of God's children as you can, black or white, just like you always have."

Jonathan eyes moistened while his irritation receded. This little giant of a woman had dedicated her life to soothing others. When her own family had vanished in that same wave of yellow fever that took his mother, he'd have shriveled up and faded away from grief had she not pretended to let him bring meaning to her days with trying to tend to her needs.

"Mama Tavie? You want some more mush?"

"Yeah, sugar bun. Best mush I ever tasted."

"Mama Tavie, you cold? You want my blanket?"

"How you know that's just what I needed? Why, you handier than a pocket on a shirt."

When all she must have really wanted was turn her face to the wall and die. And later that winter, when the ache of her horrible loss started to subside, she'd filled his nights with warmth and laughter while the cabin they shared felt like an icehouse. He leaned down and hugged her, right out in the middle of the Riverwood estate.

"You're right of course, little woman. You always are. I

couldn't very well turn down the invitation to be a guest of one of the richest planters in Natchez, now could I?"

"Naw, you can't. And didn't you say that once the furniture is put in place, all you got to do is put in some moldings and such?"

"Ummm. Something like that, yes. My workers are going to put up the bedstead today after my appointment. The armoire, chest of drawers, and canopy will be brought over from the shop Monday. It should take only a few days for me to install the trim work and be on my way."

Mama Tavie's small hand dug into biceps. "Good. Now come on back to the kitchen and apologize to Dinah like the good boy you is."

"Uh—no, no ma'am. I can't do that right now." Hating himself for having to mislead Mama Tavie further, Jonathan gave her another quick squeeze. "'Fraid I left something at the shop and I have to get back for a minute or two." He pecked her on the cheek before taking off in a jog. "But I promise to apologize to Miss Devereaux next time I see her."

"You'd better, or there'll be no more teacakes for you this year."

"Yes, ma'am. Next time I see her."

But if he had his way, he'd never see the lovely Miss Devereaux again.

Jonathan loped through the ornate gates. He'd finally decided he definitely had to look professional when he sat down with McMillan's assistant. He'd just have to make up some excuse or other for being late. It would work. It had to. From long habit, he reached for his papers—and froze.

What in the world?

What had he been thinking? He dare not go back into Natchez without his freedom papers. Jonathan stomped out a circle of frustration. Enough. He'd go back into that kitchen, and Dinah Devereaux or no Dinah Devereaux, pick up the coat that was a part of his plan toward true freedom. No matter the outcome of the meeting in the big house, he'd wear the greasy coat. The main thing was he'd have his papers back. Hopefully, he could still name his price today, but if not, he'd find a way to live with it until his next opportunity came along.

Half of this country might not know it yet, but he was already a man, had been since he was seven years old and found himself motherless and fatherless. And as long as he had papers to prove it, he had no intention of reverting to a boy now.

DINAH SLUNG the dirty mop with determination. Never had she been this furious with herself. Mama Tavie would return any second, and she was going to have to face her—and possibly Mr. Mayfield—and explain the second most stupid thing she'd ever done in her life. The first one was opening her eyes when she entered planet Earth twenty years ago.

Or was it ending up in the arms of Jack Hudson when she was only eleven?

Dinah gasped. Where, Lord, were all these thoughts coming from? The fleeting memory of what happened with that man all those years ago made her want to weep all over again. But she wouldn't. Time to plug the spigot and take responsibility for the clumsy mistake she'd just made.

"Dinah? You in here?"

The familiar cheeriness of Octavia McMillan's voice arrested Dinah's mopping in mid-stroke.

"I got wonderful news, honey. I—"

"Mama Tavie, before you say anything else, I have something to tell you."

"Yeah, Mama Tavie. You ain't gonna believe what that girl done did now."

Suppressing the urge to turn the bucket of filthy water over Violette's fat head, Dinah stood the mop into the pail and leaned it against the wall. Glancing around for Mr. Mayfield, she steepled her fingers and lifted her chin. At least she didn't have to face him quite yet.

"I'm afraid I've made a bad situation worse, Mama Tavie. I've destroyed Mr. Mayfield's expensive frockcoat, and there's no way I can repair it. But if the Lord answers the special prayer I have before Him, it won't be long before I will be able to replace it."

Dinah hadn't realized she was wringing her hands until Mama Tavie walked over and stilled them.

"Now, now. You just be easy. No need to worry 'bout trying to replace that jacket. To my way of thinking Joe-Nathan's already got more of them than he knows what to do with."

Violette shot to her feet. "But Mama Tavie—"

"Violette, what's got into you lately? You wasn't near 'bout this hateful when you first come over here from the plantation. Now go sit back down and be quiet."

Violette huffed back down into her chair next to Emerald while Mama Tavie continued.

"Anyhow, I come to tell you Joe-Nathan said he didn't know what come over him in here a while ago and he'd make it right with you soon as he could." Mama Tavie chuckled. "I expect I know what got a hold of him. Same thing what gets a hold of any man seeing a beauty like you. He love-struck. "

Dinah flushed with embarrassment. Never had she even considered herself pretty, not to mention beautiful. But she couldn't help but be heartened by Mama Tavie's enthusiastic words. Had she misjudged the man that severely? Maybe he hadn't taken the whole frockcoat thing quite so seriously after all.

She managed a peek at Violette. The girl looked like a bank of thunderclouds, loaded and ready with deadly strikes of lightning. No question but a downpour of more trouble from Violette McMillan was on the way.

A TALL WILLOWY middle-aged gentleman dressed in spotless livery intercepted Jonathan's path as he made the turn back toward the kitchen. Immediately recognizing the oldest of a pair of butlers at Riverwood, Jonathan cringed as the one known to the slaves as Mr. James scanned his disheveled appearance.

"You all right, sir?"

"Uh, yes, Mr. James. Just a minor mishap in the kitchen. But everything's fine now."

"Glad to hear it, sir."

Hoping Mr. James would one day relent from the formality of addressing him as "sir," Jonathan decided not to protest this time. Since he'd become a successful cabinetmaker, the man had taken to treating him differently in a goodly sort of way. But the unnecessary deference always wore on Jonathan's comfort. Countless times he'd asked him not to refer to him as such, thinking to himself he'd even be willing to tolerate "Joe-Nathan" if Mr. James would only stop this embarrassing reverence toward a man ten years his junior. He reached out to shake the older man's hand.

"It's good to see you, Mr. James. How've you been?" Chuckling, Jonathan motioned toward the kitchen. "You headed toward those teacakes in there, too?"

The distinguished looking butler's face split into a warm smile.

"Matter of fact, Octavia's been sneaking a batch in to me for over a week now every time she brings in supper to the big house —sir."

Jonathan blew out a sigh. A mild objection was in order. "Come on now, Mr. James. Do you have to keep on with the 'sirs'? You've known me quite a while now. What can I do to keep you from lavishing all this ceremony on me each time I see you?"

The older man took his time to answer. The tiniest light of fixed determination flickered in his eyes. "A big part of my life is 'sir-ing' people all day long, those who deserve it and those who don't." He stabbed his finger to his own chest. "No choice for this old man. So when I find somebody I can be proud of like you and I can choose to say 'sir' to him when I please, I'm going to do it. So you might as well get used to it."

Jonathan tilted his head up toward the mansion towering over him. A strange new feeling of wrongheadedness niggled at his conscience. Here he was scratching to get the respect of a man inside that house that he'd never formally met when Mr. James, a kind, godly man, was offering him a silver platter overflowing with undeserved honor.

But James was still a slave. And good man though he was, he didn't have the power to make Jonathan a respected businessman.

Shaking off the selfish implications of that disturbing thought, Jonathan bowed to Mr. James. "Thank you, sir. I am honored."

The butler honored him in kind with a deep bow of his own. "You're most welcome, sir. I've been watching out for you for more than an hour now. Don't know how I missed your entrance onto the grounds. As I'm sure you know, Master McMillan is out of town for a week or two, but the mistress has instructed me to tell you Master's accountant is going to be late for the appointment. He sent word to tell you to wait. He should be here in about two hours if everything goes according to plan."

A two-ton weight slid from Jonathan's shoulders. More than enough time to get his papers and get home to change clothes before returning. He felt like scooping the older gentleman off the ground and swinging him in the air the way Papa used to do him when he was a little tyke. Instead he nearly wrung the man's arm off.

"Mr. James, you have no idea how much I—"

"But Mama Tavie, are you sure Mr. Mayfield won't be too upset?"

The two men's heads swerved toward the kitchen as Dinah Devereaux's voice floated through the open window.

"Well, I guess I'll see you after a while," said Mr. James making his exit. "Just come on through the servants' hall right there." He pointed to the door near the end of the back verandah. "I'll be waiting to show you to the study."

Despite his resolve, the sweet sound of Miss Devereaux's voice left Jonathan feeling a mite unnerved, but he had to have his papers. He pushed opened the kitchen door.

"So what is it I'm supposed to be upset about?"

RETREATING to the opposite wall where Emerald scolded and petted her ragdoll in courses, Dinah placed her hand on top of the child's head. For some reason the nearness of this four-year-old darling always brought comfort to her. She shuddered as a line of emotions marched across Mr. Mayfield's finely chiseled face. Anger? Fear? Disgust? He stood in a stony posture before the fireplace where the coat lay in ashes. Obviously, Mama Tavie had been wrong. No matter how many suits of clothing he owned, this piece must have been very special.

"My freedom papers were in there."

His words propelled Dinah out of the shadows, panic coursing through her veins. The question slipped through her lips before she could stop it.

"D-did you say freedom papers?"

Cold silence.

Oh, Lord, no. Not that glorious thing every slave in America coveted every day of his or her life. Bile clambered up Dinah's throat. She couldn't have been more stricken had she been diagnosed with a dread disorder. Not only would Mr. Mayfield never forgive her, she'd never forgive herself. She'd just added another item to the list of missteps in her life that grated her very soul. Before she thought about it, she'd laid a trembling hand on his arm.

"Oh, Mr. Mayfield, I am so very sorry. I'll make it up to you somehow. I promise."

Eons slipped past as she waited, his profile of clenched teeth and angry jawline as poignant as his overwhelming good looks. Finally, he moved from her touch, a look of panic shading his brow.

"Make it up to me? Are you in the business of drawing up freedom papers, Miss Devereaux?"

"Well, no, I don't suppose I am, but—"

"Then how on earth do you plan to make this up to me?"

No one, not even Mama Tavie, said a word. It was the first time Dinah had seen her look this troubled since she'd come to Riverwood. A knowing glance passed between her and Mr. Mayfield.

"You sure you had them papers in that jacket, son?"

"I never go anywhere without proof of freedom on my person. You know that, Mama Tavie." At last, he looked at Dinah. An incredulous glower spread over his countenance, ending in a withering stare. "I just never counted on an act of carelessness destroying it."

A strange but powerful need to defend herself stood up in Dinah. She pulled her frame to its full height of well over five and three-quarters feet. After all, she hadn't deliberately thrown the flamboyant coat into the fire . . . *well, flamboyant might be a little beyond the pale, Dinah. Costly was a more apt description.* Whatever, she'd taken all she could for one day.

"Mr. Mayfield."

He snapped to attention as inwardly Dinah complimented herself on the decisiveness of her tone. Why, she'd just called him out with only two words!

"Don't you think you're being a little dramatic here?"

His brows flew to his hairline, just before he tried once again to melt her with a sizzling glare. But Dinah was having none of it.

"I have already sincerely apologized, sir, which you so

ungraciously flung in my face. But, I might add, I'm not the one who put your precious coat and papers in jeopardy by placing them on a greasy table next to an open fireplace in the first place. Let that sink in, Mr. Mayfield! And in the second place I can design and make a frock coat that will match or even supersede anything you've ever owned."

He stared at her as if she'd switched to speaking Chinese. "What are you talking about? I don't care about that coat."

"But I do." She pointed her finger toward his broad chest. "So I shall make it anyhow, and you will like it."

What was she saying? She had no money, no fabric, no sewing machine. No needles, thread, nothing. And besides, the papers were what really counted here. Merciful heavens. She must really look like an advanced lunatic now. The look of shock on Mama Tavie's face offered swift confirmation.

"I know you upset, honey, but maybe you should think on this before you make such a promise."

Suddenly, Jonathan Mayfield looked more defeated than angry. "Doesn't matter, Mama Tavie. My freedom to move around the countryside is now in ashes, pretty much the same as my means of making a living." He dropped his head. "I'll be leaving now. I have a meeting."

Mama Tavie's usual smile had degenerated into a grim line. "Joe-Nathan, honey, this ain't the end of the world, you know."

"For me it very well might be," said Mr. Mayfield before he turned and walked out of the room."

Mama Tavie, a glint of hard-edged resolve in her eyes Dinah hadn't seen before, didn't lift a finger to stop him.

"I love that boy as if I brung him into the world. But Joe-Nathan got some stuff in him what needs to be worked out. And if the Lord done finally saw fit to use me to help get it out of him, then I'll just be so humbled to do it." She glanced over at Emerald who, using Lucy as a pillow, had fallen asleep on the floor, then over at Violette who'd become unusually quiet.

"Dinah, Emerald acting more peaked than usual. Why don't

you take her up to the bed whilst I have a little talk with Violette? And whilst you up there, crawl on that mattress and get a little rest for yourself, honey."

"Yes, ma'am."

Rest. About as likely as a romantic proposal from the dashing Mr. Jonathan Mayfield.

4

Dinah's emotions raced around among anger and shame—and yes, pride. A tiny bit of her was proud of the way she'd stood up for herself a while ago against Jonathan Mayfield. That kind of resistance might have served her better when she had relaxed in Jack's arms all those years ago.

Lord, help me.

There it was again. Why, after all these years, was she being beleaguered today with thoughts of that evil man? In a moment of childish weakness, she'd substituted a lawyer named Jack Hudson for the father image she'd so desperately needed all her life, and he'd rewarded her by exploiting her innocence. Was she ever to get past that wretched afternoon?

Whisking Emerald's slight weight up the stairs, she entered the small room she now shared with three other people and sat down on one of the mattresses with the drowsy child on her lap. Thoroughly frustrated by her thoughts and the events of the day, she was unaware that a rush of water toppled down her cheeks.

"What's the matter, Miss Dinah?" Emerald swatted at the tears landing on her ear.

"O-o-o-o. Miss Dinah's sorry, sweetie."

Dinah pressed her cheek against Emerald's forehead. Hot!

Way too hot.

She gathered the child closer to her, the same way she'd so often longed for the Devereauxs to do when she was a little girl, and tried to figure out the best way to handle this.

"You scared of Mr. Jonathan, Miss Dinah?"

No. She wasn't scared of Mr. Jonathan. Just crushed by him. *"My freedom to move around the countryside is now in ashes,"* he'd said. How was a girl, whose sole desire was to purchase her own freedom, supposed to live with that?

"Shhh, darling. Of course Miss Dinah isn't scared. Mr. Jonathan is a nice man." She put on a smile. "See? Everything is all right."

Now what? Should she go down and tell Mama Tavie about the fever? That had to be the best thing to do, but what if Violette was back? Dinah certainly didn't want to stir her venom again by causing Violette to think she was trying to usurp her place with Emerald. She smoothed the little girl's forehead.

Emerald was past Mama Tavie's "peaked."

"I want Lucy."

"Why, Emerald, did you forget and leave poor Lucy downstairs?"

"Yes, ma'am. I want her. And I don't feel better," she said burrowing into Dinah's chest. She sounded so tiny and pitiful.

"I know, sweetheart, but don't you worry. Before you can blink, Mama Tavie's gonna be up here with Lucy and something that'll make you feel all better again."

Dinah hummed a tune and rocked Emerald until she entered a fitful sleep then laid her onto the mattress. She stretched out on the floor next to the mattress where the child lay sleeping, pondering what it must be like to have a child such as Emerald wrenched from your arms at an auction. Best not to get her heart too tied up with Emerald. Who knew how long this child would be at Riverwood anyway? What power did Violette, or for that matter, Mama Tavie have over her future?

Absolutely none.

Her stomach soured at the very notion. No matter what she had to do, she'd see to it that she never subjected a child to this kind of future. She sat up to look at Emerald once more and found her frowning in her dreams. *Lord, please don't let anything happen to this little gem. And please never let her be sold away from us. I don't think I could bear it.* She'd wait for Mama Tavie another minute or two, and then Violette or no Violette, she'd go looking for her.

Determined to blink back the horror of slavery encroaching upon her thoughts, Dinah tried to shut out her worries by closing her eyes. But unbeknownst to her, she was already asleep by the second blink.

RUNNING down the three flights of stairs, her heavy pigtails flying behind her, Dinah skidded to a stop and breathed in the smell of scented beeswax used to polish the hall furniture. Today was her eleventh birthday, and Mistress Devereaux had left shortly after breakfast to be gone for the duration of the day. Now at last Dinah stood in front of the massive arched door to Master's library, tingling with anticipation. Promising to bring her a treat, Mistress had declared today Dinah's off day from honing her sewing skills and given her free run of the floor-to-ceiling bookshelves on the other side of that glorious door.

Dinah's brain urged her to pause before opening the door. Had Mistress said something about waiting until the afternoon before exploring the library? Unaware, Dinah slid into the habit of biting the side of her lip when uncertainty hit. What exactly had Mistress said? The last word Dinah could truly recall was "library." Past that, she'd reckoned the rest inconsequential. She breathed deeply and shrugged off the nagging indecision. What did it matter, really? Master would long since have left the house, and she was here now. So what difference could an hour or two make?

About to press down on the curved brass handle, she halted at the sound of male voices. Master Devereaux? Oh, fiddle-faddle! Wasn't he supposed to be at the office this morning? This was ruining everything. Mistress had warned her never to interrupt while the master conferred with another lawyer or cotton factor, or any guest, for that matter. Then how else was she to pass off this fine birthday morning she'd looked so forward to if she couldn't have something new to read?

Shoulders drooping, she'd begun making her way back toward her attic room when Master Devereaux's voice boomed from the other side of the wall.

"That's despicable, Hudson, inexcusable. We'll not represent such a cad."

"I quite agree, sir," said Jack Hudson, a young lawyer from Master's firm. Dinah had met him only once. She hadn't liked him at all. "Treating Negroes in that manner is what's given our way of life such a bad name."

Instructions never to eavesdrop warred with Dinah's curiosity. Though she herself was a Negro, wouldn't it be safer for her dreams at night to simply walk away? Shut down her mind from what might be something ugly?

But rarely had she heard Master Devereaux get that agitated about anything. And what exactly did Mr. Hudson mean by "our way of life?" She tiptoed back toward the library, inching along the wall until she stood next to the door.

"I've never subscribed to that kind of behavior toward neither my hired household workers nor Dinah." Conversation ceased for a moment while Dinah's master put forth a long throat clearing. "You know, of course, Mrs. Devereaux and I have never been able to have children."

"Right, sir."

"But our little slave girl Dinah has proven a comfort to us as we grow older."

Dinah's heart swelled with gratitude. Though they'd never embraced her, or even cupped her face the way she'd seen Cook do with her children, they did care for her as much as she ought to be cared for. Resignedly, she sighed. Hugs were simply too much for a little black girl to hope for, she supposed.

"I can't help but wonder what life would have been like had I not found her that morning in early June of '40. I was taking a sunrise stroll when I came upon her at the entrance to an alley near the Cathedral. That was before we built here in the Garden District. She'd just woken up and started to cry, straining against the gaudy red shawl she'd been carefully wrapped in. I never even considered leaving her there. My first thought was to try to find the nearest orphanage, but then I reached down and picked her up. One look into those wide eyes the color of a fawn and I simply couldn't walk away. I took her home to Mrs. Devereaux."

"She does have lovely eyes, sir."

A knot of fear formed in Dinah's stomach. For some unexplained reason she didn't like the idea that Mr. Hudson thought her eyes pretty. Maybe it was the way he'd looked at her the other day.

"Our cook who has children of her own helped us settle her in. Two days later I happened upon a newspaper article about a local prostitute who worked exclusively for a bordello called The Gentleman's Caller. Turns out, she'd been a fieldworker and a breeder on a nearby plantation who'd been sold to the Gentleman's Caller."

Suddenly, all Dinah's senses were on alert. She could almost smell evil in the air. She should leave. Now. Escape these ominous words the way she always did when she was excited or hurt or lonely. But she couldn't this time. And besides, hadn't Cook warned her for years about not getting the whole story?

"The woman had gotten herself with child by some lewd rascal," continued the master, "and been forced to get rid of it the very night the baby was born. She died on the streets after leaving our little Dinah. Though Dinah has the blood of a prostitute and a rascal running through her veins, we've done our Christian duty by her. We call her our little pet slave."

"My congratulations to you sir, for such a noble sacrifice—"

"What? What's wrong?" Dinah felt a hand on her shoulder as she bolted up from the floor still mired in the dream.

Dear Jesus. What a pity I didn't hear a thing Mistress Devereaux said past the word "library." I might have saved myself from Jack Hudson. Then again, if she'd just shut down her curiosity that once, just returned to her attic room before she'd heard . . .

"Where your mind at, honey?" Mama Tavie's face was a palette of concerns. "I called up them stairs three times, and you didn't answer nary a one. Thought you might want to come down and sample a little of the soup I made. Lord knows them bones could use some meat."

"S-sorry, Mama Tavie. I'm not hungry, and somebody has to stay with Emerald. She's hot as a furnace."

Mama Tavie hastened toward Emerald's bed, her face quickly turning into a scowl. "Hmmm. You right. Why come you didn't tell me sooner?"

Dinah shrugged a lie while Mama Tavie riffled through a bag from beneath her bed until she produced a small brown bottle. "This quinine oughta back that fever off. Mind giving me a hand, Dinah?"

Where *was* Dinah's mind? The dream. She was still choked by that dream.

"Oh! No, ma'am. Not at all."

The remarkably agile forty-year-old lifted the sleeping child into her arms and passed her to Dinah.

"What was you doing down there on that floor anyways? Should 'a been resting yourself on that mattress like I told you. You look as peaked as Emerald."

"I meant to keep an eye on her until you got here. I must have dozed off, but my sleep turned out to be . . . well . . . not so restful. Lots of dreaming, you know."

Mama Tavie deftly began pouring the liquid medicine into a spoon.

"You worried about them papers, ain't cha."

"A little." *I'm worried sick.*

"Don't be. I told you everything gonna work out just how it's supposed to for Joe-Nathan. He just got some yielding to do."

"Thanks. Where's Violette anyway? I thought she'd be back by now"

"I took her back of the 'pendency. Had me a good talk with that one, but I still don't know what's got her so mean lately, 'specially toward you. Anyhow, she's down there finishing tidying up the kitchen before supper." Mama Tavie ran her hand across Dinah's forehead. "I hope you ain't catching whatever the little one's got. Lord knows when I walked in here, your face didn't look like you just come out of a dream but a real long nightmare."

A breeder. A prostitute.

Dinah blinked away the traitorous tears. How could she ever explain to this lady or anyone else how she'd hidden in the drawing room that day so many years ago, waiting for her master to vacate the library so she could seek out the meanings of those foul-sounding words in his dictionary? How could anyone ever understand how over the years those words had become specters in a lifelong nightmare that had invaded her, shaping whom she was, whom she'd always be?

There was no getting around the misfit she'd proven herself all day long today. She was cursed from the day she was born. She could only continue to fight to make sure she'd get her freedom and not end up a field worker. And a breeder. And a prostitute. Along with whatever else Jack Hudson had ultimately turned her into that day. Dinah wrung her hands around a bit before starting for the door.

"Oh, I'll be fine, Mama Tavie. I just need to catch a breath of air." She hesitated before turning around. "Mama Tavie? Shouldn't even a pet slave be hugged once in a while?"

JONATHAN GLANCED over his shoulder to see if anyone was following him. He felt naked, lonely, and afraid. Though, unbeknownst to Thomas Day, the freedom papers he cherished had been meticulously forged by an abolitionist-apprentice in North Carolina, they'd been the most real thing in his life for the last nine years. Warding off danger. Completing his manhood.

Not quite ready to brave the emptiness of his two-storied brick home in the heart of Natchez, he'd strode right past it and made his way toward his private sanctuary, the bluffs of the Mississippi River. But now that he was here, he felt lonelier than ever. How could this be, when hours ago he'd gotten everything he'd ever hoped for?

The meeting with Mr. McMillan's accountant had gone smoother than Jonathan could have imagined. Though he'd made up a story as to why he was coatless, he'd stood like a man, named his price, and received it without so much as a raised eyebrow. For the first time since becoming a cabinetmaker, he'd been treated like a valued artisan instead of a talented boy who didn't have sense enough to count his own money. It seemed Mr. McMillan truly was a fair man after all, and when other planters learned of the respect he'd tendered toward Jonathan, hopefully, they'd behave likewise.

So why was his gut roiling like a pot of week-old stew? The papers. Of course.

He looked over the precipice of the towering bluff, down at a spindly tree he'd been watching for the last several years. Struggling to put down lasting roots, the tree had become like an old friend. After all, wasn't that what Jonathan had been fighting to do all his life? Put down impressive roots?

Jamming his hands into the pockets of his smoke-tinged pants, he watched as the sun made a rapid free fall behind the town of Vidalia, Louisiana. The many sets of clothing he had purchased over the last few years could easily meet the fate of his frockcoat, but the operations of the heavens God so generously provided never failed. He lifted his head in adoration.

Great is thy faithfulness, dear Lord. You never forget to turn on that great light we call the sun, and you always know when it's the perfect time to turn it off.

A joy-filled whistling tune escaped from Jonathan's soul out across the chilly waters.

Face it, Jonathan. Dinah Devereaux is the most delightful woman you've ever met, and she's got some fire in her too. Stood up to you like no other slave except Mama Tavie in a long while.

Instantly, the tuned died on his lips. Truth was he wanted more of Dinah Devereaux than a curtsey or a hasty goodbye or even a good dressing-down like the one she'd given him a few hours ago. He wanted to see her again. And again and again. And that truth distressed him more than the loss of papers could ever do. In fact, he wondered if he was strong enough to lay eyes on that skittish beauty again without—

"Not true! Not true. None of it's true."

Jonathan stomped around and yelled bolstering-up stuff at himself in the quiet darkening of the old river until he ran out of steam. Hoping no one heard his outburst, he looked around before continuing his self-talk in a more tame voice.

"All right, so . . . it *is* true that she's beautiful, and so very charming when she bites her lip in that innocent way. But it isn't true that any of those things mean anything to me. It is true that the beguiling woman with those majestic cheekbones and large liquid eyes the color of an amber creek and braids that, when loosed, must graze the small of her back and skin like midnight velvet . . . . Wait, wait! Jonathan, wait. The woman has yet to be born who can sink you into marriage."

Marriage? Who said anything about marriage? And why was he even thinking about marriage to a woman he'd known for three hours, one who'd come close to setting Riverwood afire, destroyed his proof of freedom, and had the effrontery to blame him for it?

Jonathan was losing his mind. Plain and simple.

Downriver, a stately sternwheeler, bejeweled with lights,

pulled away from the docks under the hill and paddled toward New Orleans. Dinah's home. Blast! Was there no escaping this girl tonight?

Jonathan placed a foot on a nearby stump and splayed his hands onto his sides. This whole thing was ridiculous. So-o-o ridiculous. He would only be at Riverwood for a few days, and he'd basically be working alone, except for some out-of-town seamstress Mrs. McMillan had, at the last minute, decided she wanted him to work with. He wasn't worried about that.

So long as he could avoid Miss Devereaux.

Taking his meals in his room, he'd probably not even see her while he was at Riverwood. And if he did, he knew what to do. He'd clamp down on his feelings like a vise. He did it all the time with the rest of the slaves. Why not with the gorgeous Miss Devereaux?

God forgive him, but unlike Papa, he'd protect his heart at all costs.

He started back toward his townhouse only to be nearly undone by the idea of the stark emptiness awaiting him there. Glancing southward, he decided to take a turn down Silver Street toward an alternate world from the glory of upper Natchez. Before retiring for the night, he'd risk a few minutes down at the landing, check on a shipment that was past due. Maybe then he'd feel more like trying for sleep.

JONATHAN PICKED his way through the flimsy shanties thrown up along the shelf of land called Natchez-Under-the-Hill. From years of habit, he slid his hand over his heart and tapped outward, feeling for the proof that he was a free man.

All in vain.

Prickles of panic plied their trade among his thoughts. Every unsavory character looked like a heartless slave catcher. Mentally, he shook himself. He was a better man than this. He was as familiar with this town as birds were with the air. And just about everyone in Natchez knew who the black cabinetmaker was. There was simply nothing that called for these jitters.

Trying to beat the habit of checking for his papers, he clasped his hands behind his back as he maneuvered his way through the maze of homeless drunks and rebellious heirs of cotton planters, sallow-faced children and starving animals toward the places of commerce teetering on the water's edge. Down here on the underside of Natchez's gilded estates, the echoes of godlessness coming from the raucous laughter and profane speech of the barrelhouses showed no signs that anyone was interested in the God he'd felt so strongly just minutes ago on the bluff.

Jonathan glanced back over his shoulder. What had possessed him to come down here this time of evening anyway? Oh, yes. He remembered now. He'd come to check on that delayed shipment of materials from the islands.

Sure, he had. As though he couldn't have waited until next week. Chances were the warehouse would be shut down by the time he made it there anyway.

Jonathan muttered under his breath. "Nothing like a restless spirit to make a body take silly chances."

"Ain't that the truth."

Fists at the ready, Jonathan wheeled around to a familiar voice breaking through the surrounding racket.

"Benjamin? What are you doing down here?"

Benjamin Catlett, Jonathan's right-hand man at his furniture shop who'd been born free in northern Virginia, crossed his arms and chuckled.

"Have you forgotten, sir? You commanded me, since you were going to be hobnobbing with the nabobs out at Riverwood all afternoon, to check on that delayed shipment."

"And did you?"

"Tried to. But I was a few minutes too late. They'd already shut down for the evening."

"Why'd you wait so late?"

Benjamin's brow flew upward. "And what brings you down here, sir?"

Jonathan decided to ignore the "sir." The man could be as bad as Riverwood's butler, Mr. James, except Mr. James was in earnest and Benjamin merely enjoyed witnessing Jonathan's discomfort with all that fluffy respect.

"Frankly, the shop was unusually busy this afternoon when Henry and I returned. We even had a couple of new orders for entire rooms." A worried look passed over Benjamin's face. He relaxed his stance and rubbed the top of his head.

"What's the trouble, Catlett?"

"I don't know. Probably nothing. It's just that Henry spoke of a couple of men from the North who's been prowling around Natchez trying to catch black men without passes or papers."

A red-hot poker of fear stabbed Jonathan's heart reminding him of the feeling of being watched on the road to Riverwood.

"Truly? When did he see them?"

"Said he'd not seen them himself, but he'd overheard whispers about them from the overseer on the plantation where he lives. Said they're claiming to be setting up a business on the order of what Franklin and Armfield once had in Virginia."

Franklin and Armfield? Who in the world were they? Whether from shock, fear, or plain old pride, Jonathan decided to forego asking. And he wasn't ready yet to discuss with anyone that he'd just had his freedom burned to a crisp, not even to Benjamin. But knowing his friend to be a bit careless at times about his own proof of freedom, often accusing Jonathan of being too vigilant about his papers, Jonathan clapped Benjamin on the shoulder and offered a muted warning.

"I suppose you and I had better be diligent in keeping our papers on our person, then. Agreed?"

Benjamin reassumed his usual knowing smirky grin. "Yes. Sir. I suppose we had."

5

Dinah carefully dipped the exquisite breakfast serving dish into the rinse water and passed it on to Violette to dry. Lately she was loath to ask the girl anything about her little sister. But remembering how that poor baby upstairs had retched and groaned and whimpered last night pushed her toward the risk.

"How's Emerald this morning?"

Violette brightened as though happy about the inquiry. "She better. No more fever. She sleeping now. Whatever it was, look like it didn't come to stay."

A prayer of thanks slipped through Dinah's lips, "Lord, we do thank you for mercy on the little one."

A lone tear slid down Violette's cheek. Surprised and deeply moved, Dinah dabbed her forehead with the back of her sleeve, wondering how to proceed. Never able to read the girl, she fluffed the skimpy skirts of her shapeless slave-issue dress and decided on a subject change. For now.

"Wonder how Mama Tavie has been able to stand this kind of heat all these years."

Violette hiked a brow. "This kind of heat? What kind of

kitchen did you cook in before you come to Riverwood anyhow? Was you in the big house or your own cabin in the quarters?"

Quarters? In the exclusive Garden District? If Violette wasn't so easily irritated, Dinah might have laughed out loud. Though there were several cabins here at Riverwood to house the slaves who handled the grounds, gardens, and orchards, the very idea of dropping a cabin into the manmade paradise of every flower imaginable surrounding the Devereaux's three-story mansion was anathema.

"Violette, hasn't anybody ever told you about—"

Dinah halted, once again sensing a hollow core to Violette's constant swagger. Having spent her entire existence on one of the McMillan plantations before being transferred to Riverwood, the girl would know nothing about the exclusive section of New Orleans where Dinah had spent every day of her life. A gentle admonition swept past her ear.

"Do not humiliate her, dear one, for her needs are many."

A swell of sympathy for what Violette's short life might have been like so far cooled Dinah's usual feelings of annoyance toward her. She swallowed down the hasty correction about to fly from her mouth and stepped back from the pan of soapy water, slowly sizing up Violette McMillan with a soft eye. Though somewhat plump, she had a heart-shaped persimmon-colored face complimented by deep brown eyes. In truth, she could be lovely to look upon if she'd only give herself a chance. What was it that drove this young motherless girl who—

Clap! Clap!

The pudgy object of Dinah's compassionate musings jolted her back to her oppressive surroundings.

"Well, Miss Lady? You gonna answer my question today or next Saturday? What kind of kitchen did you cook in?" Violette laid a finger to the side of her face. "Ha! I bet you wasn't no cook a'tall, one of them pets what gussies up her missus's hair all day. I got a good mind to talk to Jethro about you myself. Nothin' he'd like better than to break you in on one of them long hot rows and who knows what else."

Anxieties circled back with gale force. Dinah felt the air sucked from the momentary good will she'd felt toward Violette.

"Wh-who's Jethro?" As though the slave driver's very name hadn't haunted her dreams more than once.

"Don't try to act like you don't remember. One of Massa's drivers, that's who." Violette glanced out the window, a wide grin splitting her face. "Matter of fact, he outside right now."

Dinah's heart wobbled between fear and relief. At least, she'd be able to put off this spiteful girl's probing if Violette was occupied with the dreaded slave driver. But what if Jethro's reason for being here was her—Dinah? What if Mr. McMillan had ordered him to remove her to the plantation and Jethro was here to claim her? Perspiration trickled down the center of her back causing her to recall Master Devereaux's hunting stories. So this was how one of his "treed" animals had felt.

Calm yourself, Dinah. Master McMillan's not even here to give such an order. And even if he was, winter is approaching, not the time for cotton farming. From nervous habit, she pointed her toes in, bit the side of her lip then forced herself to meet Violette's gaze. Trying not to blink, she silently prayed.

Dear Lord, I know I've neglected you lately, but I could truly use some direction right now. You know, more than all else, I cannot survive the fields.

She felt a telltale twitch pulsing beneath her eye. She had to think of something quickly, or this shrew could begin building a case for Dinah's eventual removal to the plantation, to begin the cycle of planting, chopping, and picking cotton—breeding children to build up the master's inventory—until she ended up scouring the streets of New Orleans for customers just the way—

Jesus, no! Before it came to that, she would flee in the dead of night, alone toward Canada.

And be eaten by a pack of dogs before you get to the Mississippi River?

She pillaged her brain for a way to keep this heartless girl, who'd set her wrath upon Dinah from the moment she'd stepped over the threshold of Mama Tavie's kitchen, from feeding this Jethro fellow's curiosity. Fumbling at the back of her neck, Dinah tried to pin the thick ropy braids that had once again come loose. Guilt spiraled through her. *God forgive me. I'm about to tell a half-truth.* The words of her old mistress sprang to life.

"More often than not, half-truths are but poisonous herbs coated with sugar."

"I am not a pet slave, Violette." Not anymore, at least. "Since Master and Mistress were both scant eaters, I-I guess you could say we cooked a little differently in New Orleans." She nonchalantly waved toward the table with dozens of apple pies waiting to be fried. "Not quite in these quantities, at one time, that is. Th-that's what has me a little awkward still."

Looking most unconvinced, Violette walked over to the window and looked out. She crossed her arms and cocked her hips to the side. "Now, I wonder where did Jethro get off to so fast?"

"Miss Tavie? Y'all in there?"

Violette's face lit up with malicious intent. "Well, if this don't take the cake. Just when I thought he'd disappeared. Come on in, Jethro."

Dinah stared in disbelief at the scrawny ogling high-yellow man standing just inside the door. She hadn't felt this contaminated since Jack Hudson. Yes, this meeting could very well be about to take the cake and perhaps her whole existence along with it to the fields of the McMillan plantations.

"Name's Jethro."

"Dinah Devereaux."

"Pleased to meetcha."

Chin lowered and shoulders shrugged, Dinah recoiled from the beyond-brazen pressure of Jethro McMillan's ham-sized hands resting there. How dare he touch her without permission? Short in stature but oozing self-worth, this crass wiry man sent icy fingers along her spine.

"You must be that Dinah everybody talking about." He grinned showing a picket fence of tobacco-stained teeth. His eyes turned her coarse slave dress into mosquito netting. "Now I see why."

"What can we do for you, Mr. Jethro?"

He guffawed as though she'd called him President Buchanan. "Now ain't that somethin'. 'Mr. Jethro.' Hmm. I think I could learn to like it." He tugged at his scruffy beard. "And about what you just said, I think we can do something for each other."

"Hey, Jethro. What you doing over here on a Saturday?" said Violette.

But Jethro never took his eyes off Dinah. "Jes making my rounds trying to figure out ways I can help my massa."

Dinah could only imagine what that would be, but she suspected it rested under the tent of tormenting other slaves. What she didn't want to imagine was what *she* could possibly do for him.

"Oh yeah, 'course you is, Jethro." Violette allowed an earsplitting laugh. "Here to help Massa out, huh? And just when did Jethro the important driver man ever do anything that wasn't going to help his own self out first?" She waved him off before he could answer causing him to look her way for a second. She motioned her head toward Dinah then winked at him.

"Looking for more hands, maybe—for the spring of the year?"

"Naw. Not exactly. Just been curious 'bout what's cooking up in Mama Tavie's kitchen these days. Thought I might find me something to nibble on in here. Somethin' real sweet, don'tcha know." He returned his sights to Dinah, reminding her of a salivating dog. "That is if I can work something out with the sweet thing here."

He was baiting Dinah. The urge to risk jumping into the trap and trying to bite Jethro's head off before she was injured nearly overpowered her. But this was no gentle and humane trap. It was potentially deadly. As much as it sickened and frightened her, this slave might just hold her future in those disgusting hands of his. She held his gaze hoping to signal to him that she understood his poor attempt at metaphor but refused to answer.

"All I need is a little company now and then. That way I can make sure Mama Tavie keep the kitchen full up with staff and running like it is, and Massa's lady is satisfied with the help. Wouldn't want to break up y'all's little threesome if I didn't have to."

Dinah's blood ran cold. Though her experience with men was limited to the nightmare of Jack Hudson, she knew this louse was trying to proposition her, no, threaten her, with the cotton fields if she didn't keep him "company." Violette darted her eyes from Dinah to Jethro and back again, her look of triumph fading toward something akin to concern.

"What kind of sweet things you talking about, Jethro? Like some teacakes or somethin'?"

"Uh umm. Don't think so. This here gonna be better than teacakes."

Dinah started to back away. Was this man about to try to hurt her right here in Mama Tavie's kitchen? With Violette witnessing the whole thing? Would Violette even try to stop him? Suddenly, he snatched up her arm.

"Don't you touch me!"

"Whoa, there little lady. Where you going? Ole Jethro ain't gonna hurtcha. I just want to talk to you."

Violette smacked away the huge hands grabbing at Dinah. "Now looka here, Jethro. I thought we was just teasing her. But you going too far with this. Mama Tavie ain't here, so I think you best be leaving."

He turned toward Violette obviously snarling with disbelief. "You done forgot who you talking to, Violette? I can have you back on the plantation by nightfall, and I got a mind to do jes that."

Violette dropped her hands to her sides and studied her feet. "I-I didn't mean to insult you or nothin', Jethro. Just thought you was having a little fun was all."

Dinah backed her way toward the iron skillet hanging on the wall. No matter what Violette decided to do, she would never let another Jack Hudson touch her.

"Next time you be careful who you rare up at, Violette," continued Jethro. "As for you, sweet thing—"

"I think you'd better leave now." Dinah waited with the skillet in her hands. "I might not fry the best chicken yet, but I'm confident I can use this skillet to heat you up."

"Hey now! I like that! A spunky little thing." His smile curdled into another threat. "Have it your way for now, Little Miss, but remember, I'll be back to finish up our fun."

Heart pounding against the skillet she'd brought close to her chest, Dinah said nothing as he moved out the door.

DINAH BALANCED the load of empty dishes on her arm as she hurried from the slave hall in the main house into the rapidly-dropping temperature outside. She harbored no regrets about the way she'd handled Jethro. But a thousand times since the day of the grease fire, she'd regretted the way she'd mouthed off at Jonathan Mayfield. How could she have shown such unmerited effrontery after he'd saved her life? And what if he lost his livelihood, or even his life, because of her clumsiness? No. She couldn't live with that.

Pausing at the bottom of the back steps, she looked up into the early evening sky. Tonight promised a splendid sparkling canopy, and she wished with all her heart she could remain outside for a while and enjoy it. Though she'd learned quickly that the slaves on estates like this were to keep out of sight as much as possible, it was nighttime and she longed to enjoy the nocturnal heavens and the beautiful gardens as she'd so often done from the terrace of her master's home in New Orleans.

Surely Riverwood, the grandeur of it all, was made to be absorbed now and again. Not rushed through every day from sunup to sundown. She shivered at the thought she may never be free to enjoy the night skies again. More and more she'd begun to wonder what it must be like to be free to sit beneath the stars for as long as she liked, with a husband and a darling like Emerald by her side?

Someone like Mr. Mayfield, perhaps?

Warmth crept along Dinah's neck as she locked her gaze onto the heavy tray of dishes resting on her forearm. She knew how futile this kind of thinking was. Despite Mama Tavie's suggestive introduction the other day, a man as well-spoken and fine-looking as Jonathan Mayfield had to be already married if not betrothed. Besides, she'd literally set fire to his freedom. How likely was it that he'd even abide the same room space with her? A shrill voice cut into Dinah's thoughts.

"Dinah? What's keeping you, honey?"

Dinah flew down the walk and ducked into the kitchen. Toes pointed in and shoulders drooped, she lowered her eyelids. "Sorry, Mama Tavie. I suppose I was woolgathering a bit. The night promises to be so beautiful."

Mama Tavie grabbed Dinah's wrist and tugged her into the tiny servant's dining room on the other side of the double fireplace.

"Honey, I got news that's go'n lay you with the peas. Miz McMillan done found out from somebody in Louisiana what a fine seamstress you is. Why come you ain't said nothin' to Mama Tavie before now?"

Dinah's hand flailed around in search of her heart. She had stopped breathing. If she didn't get a hold of herself, she was going to die of hope right here on Mama Tavie's immaculate brick floor.

She simply cannot mean . . .

"Anyways, she wants you to make the drapes and such for that room Joe-Nathan's 'bout to fix up with new furniture. She thinks the world of Joe-Nathan's work, and I 'spect he's built every piece of that furniture for that bedroom all by his self. So this is a real honor. You 'bout to be fetched from the kitchen to the big house. Ain't you glad about that, having a chance to do what God gifted you to do?"

A delightful shiver vibrated Dinah's body back into commission at the mention of working with the cabinetmaker. *I'm to work with Mr. Mayfield?* Staring open-mouthed at Mama Tavie, Dinah tried to shake off the various unsettling thrills having their way with her.

"But why? Why would the mistress choose me when she must know dozens of good seamstresses?"

Octavia McMillan quickly turned thoughtful. "Well, for one thing, you hers. She can do with you whatever she please. Then again, that's just the kind of lady the missus is. Why, she once lent one of the kitchen girls a piece of her own jewelry to get married in. And even with losing several babies in childbirth, and worse, now watching her beloved son slip away from her, she still got a heart for others."

Dinah gasped. "Oh! How awful for her. I didn't know."

"I know, honey. We don't discuss it too much 'round here. Truth is, I believe young massa's failing health is the reason Massa Theodore hired Joe-Nathan in the first place. Somethin' to try to relieve Missus's mind from her child's condition a bit."

And to think, in the midst of all this, he'd taken Dinah in. Sorrow and confusion shadowed the hope Mama Tavie had just given her, not the least of which was whether she should be working with the intriguing Jonathan Mayfield at all.

"I-I don't know about this, Mama Tavie. Is Mr. Mayfield . . . I mean . . . is he betrothed or married? My old mistress always said it's improper for an unmarried woman to work that closely with a man unchaperoned."

"Betrothed? Who said anything 'bout Joe-Nathan being betrothed?"

"Well, I just thought maybe—"

"Honey, that boy runs from the ladies 'round here like a rabbit on a mission. But trust me, the way he was looking at you the other day, he ain't long for this world, this unhitched world, I mean to say."

Dinah felt lightheaded. "I—I think I need a bit of air, if it's all right with you."

Mama Tavie chortled and tossed her an old threadbare shawl. "That's fine, sugar, but don't wander too far toward the cabins. You wouldn't want to get yourself caught out there, 'specially by the likes of Eli Duggan. Plus, you know us slaves supposed to make ourselves scarce as much as we can. Go on with you, now. Me and Violette can finish up in here. But don't forget. Tomorrow morning early you report to James—you know, the tall butler inside the big house."

Dinah turned aside to hide her smile. She'd noticed it before, that hint of joy in Mama Tavie's voice when she mentioned the butler named James.

"Yes, ma'am. I know the one."

6

Skipping like a six-year-old from the dependency to where the butler was waiting for her didn't seem an option, so Dinah schooled her features and greeted Mr. James on the back verandah like the lady she was trained to be. Never having been past the servants' hall, she was delighted when the kind butler insisted on surreptitiously giving her the grand tour.

Dinah was speechless. Riverwood's interior matched every whit the exterior and grounds she'd admired for weeks. The finest Rococo furniture, expertly arranged atop endless carpet punctuated the grandeur, while Ionic columns surrounded the pocket doors separating the rooms. She followed the graceful butler as he slipped from room to room scarcely able to absorb it all. She ventured a question as the butler pointed out art pieces worth a fortune.

"You like art, Mr. James?"

Understatement. The man's eyes fairly shone as he looked at artwork as though he were seeing it for the first time all over again.

"Under different circumstances in another world, it's what I was meant to be."

The finality of the answer cautioned Dinah against further

probe. Someday, she'd find the right moment to ask him about his work. She felt sure he had some hidden somewhere.

DINAH WAS COMFORTED by Mr. James's presence outside the door of the drawing room as she struggled to stay focused before the mistress of Riverwood. Lost in thoughts of why anyone would need this much opulence, she was stunned by the first words from the mouth of Sarah Susan McMillan.

"I'm informed that we almost lost our kitchen to a fire a few days ago, a fire for which you're responsible."

Dwarfed by the fourteen-foot ceiling, the wisp of a woman sat at a table strewn with writing tools and fine stationery, while Dinah's knees turned to liquid that must rival the consistency of the ink in the exquisite French porcelain inkwell. Dinah swallowed against the drought threatening to claim her mouth and answered with all the aplomb she could muster.

"Yes, Mistress. That is true, but—"

"Your master and I can't simply ignore such an occurrence."

Having often thought of how freeing it might be to wear skirts above the ankles, Dinah reneged. Her legs trembled so fiercely right now that she was ready to hug whoever invented long skirts. Here she'd been expecting to be promoted to doing something she loved, while in truth, this was looking more and more like an investigation that could lead to Jethro and the cotton fields.

Calling upon every bit of poise she'd been taught by Mistress Devereaux, Dinah prepared to engage. She didn't know if it was best to study her feet or square her shoulders. She chose the latter.

"And I do apologize, Mistress McMillan. It was purely accidental. I'm working hard to improve my kitchen skills. Mama Tavie will attest to that."

"Then losing you won't put Tavie in further straits. I worry about her. She tries to do too much."

Dinah's mind searched for every possible refutation. She barely grasped her mistress's words. All she could hear were her chances as a seamstress tripping away like a teasing dream. But if she was to be denied the joy of doing what she loved right away, she simply must be allowed to stay in the kitchen until she could somehow find a way to demonstrate her skills.

"Perhaps I'm not the best at cooking right now, ma'am, but I think Mama Tavie would agree that though progress has been rather slow, I—"

The mistress held up a delicate hand. Dinah's hope plummeted.

"I happened to run upon an inset for a canopy cover in Newport, Rhode Island recently that you designed and created. In the east, your work is being inquired about, and I understand it had become quite sought after downriver before the tragedy with the Devereauxs. It's a wonder your former mistress never spoke of it to me, or perhaps she did, and I simply don't recall. In any case, you're relieved from kitchen duty."

Kicked out of the kitchen. A pause stretched into eternity. Dinah was about to be banished after all she'd done to save herself from her mother's fate. She would not go down without a fight. "Yes, Mistress, but may I—"

"I'd like you to work on a canopy of mine, and perhaps, a set of draperies."

All decorum chased away like a bevy of startled birds, Dinah's heartbeat slowed to naught. She'd done it again, focused so hard on what she'd say next that she missed what God was trying to say to her. When would she ever learn?

"Jonathan has already been instructed to discard my original choice of upholstery for the canopy."

Somehow, perhaps from years of experience, Dinah's brain managed to record her mistress's instructions for the pieces she wanted her to design. Renegade tears made their way down her cheeks. God was truly amazing.

"I-I do thank you, ma'am, with all my heart."

"James will take you to the room in question, and Dinah?"

"Yes, ma'am?"

"I await the results with high expectations. If they're as pleasing as I anticipate, you'll be doing much more."

As she curtseyed and backed out of the palatial room, Dinah felt sure she glimpsed a smile from the mistress of Riverwood. She wouldn't let her down. Now more than ever she had to succeed.

FINALLY, they climbed the wide stairs and stepped across the upper hall to the room assigned to Dinah and the cabinetmaker. Cupping her cheeks in her palms, Dinah squealed with joy.

"A sewing machine! Oh, Mr. James. I thought I'd lost access to a sewing machine forever."

James harrumphed before setting forth a gentle warning. "Do try to contain yourself, miss."

Instantly, Dinah transformed back into the lady she'd been trained to be.

"I beg your pardon, sir. I forget myself, and I should like to thank you for your courtesy and indulgence this morning."

Lifting a brow, this man who'd molded himself into a butler rivaling any she'd ever read about offered a hint of a smile. "Somebody surely has trained you well, miss. Would there be anything else?"

Dinah returned the smile. "No, sir. I thank you."

There was a kindness behind that starch that could easily account for Mama Tavie's attraction to Mr. James, though they appeared polar opposites. Dinah's mind lit up with an idea. She wondered if Mama Tavie might like to learn to read and perhaps articulate a little better. How she'd love to give back to this woman who'd given her so much.

As soon as James was out of sight, Dinah sashayed about the room, her mind flying ahead with abandon like a wild mustang. It was turning out to be a most delicious morning. In detailed fashion, Mrs. McMillan had explained what she wanted her to do, and Dinah was certain she'd understood it all. Now she stood in a room with the most exquisitely crafted bedstead she'd ever seen.

Had the dashing and mysterious Mr. Mayfield really done all this by himself? Dinah heated up with embarrassment. Daydreaming again.

Bolts of rose-colored silk lay atop a daybed along with all the sewing needs and notions she could ever desire, just waiting for her to weave her special magic among the delicate carvings and stately bearings of the cabinetmaker's artistry. Fresh anticipation of working with him, only working with him she reminded herself, wended its way into her heart as she closed her eyes and took a moment to thank the Savior for this enormous blessing.

"Lord Jesus. I've always known you loved me. But until this moment, I had not a notion of how much. Please help me to show myself worthy of Your trust, and Lord, please soften the heart of—"

Another harrumph, more pronounced than before, interrupted her prayer. Mr. James again? She opened her eyes to a doorway filled with Jonathan Mayfield, his gray eyes hooded beneath a scowling brow, his imposing height and broad shoulders holding their own against the large and lofty entrance into the bedroom.

"Mr. Mayfield. I-I didn't expect you quite so early."

An inscrutable shadow crossed his face.

"How interesting, Miss Devereaux. I didn't expect you at all."

JONATHAN TENSED as she stared up at him like a panicked deer. This could not be the seamstress that the accountant spoke of. It simply could not be.

He could swear she was more striking than she'd been three days ago. Mr. McMillan's accountant hadn't mentioned the name of the woman assigned to work with Jonathan. He'd only said she was a slave and a fine seamstress.

It just wasn't possible. How could a quasi-renown designer from New Orleans end up in Mama Tavie's kitchen?

Jonathan couldn't honestly say he was surprised Dinah Devereaux's name hadn't come up in his conversation with the accountant. He understood only too well that unless she'd caused trouble before, the name of a slave wouldn't have been that important. That was simply the way of it.

He hadn't been this nervous since his master called him into his study nine years ago and presented him with his freedom papers, papers that would be ripped to bits and dropped into the Atlantic in a matter of weeks. He'd been clever enough to regain a set of papers and his life back, and he would never let Dinah Devereaux see his momentary discomfiture. Over the weekend, he'd worked hard to come to his senses about this achingly beautiful and mysterious girl who'd cost him his peace and perhaps his freedom. And he meant to keep it that way. Her words from the other day returned with fresh meaning.

"I can make a coat to surpass the one I've destroyed."

"Please say you're not the seamstress."

Glaring at him unabashedly, the girl eased into a chair. Was his shock that transparent, or was she the one who was shocked? Or did she simply think him the bumbling oaf he was feeling right now?

"Sir?"

"I asked the whereabouts of the seamstress. I was told I'd be working with an accomplished seamstress, not a kitchen girl."

She stood to her feet, eyes turned to slits, slender shoulders squared, chin elevated. "I regret to inform you, Mr. Mayfield, but you're looking at the both of them."

Hmmm. Not quite the terrified girl he'd first seen mesmerized before the grease fire the other day.

"I see. Well, I must insist you explain how you came to be such a celebrated seamstress in the first place and what you're doing at Riverwood." Jonathan stepped over the threshold, spread his feet apart, and clasped his biceps. "I rather like to know with whom I'm working, if you don't mind."

"As a matter of fact, Mr. Mayfield, I do mind. May I remind you that it is Mr. McMillan who owns both Riverwood, and unfortunately, me." She stabbed her chest with her pointing finger. "And even human property like me have feelings. Or have you been so busy building fine furniture all your life that you haven't noticed?" Her voice shook with anger. Clearly, she struggled to stay back the tears. "Insofar as I know there's been no order for this particular piece of property to explain herself to you."

Jonathan scrambled to rectify his intentions. "Miss Devereaux, you misunderstand me. By no means was I speaking of your—uh—slave status. I myself was once a slave."

"Then what were you speaking of, O great one?"

What a little spitfire! Jonathan could hardly restrain a chortle.

"Furthermore, if you'll stop to think, you'll know I couldn't be referring to your life as a slave since you essentially reduced me to that station when you threw my freedom into the fire."

Her own fire seemed to go as flat as a flapjack. Despite a valiant effort to corral it, water pooled in her eyes. Jonathan's insides melted. Now he'd gone and done it. He'd hurt her, really hurt her, again. Why did this girl make him act such a boor?

"Miss Devereaux, if you'd just give me space to explain what I—"

"Take all the space you want. I have work to do." With the tips of her fingers, she dabbed beneath her eyes. She strained to lift the bolt of fabric from the daybed and flung it to the floor. Never once looking at Jonathan, she knelt to unwind it.

"I'm afraid you'll have to move that. My men are on their way up here now to complete the delivery, and they'll surely step on it." Either she'd gone stone deaf, or he was being soundly ignored. "Miss Devereaux? Did you hear me?"

She stood and glided across the floor toward the window, in that graceful maddening way of hers, and sifted through a basket of sewing sundries. She tilted her head to the side and bit the side of that disturbing luscious-looking lip again.

"Now let's see. Where could the scissors be?"

Torn between feeling the complete fool and wanting to wipe away the stray tears that seemed to accuse him of some villainous deed, Jonathan turned and left the room. He had to figure something out. Much as he cherished this one job, had worked on it with every drop of the gift God had given him, there was no way he was going to operate in these close quarters with this woman.

Absolutely no way.

HEAVY FOOTSTEPS RETREATED down the stairs while Dinah pressed her forehead against a windowpane and drew long breaths. Anger and confusion combined to choke her, releasing the sobs she'd been desperately holding on to.

The unprecedented gall.

She swiped away the rivulets rapidly coursing down her cheeks. "I will not let that arrogant lout mar my chance to stay at Riverwood."

Hadn't Violette warned her? The man was going to be impossible to work with. All those years in New Orleans she'd worked alone, and liked it. Why Lord, on her first assignment to prove herself here at Riverwood, did she have to be thrown into the same space with a cold, selfish, conceited . . . She'd simply have to request another place to work. Yes, that's what she'd do.

But where? As a slave, what other place in this mansion would be suitable for a slave to work? Would she seat herself comfortably downstairs next to one of the Italian marble fireplaces? Or, perhaps, recline on the revolving sofa in that drawing room she'd just seen? Or maybe she'd set up shop in that voluminous library—close the pocket doors so she could have her privacy!

"For heaven's sakes. Wake up, girl."

Even if by some miracle she found a nook somewhere befitting a slave's workplace, whom did she know well enough to ask the favor of hauling down that sewing machine, should Mistress McMillan agree to such an outlandish idea?

One of the many bells positioned in the rooms of Riverwood rang, startling Dinah and summoning a house slave to do only God-knew-what. Perhaps clean up a spill, or adjust the stays of a corset, or empty a chamber pot or . . . Shame flooded her.

Who do you think you are? The Lord has just given you an opportunity to walk in the gift you love so much. He has also rescued you from not only living your life at someone's constant beck and call, but a backbreaking thankless job in the fields. Or worse, having to leave a motherless child to the side of a church, while you wander away and die like your mother did.

Using the folded pristine rag she'd forgotten Mama Tavie had poked up her sleeve this morning, Dinah tried to control the freshet of tears curling underneath her chin. She glanced at the intricate carving on the mahogany posts and sides of the bed. Beautiful as it was, the bed was indeed unfinished. It longed for the canopy for which she would supply the delicately pleated sunburst pattern. In her silly romantic notions about the free cabinetmaker, she'd overlooked how important it must be to him to have his work properly complemented. She'd let herself hope for at least a warm conversation with him. Something to relieve the heartache and loneliness, the abject fear, she'd lived with for weeks at Riverwood. For years in the Garden District.

But Jonathan Mayfield was a meticulous cabinetmaker with a reputation to protect. How could he possibly know of her schoolgirl dreams about love and marriage, something her heritage and Jack Hudson had made her unfit for anyway? She'd been too hasty in her reply to him.

Dinah looked out at Mrs. McMillan's magnolia tree, the one Mr. McMillan had planted just for her. The one Mama Tavie said his wife loved so much. Perhaps theirs was the perfect love Dinah so desired. But they were free and she was a slave, a slave who was done with her brief tryst with the idea of romance. Mr. Mayfield wanted to know with whom he was working. When he returned, she would most certainly tell him. And then she'd return to her quest for freedom and forget he'd ever existed.

HIS NERVES IN A TANGLE, Jonathan led his workers up the stairs he'd exited just minutes ago. In truth, Benjamin Catlett, who had somehow wormed his way into an odd friendship with Jonathan, and the young apprentice named Henry could do this job of placement and trim work as well as he could. And he couldn't wait to turn it over to them. A few instructions to these fine woodworkers God had blessed him with, and he would return to his shop, never to see this room and Miss Devereaux again.

He hated the way he'd behaved earlier, causing her to believe he thought himself better than the slaves when the opposite was true. If he was honest, he'd admit to being less than they. Though he'd worked the fields as a child, he wasn't sure he was man enough anymore to survive doing something every single day other than what he loved. Just as he'd not been man enough all these years to demand better payment for his work. Just as he had failed to defend himself on that ship so long ago when his first set of papers was destroyed.

Jonathan shook off those haunting thoughts of failure. Miss Devereaux had shown remarkable mettle in there. He'd give her that. Calling him out on the hurtful things he'd said then going ahead with her assignment as if he wasn't there. If Jonathan should ever even think of marrying someone, which he never would, it would be a woman with spirit, like Dinah Devereaux.

He grimaced. There he went again, thinking of marriage. All the more reason to bank his feelings and get away from this job as soon as possible. Stopping at the door, Jonathan bellowed orders as he directed Benjamin and Henry into the room.

"Careful there, my man! Don't scratch the finish on the armoire before the puzzle is even pieced together. You, sir." He pointed at Henry. "Gently, if you please."

Gracefully lifting herself from the place on the floor where she'd begun creating the sunburst, the girl arrested his gaze.

"Mr. Mayfield. May I have a word with you?"

Jonathan stared at her. He could swear his heart leapt to the other side of his chest at the sound of her voice. He resisted the urge to place a hand over it to try to steady it. Back straight, tears vanished, she owned him with those liquid almond eyes of hers.

"It'll only take a few minutes if that's what you're concerned about, then I'll . . ."

Determined to maintain his façade, Jonathan dragged his gaze away from her and halted her words with an outstretched palm. He noticed the tiniest muscle twitching beneath one of her eyes. But she folded her hands across her midriff, kept her head high and waited just as he'd ordered. He sensed that again he'd belittled her. Chances were she was about to even the score. He decided to seek a truce or at the least, a stall.

"If it's the canopy you're concerned about, we're about to place it within your reach." He reached in his shirt pocket. "I've taken the liberty of writing down the measurements of the sunburst, and my men have already removed the fabric design that wasn't to Mrs. McMillan's liking, so—"

"Pardon, sir. But I know my job. Mrs. McMillan already gave me the dimensions. It's not my assignment here that I want to speak to you about. I need to ask a favor." Her voiced thinned as embarrassment about whatever she was about to ask seemed to swallow her whole. "I-I need to speak to you alone."

Alone? Lord, what have I gotten myself into? I've acted in an ungentlemanly, ungodly way this morning, and I don't know how to undo it without letting down my defense.

But though he couldn't think of a single reason to refuse her, maintain his defense he would. Besides, in a few minutes none of it would matter because he'd be headed back to his house and shop in town for good. He gestured toward the two men.

"If you'd be good enough, fetch the canopy from the wagon." When the men's footsteps died on the stairs, he turned toward Miss Devereaux, heart pounding against his chest like the thud of a lumberjack's axe. "Have your say."

"I'd like to apologize." Courage bled through her trembling voice, causing an absurd desire to comfort her.

"Apologize?"

"We both have jobs to do and you deserve to know with whom you're working. Like all good artists, you value the integrity of your work more than the living it brings you. Am I not correct?"

Jonathan was afraid to try his voice, afraid its sound would ring true to the ugly frog he felt like right now, that is, if it didn't come out sounding like a beardless youth. So he dipped his chin in agreement.

"I was a foundling, laid near the steps of a church shortly after my birth, a birth I was later to discover that killed my mother. My former master always said his finding me had been an act of God. I must have slept through the night. Had I cried out and been heard, I surely would have been delivered to an orphanage, or worse, thrown into the Mississippi River. He set out before dawn that June morning simply for a walk. I must have gotten hungry at the right time, for I began to cry just as he passed by."

"Are you saying a white gentleman simply took you home?"

She lowered her head and stumbled over her words. "Master Devereaux said he took one look at me and decided I was too beautiful to ignore."

Your master was quite discerning. Jonathan crossed his arms again and tried to shore up his no-nonsense stance, which was flagging desperately.

"So why did he sell you to Mr. McMillan?"

Dinah's head jerked up. "What? Who told you that? He did not *sell* me. It wasn't like that at all."

"Really? Then how did you end up at Riverwood if you weren't purchased? Did you simply sail up river and apply for the job?" Jonathan couldn't believe how small and nasty that comment came out. A shadow fell over her lovely face.

"No need for sarcasm, sir."

Determination rested upon that perfectly-lined brow of hers as she redoubled her efforts to remain calm. Who was this woman, anyway? A runaway somehow able to escape the usual checks from a family like the McMillans? And how had the usually astute Mama Tavie become so completely taken with her, when obviously Miss Devereaux was about as skillful with a mixing spoon as a yearling child? Ah, but she was elegant and beautiful enough to fool the most experienced in discretion, even Jonathan himself if he'd allow it.

Talons of suspicion raked over him. Could she be a discarded worker from a brothel in the Under-the-Hill district who'd somehow wheedled her way into Mama Tavie's kitchen?

"By chance, did you happen to come from one of the . . . ahem . . . houses under the Hill?"

She gasped, while Jonathan cringed at his own stupid bumbling attempt to garner an excuse to dismiss this lovely, intelligent, available woman from his thoughts and his workplace. Whoever heard of a runaway dropping in on a plantation? Or a prostitute deciding to try her hand at being a kitchen slave? Without a doubt, desperation had taken him over. Between finally being able to negotiate his own finances and losing his papers, had he become so addlepated?

Eyes snapping, hands fisted to her sides, Dinah Devereaux's fury rammed into Jonathan straight on. "What did you say?"

She looked as though she was trying to decide whether to lam him upside his head with one of the tools lying about or simply spit in his eye. Clearly that remark about the possibility of an unsavory profession under the hill had hit a nerve. Jonathan was beginning to really dislike himself.

"Miss Devereaux, I'm so very sorry. I sincerely ask your forgiveness. I've been unkind. I don't know what's come over me lately. Please, have a seat and go on."

She trembled so violently that he wondered if perhaps someone should be notified.

"Are—are you going to be all right? Should I fetch Mama Tavie?"

She shook her head, obviously deliberately calming herself.

"Next time, sir, you should verify your information before making such dreadful assumptions."

She found a chair and released a tremulous sigh, the visible anger replaced with a hint of dread in her lovely eyes.

"Last month, I was in my attic room in the middle of the night, bent over the final hand-stitching details of a set of draperies, when I decided to go down to the next floor to one of the terraces to enjoy the night skies for a bit." She smiled at that revelation.

"So you're a stargazer, are you?"

"You might say that. At any rate, just as I was about to leave, I detected a parched smell unlike anything Cook had ever prepared. I looked toward my door and saw tendrils of smoke crawling from underneath.

When I opened it, smoke came after me from both ends of the short hall. From habit, I suppose, I closed the door behind me before I ran for the stairs. But I was met by a wall of flames. I screamed, but the fire was so loud and hot it practically choked off the sounds coming from my throat. I heard the noise of a crash and knew the attic stairs were going. All I could think of was the childless old couple sleeping beneath me on the front side of the house. I prayed they had escaped—that they hadn't been overcome by the fierce smoke that was sucking the very air from my lungs."

Dinah paused. That same look of terror Jonathan had seen in the kitchen the other day settled in her eyes. Now he understood. Again a fierce urge to comfort this elusive girl swept over him. But he mustn't go near her. Not now. Not ever.

"Instinct sent me scrambling back into my room, but it took the voice of the Lord to jar my memory as to what to do. There was a set of backstairs leading from the attic room, stairs I rarely even thought of, since I'd always been given the run of the house except on occasions of company. As I fled down those outside stairs, flames appeared in every window. My lungs ached. My eyes burned. But I managed to make it around to the front of the house hoping to find the Devereauxs waiting on the outside for me. They'd be devastated, I thought, but safe. They had to be, they were the closest thing to a family I'd ever had. But they were nowhere to be found.

"I screamed again but nothing came. I was running toward the front door when . . . when Jack . . ." Her voice shrank to a whisper. Her hands flailed as she seemed to choke down some horrid recollection. "A f-friend of my master's arm caught me, forcing me back toward the front gate. I fought as hard as I could to get away so I could try to get them out. And, at length, I freed myself just before tripping on the cobblestone walk and hitting my head. When I awakened, I was in the police station. Late the following day, I was put on a boat bound for Natchez."

Jonathan thought she looked about to collapse. But something—pride, fear, he knew not what—wouldn't let her. All he could think of was how awful he'd been to her after all she'd been through. He never even offered to help her earlier as she struggled with the bolt of fabric, and then to randomly accuse her of being a lady of the night!

Out of nowhere, she started to cry again, demolishing the little remaining defense he held against her vulnerability. Before good sense could intervene, he was across the room holding her, speaking soothingly to her.

"Please forgive me, Dinah. I am so sorry. I had no idea."

She burrowed her face into his chest, babbling about the "bit of air" she'd taken last night and how, for a moment, she thought it might have cost her the place she so desperately needed in Riverwood's kitchen. Instead, Mama Tavie had made her the happiest girl in Mississippi.

"I-I love the night skies and the gardens. M-my old mistress always allowed me t-to get a bit of air on the terrace."

Shuffling feet and grunts in the stairwell signaled the reentrance of Benjamin and Henry. He'd meant to gently take hold of her shoulders, ease her back a bit. But before he could, she shot away from him with the force of a cannon.

She was terrified. Had he done something inappropriate that he didn't realize?

She pulled a plain square cloth from her sleeve and tried to wipe away the imagined damage to her flawless face.

She should have real handkerchiefs. Lacy, frilly ones—dozens of them. All shapes, colors, and sizes . . .

Jonathan blinked away the ridiculous musings. What had happened to him these last couple of days? He was beginning to daydream like a mindless young girl swept away by an ill-fated romance. He strode over to the men who carefully hefted the wood pieces through the door.

"Careful." He moved in closer to help them angle the circular half-tester piece. "This is a one of a kind piece."

At this point he hardly cared. But barking needless orders was one of his time-tested mind-numbing techniques, and he knew Benjamin and Henry knew that. He blew out a breath of relief. Good. Back in control.

"Do you still want us to take over here, sir?" Benjamin's teasing voice got his attention.

Sheepishly, Jonathan sneaked a glance at Benjamin and Henry. How could he just up and leave the girl after what she'd just revealed and all he'd put her through?

"Uh, no. I suppose you should . . . go back to town, that is."

The men could barely contain their snickering as what must have sounded like foreign halfhearted words flew out of Jonathan's usually decisive mouth. Jonathan was going to have to be extremely careful around this woman or she'd make him the laughing stock of Natchez.

7

Dinah sidestepped as Mama Tavie nearly collided with her at the door of the kitchen.

"Oh, 'scuse me, honey."

Barely regaining her balance before hitting the pavers, Dinah straightened her skirts and laughed. "No harm done, Mama Tavie, but it looks like you're in a bit of a hurry." She followed as the older woman darted back inside the kitchen and planted a kiss on Emerald's cheek.

"Now, you mind Violette and Miss Dinah whilst I'm gone. I'll be back in a few minutes."

"Yes'm."

"Dinah, honey, you know you don't have to do this, but I left you a job right there on the cutting table since you mean to do it anyways. Keep this up, and you gonna be a right good cook one day soon, you know that? I just need to check with James about tomorrow's supper. I'm leaving the door open to let off some of this heat."

"Yes, ma'am."

Dinah smiled as she picked up the paring knife. It seemed James and Mama Tavie found more and more they needed to talk about these days. Was love in the air? The thought of the two of them together warmed her. Given a chance, her mother might have been like Mama Tavie. But her father? The very idea of him alongside Mr. James's name made her sick.

She wiped her brow and began peeling the potatoes as carefully as she'd worked on the rose-colored silk all day. Though relishing every minute of her new assignment, Dinah hadn't failed to help out in the kitchen when she could. She'd peeled potatoes near perfectly this weekend, and she didn't want to mar her improving record.

"Violette, would you mind taking a look at these to see if I'm leaving too much potato in the peel?"

Behaving as though Dinah had never entered the room, Violette continued to poke into the pot of boiling pig feet as she stretched her neck toward the pot of beef roast Mama Tavie'd left simmering. She directed a smile at little Emerald who strutted around the kitchen pretending to be the lady of Riverwood.

"Reckon what it would be like to eat your fill of that beef Mama Tavie cooking for the big house 'stead of pork all the livelong time, Emerald? You ever thought about that?"

Emerald took a seat on the floor. "Dunno," she said, her face alight with wonder. "But Mr. James told Mama Tavie lots of beef be left over after supper sometimes." She crossed her legs and rested her chin in her hands. "Violette?"

"Hmmm?"

"Where beef come from?"

Violette let loose the trademark snort she always offered when a good answer wasn't forthcoming. "Must be something real special, since me and you ain't never had it in our lives."

Truly, Violette? In the short time Dinah had been at Riverwood, she'd seen Violette squirrel away enough beef, and every other conceivable edible, to feed the Roman army. Emerald continued to press for answers.

"Thought you said that was beef wrapped up in your head rag

the other night." Dinah fought and failed to suppress a giggle as Violette flushed crimson.

"What's got you so tickled, Miss Lady? You ever had your fill of beef?"

Emerald bounded up from the floor like the sun at dawn. "Have you, Miss Dinah? Where beef come from, Miss Dinah? Tell us who makes it!"

Fearing Violette's retribution if she dared answer the little girl, Dinah hesitated. "Well, sweetheart, I don't think—"

"Pleeez, Miss Dinah? Tell us."

Dinah loved Emerald's pure curiosity. Despite her best efforts to hedge her heart, this little golden-colored girl with coarse wiry plaits thick enough to rope a steer delighted her in ways different from any one else at Riverwood.

"Oh, all right, then. Well, you see, beef comes from a cow just as milk does."

Shock doubled the size of Emerald's honeyed eyes.

"Folks eat the milk cows?" She waggled her tiny finger at Dinah. "That's mean, Miss Dinah, taking their milk and then eating the poor cows." She shook her braids from side to side. "God don't like us to be mean. Anyhow, if folks kill up the cows, what they go'n do when they need more milk, Miss Dinah?"

"Humph," smirked Violette. "Sew that one up to suit us, Miss Seamstress."

Dinah laid down her paring knife and scooped Emerald into her arms. Pulling up a chair, she placed her on her lap and snuggled her close. Despite Violette's objections, she snuggled this precocious little bundle as often as she could. Mercy, me. The sweetness of her touch was as rare as . . . an emerald? My, but this felt good—right. She gave her an extra little squeeze. Maybe she'd start telling her stories each night if Violette let her.

"When God made little girls like you and me and Violette, He meant for—"

A string of giggles filled the tiny kitchen. "You and Violette ain't no li'l girls."

"True. But we once were. Anyhow, God meant for all of us, girls and boys, men and women, to have plenty to eat so we can grow up strong."

"Colored people, too?"

"That's right, God meant for us colored people to have enough, too. And yes, little Miss Curious, I've had beef and it's very, very tasty when someone like Mama Tavie cooks it." Emerald tittered and squirmed as Dinah lovingly poked her sides. "The Bible, the very best book on earth, says it's all right to eat animals if we're hungry. He told the first humans they were to be in charge of animals. But you're right, He doesn't want us to be mean to them. If we're hungry, we may use them for food, but we shouldn't mistreat them just to be mean. The good thing is He keeps producing them so that we can have enough milk and meat at the same time. Understand?"

Dinah paused, praying Emerald would accept her less-than-stellar answer. "Yes'm. I think so. Now where do hogs come from?"

"Cincinnati, you little squirt. Where else?"

Dinah's breath caught, as the aroma of wood and varnish, mixed with the distinct smell of a male laborer, wafted into her space. There in the kitchen door stood Jonathan Mayfield, arms crossed, one hip slacked, a boyish grin on his face. Though he obviously hadn't had time to freshen up after the day's work, to Dinah he looked more regal than ever. Visions of her own kitchen, her very own "Prince and Emerald" waiting for supper, enfolded her like a priceless counterpane as the child slid from her lap and ran toward Jonathan.

"Mr. Jonathan! You comed to see me?"

"Indeed I did, Squirt."

Stooping to Emerald's height, he wrapped her in a hug. Other than with Mama Tavie, Dinah had never seen him this relaxed. She smiled. Her lap was empty. But her heart was full of what might have been had she been born free.

Violette laid down her turning fork and rushed over to greet Jonathan.

"Hey, Mr. Mayfield. Mama Tavie made teacakes. You want some?" She hurried to the sideboard, picked up a bowl of teacakes, and poked them toward his nose. "I know she don't mind you having some."

"Matter of fact I do mind." Mama Tavie came through the door, a wide grin enveloping her small face. She swept the bowl of cakes from beneath Jonathan's chin. "Joe-Nathan, when the last time you had a decent meal?"

"Well, actually I—"

"That's what I thought. So you just sit down over there 'til supper's ready. After supper, then you eat your bellyful of teacakes. Supper already fixed for the big house." She looked at Dinah. "All we have to do is take it over to the warming room and let James's bunch serve it. Then we can all sit down and eat together."

A frown cut furrows between Jonathan's brows, shouting his resistance to that suggestion. Dinah couldn't help noticing he'd not once looked at her since he entered the kitchen, though they'd just finished working together less than an hour ago in what she'd imagined as sweet silence.

"As I was saying, Mama Tavie, I actually stopped in to say I'll be taking my supper up to my room tonight. If you'd be so kind to fix a tray for me."

Mama Tavie jabbed a fist onto her waist. "Well, that's the only way you gonna get it. You go'n have to take it 'cause I ain't giving it to you. I hardly get a chance to see you as it is, and now you go'n come out here, sleeping in a room close enough for me to spit into, and not even set down to supper with me? Nope, I ain't having it."

Jonathan looked completely bewildered, his easy manner from moments ago locked in a rigid shrug. Dinah couldn't help but feel sorry for him. He had, in fact, worked very hard today and most likely simply wanted to go to bed early. Perhaps she could help him this once.

"Mr. Mayfield, how's your shoulder?"

Jonathan looked befuddled and a little cautious. "Shoulder?"

"Mama Tavie, did you know Mr. Mayfield's shoulder's been bothering him?" She locked gazes with him.

"O-o-oh. Yes." Gingerly, he moved his shoulder back and forth. Very convincing. Dinah dipped her chin signaling her approval.

"Probably too much lifting lately." *I know, I know, Lord. We're way shy of the truth. But I did see him rub his shoulder once or twice today.*

"Where? Lemme see. How'd you do that, son?" Mama Tavie bustled over to Jonathan and pressed hard into his shoulder, while Jonathan duly winced. "Well, why didn't you say something? You can't be expected to sit up at no table with your shoulder all achy like that! Violette, go get the liniment. We gonna have you fixed up in no time."

Dinah had never been so tickled in her life. My, how Mama Tavie loved this big hunk of a man. Smart as she was about everything else, she obviously hadn't stopped to think about this one. Surely, if he'd put up molding all day with that shoulder, he could manage supper. Any second now, she would burst with laughter if she didn't find something to distract her.

"Now you just go rest yourself for a while," said Mama Tavie, shooing Jonathan toward the door. "I'll get one of the yard men to bring you a plate directly."

Good. Jonathan must be relieved Mama Tavie had forgotten the liniment.

"Yes, ma'am," he said looking back over his shoulder. Dinah glanced up in time to see him wink and mouth, "Thank you."

Too surprised to speak, she wasn't able to whisper the customary, "You're welcome." But she guessed the involuntary smile splitting her face said it all.

"He just don't want to eat with us slaves is all." Violette's voice sliced into Dinah's exhilaration.

But relishing the friendly gesture sent her way by the most maddening man she'd ever met, Dinah chose to ignore her. And for the first time in weeks, she felt really hungry.

"Anything else I can do, Mama Tavie?"

"Yep, sure is." Mama Tavie pushed a plate of fixings onto Dinah's arm. Plastering a firm hand at Dinah's back, she hastened her toward the door. She practically threw her over the threshold. Something was fishy. Just outside the door, Dinah balked.

"What are you doing?"

"Giving you something to do. Take this here plate to Joe-Nathan."

"B-but Mama Tavie, didn't you say one of the men would take Jonathan's supper up to him?"

"You see any mens around here? Plus, they don't take too kindly to Joe-Nathan yet. Poor little thing. He probably starving up there by his self."

Dinah stifled a chuckle. Poor little thing? This slip of a woman looking up at her could almost fit into one of Jonathan Mayfield's pant legs. Yet here she was angling back into the past for the little boy she once knew.

"And take this with you so you can see 'bout that shoulder whilst you there." Mama Tavie winked and shot Dinah a knowing grin. "I figure since he didn't know he was hurting 'til you told him, you ought to be the one to rub that liniment into his shoulder."

Dinah's hand flew to her mouth. "Mama Tavie!"

"You don't mind doing this for ole Mama Tavie, do you, honey? Hurry on, now. The mens be here any minute for supper."

"Yes, ma'am." Clearly she, Jonathan too for that matter, had been outfoxed.

STANDING at the foot of the stairs, Dinah gripped the edges of a wooden platter and tried to temper her erratic breathing. Was it the aroma coming from the plate of steaming pig feet, onions, skillet cornbread, and boiled potatoes that had her feeling woozy? Most assuredly not. All she had to do was knock on the door and leave the platter. But not quite yet. She placed the covered tray, along with the bottle of liniment, on a stair step of the twin dependency and looked back across the square toward the one she'd just left.

If only you'd kept your mouth shut in there.

She caught her lip between her teeth and stared up into the narrow curved stairway. Mama Tavie's sweet little ploy had given her a full case of the jitters. No matter how uncomfortable it might've been to sit at supper with Jonathan Mayfield, certainly it would have been better than being alone with him in that room up there, if only for a matter of seconds. Deciding she needed a few minutes to compose herself, she backed away from the steps.

The diamond-studded twilight arcing over the sprawling estate was balm to her nerves. Her heart rate eased into a steady rhythm as she slipped to the edge of the back verandah stretching the entire length of the house. With proper care, this home would last for centuries.

From the widow's walk that crowned it to the Doric columns that seemed to proudly bear it up, Riverwood breathed precision. Dinah's eyes fastened onto the imposing twelve-paned windows, now turned into liquid gold from the many lamps and chandeliers behind them streaming into the darkness. A whisper of wonder escaped her chest as she observed the elegance once again.

Yet as lovely as it was, if she owned a house and property this grand, she'd trade it all for just one person to treasure her and be treasured by her in return. Just the thought of a family to hold and care for made her want to fly to the front of Riverwood, embrace one of the splendid columns, then chase herself around it with the abandon of a child. Arms wrapped around her waist, she closed her eyes and reveled in the vision.

Other arms stout and sweaty, tightened around hers.

"What—?"

A sticky hand clamped down over her mouth, while a stream of hot breath coated her neck. Jethro?

"Hey, there, Sugar."

Dinah recognized that voice. It wasn't Jethro's, but it was equally as nauseating. Eli Duggan, who'd been throwing suggestive remarks her way ever since she'd been here, sheathed her body like a greasy glove.

"Don't you know it's against Massa McMillan's rules for you to be out here like this? Sassy thing like you might just try to run away."

He eased his moist palm from her mouth. Dinah wanted to spit. "Now don't you do nothin' crazy like scream. Do, and ole Eli might have to hurt you. Too, the mistress might hear you, and you just might end up in the fields." Barely releasing his clutch on her shoulders, he wheeled her around to face him.

"Taking your new man some supper?"

Resisting the urge to scream, Dinah bit out a low deliberate retort. "He. Is. Not. My. Man."

"Aw, c'mon now, sweet thing. Don't take ole Eli for a fool." He jerked his head toward the dependency where Jonathan was housed. "Been standing in the shadows over yonder watching how nervous you is 'bout taking up that food. Seen you earlier today too, giddy as a filly on your way to the kitchen after you was shut up in that room with Mr. Biggity all day."

"Why you, foul-minded scoundrel. Turn me loose or I'll—"

He caught hold of her raised wrist with one of those damp

smelly hands. "A little cheeky there, ain't cha? Now you just calm yourself and think on what I just said about them fields. It ain't no fun. Take it from somebody what knows."

Dinah felt faint, the tips of her fingers tingling with fear. Thinking he might be right about the fields and wondering what he was going to do to her right now, she willed herself quiet and inwardly sought heaven.

What time I am afraid, I will put my trust in you.

"That's it. Just settle on down. This be just a warming up of what you got to look forward to in the future. Ole Eli go'n let you go ahead and deliver that supper tonight." Eli nodded toward the kitchen. "Don't want that tattling bossy cook in there asking about why I ain't at the table and then reporting it to Massa, so I'm going on in to supper. But remember, sooner or later ole Eli gets what he wants. And I declare if these days he don't want you worser than anything he's wanted in a long time."

As quickly as he'd come upon her, Eli faded from view. Just like Jack. Talking about himself in third person as though he had some type of mysterious other royal self. Just like Jack. Suddenly she felt she'd been cloaked with something soiled yet familiar. And just like with Jack . . . and Jethro, guilt and shame sidled up to her consciousness, sending her thoughts spiraling downward. She gripped the stair rail of the verandah aware of how close she'd come to a repeat of her ruin. Although Natchez had only shown signs of true winter, Dinah's teeth chattered.

"Lord, why did you send me to Riverwood? To remind me of how flawed and base I really am?"

An answer too ready to be God's truth whispered to Dinah's soul. *Don't you see? A man like Jonathan Mayfield would never take a second look at you. You were born to your mother's fate to attract beastly men. It's in your blood. You'll never escape it.*

Yet she couldn't shake the lie, couldn't send it back to hell where the God in her knew it belonged. Hyperventilating, she cupped her hands over her face, breathing deliberately until the rhythm of her lungs evened out. She had escaped Eli's advances

tonight but how about tomorrow? The day after? A week
from now?

Slowly she made her way back to the stairwell leading to
Jonathan's room and placed the bottle of liniment on the edge of
the tray. Holding on to the wall, she took the first step toward
the top of the stairs. Time to get this over. Once he found out it
was she, he'd probably make her leave everything at the door
anyhow.

THINKING he'd heard a noise below, Jonathan searched the
outside darkness from his small window. But there was nothing,
at least not that he could see. He stripped down to his trousers
and stretched out on the lumpy mattress to wait for his supper.
Hands clasped behind his head, legs dangling over the edge, he
gazed at the low hovering ceiling. Violette's words about his not
wanting to mingle with the slaves were running a loop in his
mind.

"He just don't want to eat with us slaves is all."

Problem was the words were true. For six long years, each
time he'd had to come to a plantation to install an order, he'd
seen himself in every worker in every field. A matching self that
he was powerless to rescue. A self that no less deserved a chance
at freedom than he. The familiar prayer from David plumbed
the depths of his soul.

*"Who am I, O Lord GOD? and what is my house, that thou hast
brought me hitherto?"*

Who was Jonathan to actually *earn* a living when his brothers
and sisters worked twice as hard for naught?

Unbidden, his thoughts shifted. Jonathan found himself half-
smiling. Yes, Violette had been right tonight. But not for the
reasons she supposed, nor ones he cared to admit. Tonight,
Jonathan's not wanting to join Mama Tavie and the rest of the
slaves at supper had more to do with a riveting yet sweet, strong

yet heartbreakingly vulnerable woman named Dinah Devereaux than anything else.

Each day with her would mire him deeper and deeper into feelings he couldn't afford. Why hadn't he just turned this job over to Benjamin and Henry and returned to the safety of his shop in town when he'd had the chance? Why did he always have to try to take the high road and prove what a confident man of integrity he was?

He ran his fingers through his untamed curls. What was keeping Mama Tavie's tray? He was bone tired and couldn't wait to eat his plate of food and fall into a dreamless sleep. He felt isolated up here in this little box of a room. But at least he didn't have to stumble all over himself at supper trying to avoid Dinah. He turned his back to the door and beat the already-limp pillow into what looked like an ill-constructed washboard.

A timid womanish-sounding knock pecked at the door. But Mama Tavie had said a man would bring his supper, and Mama Tavie always did what she said. Jonathan burrowed into his wavy pillow and groaned a muffled invitation.

"Come in."

Sounding almost infantile, a voice called softly to him. "Mr. Mayfield? I have your supper."

Dinah?

Jonathan leapt from the bed and scrambled for his shirt. Too late. His doorway was already aglow with the vision of Dinah Devereaux. Holding her head in that tilted way of hers, her high ebony cheekbones and oval eyes shone with moisture. Had she been crying? Toes pointed in, the only thing that mollified the ingrained elegance she exuded, she gripped the tray as though it were a lifeline.

"Miss Devereaux! I . . . I didn't expect you."

Quickly, she withdrew her gaze, looking past him toward the darkened window. "Seems I heard that from you once today already." She placed the platter of savory smelling food on the tiny table next to the wall and started toward the door. "Well, I'll be leaving then."

"No! I mean . . . I didn't mean it that way. Stay a bit. Please. You saved me in there. I want to thank you."

What irony. She'd saved him from herself, and now here she was.

"I'm sorry but I promised Mama Tavie I'd be back shortly, and I've been gone much too long."

Jonathan scrambled to lighten the mood and secure his pants. "A bit of stargazing perhaps?"

She averted her eyes. "S-something like that."

First the tears. Now this despairing look. Something had happened since they parted. She was definitely not the same girl he'd winked at a half hour ago. Jonathan longed to at least inquire. But he couldn't afford a repeat of what happened earlier today when she'd ended up in his arms.

"Besides. It wouldn't be proper for me to remain here overlong."

"Of course. You're right. Forgive me." A little voice whispered he must be looking a fright just now, standing in his stocking feet, the buttons of his shirt feeling misaligned. "Anyhow, I'd like to thank you again for what you did in there, easing me from beneath Mama Tavie's thumb."

Back turned, she took several more steps, her graceful body gliding beneath the slave issue dress she was forced to wear as though she'd practiced at the king's court. "Good night, Mr. Mayfield."

"Wait, please." He couldn't let her go. He had to ask the question that had been on his mind for three days.

"Yes?"

"I'd just like to know, why has a lady as exquisite as you . . why have you never married?"

Finally she turned to face him. Something near what he'd seen when he'd accused her of being a prostitute passed over her visage. Only this time it was fraught not with anger but sadness.

"Numerous reasons, sir, not the least of which is the so-called institution of slavery." She paused as though struggling with whether to add another of the myriad reasons or simply leave it there. Her voice faltered. "But then, Mr. Mayfield, perhaps I'm simply not fit for that other God-ordained institution called marriage."

Again, she turned away, softly closing the door behind her. Jonathan listened to her steps descend into the night. He'd never met the likes of this woman. Somehow he had to learn more about her. Just out of curiosity, of course.

8

Blessedly, Dinah had managed to return to the kitchen last night unscathed by Eli. But for how long? A chill blew across the lovely spacious upstairs room of Riverwood as the memory of Eli's probing hands tried to seize her.

"Lord, deliver me from this lurking evil."

Resisting the thought of Eli's threats, she crawled around on her hands and knees holding several pins between her lips as she meticulously formed the silk pleats into a perfect disc. She glanced over at the canopy propped against the far wall. Pins bounced up and down as she muttered her growing excitement.

"This soft rose color is going to be simply perfect against that mahogany."

The circular sunburst pattern to be set into the exquisite canopy Jonathan Mayfield had created was taking shape. She hadn't felt this energized in weeks. Could a certain ruggedly smooth furniture maker have anything to do with this feeling?

She warmed inside. Upstairs in his room last night, there'd been a guarded sweetness about him. But earlier yesterday, when they'd been alone together in their workroom, he'd done something that had endeared him to her forever.

He'd hugged her.

Struggling to keep from dropping the pins from her lips, much worse, swallowing one of them, she fought to keep a burst of laughter from escaping her soul.

Calling her Dinah, he had actually held her in his arms. Thinking on it made her shiver from embarrassment. She hadn't planned the sudden unraveling in front of the poised cabinetmaker. But the feeling she'd experienced when he held her close had taken her to a place of caring she'd never experienced before, the thing she'd been searching for that day when she'd allowed herself to cry in Jack Hudson's arms. Never once had her former owners touched her. Never rocked her nightmares away. Never kissed away the hurt when she'd snagged a fingernail or stubbed a toe.

But she understood why. Physical affection between slave and owner was practically unheard of. Except for the fleeting seconds when Mr. Mayfield had held her in his arms, she'd never known how utterly precious the human touch could be. Nothing like the feel of Eli's hands last night and nothing like that afternoon in '51 when Jack . . . No! . . . No! No! No!

She chased the thoughts of unwanted touches back into their filthy corner. It was a luscious morning, calling for only sweet thoughts. And a caring embrace from Mr. Mayfield was a very sweet thought.

"Good morning, Miss Devereaux."

Miss Devereaux? What happened to the girl called Dinah, the one he'd so sweetly embraced yesterday? Her spirits dipped. She'd hoped today he would ask to call her by her first name. Then perhaps she could call him by his.

"Good morning, Mr. Mayfield."

Noisy silence set in as she tried to return her focus to the sunburst, while Mr. Mayfield retrieved more unhung trim work from the corner. He set about examining the ceiling. Nothing Dinah could do but follow his lead and apply herself to her own task. Her favorite thimble slipped from her hands and rolled beneath the armoire.

"Oh."

Wordlessly, Mr. Mayfield strode over and lifted a side of the armoire, while in a futile attempt to remain modest, she knelt to get the thimble from beneath the massive piece.

"Thank you."

He lowered the armoire and offered a barely perceptible nod before placing a ladder against the wall furthest from where Dinah worked. Setting his project in order, he climbed the ladder and began nailing the intricate molding at right angles to the ceiling.

"Ouch!"

Dinah dropped her sewing notions and rushed over as he backed down the ladder and made a wide berth around her to his toolbox where he stooped and pulled out some bandages. He flexed his left thumb as Dinah hovered.

"What happened? Here, sit down and let me help you."

"I don't need to sit down, Miss Devereaux. All I need is to stop squandering time and get back to work, as I'm sure you do."

Oh, dear. The old Jonathan Mayfield was back with added support, and Dinah had just about had her fill of the big proud churlish spellbinding cabinetmaker. She folded her arms across her chest and tapped her toe on the polished floor.

"You will sit down and let me look at your thumb, Mr. Mayfield, or I will call for Mama Tavie and have her do it."

One brow shot up before settling in to a deep scowl. "What did you say?"

"I think you heard me. Now sit."

Sulking like a six-year-old, he eased his muscular frame to the floor. "Is this some kind of exacting of payment for making up that lie about my shoulder last night?"

Dinah cringed. "It wasn't exactly a lie. I did catch you exercising your shoulders a couple of times yesterday."

"Habit. That's all."

He scooted back toward the wall and jutted his thumb toward her. The stiff way he held the rest of his body made

Dinah almost wonder whether "quarantined" had been stamped across her forehead without her knowledge. Kneeling before him to get a closer look, she noticed a deep scar in the center of his palm. Strange place to have a scar that long and prominent. Maybe she'd ask about it someday.

"Mmm. Doesn't really look that bad, but I would think you might need to apply a little liniment?" Dinah's attempt at humor sank like a basket of rocks. "And a light bandage if you're to continue with the trim work."

Cautiously moving his head in closer to inspect the redness, he grunted, his rhythmic breathing softly warming her brow and sending unfamiliar prickles along her spine.

"Don't know how I managed to get so careless. The last time I missed a nail and struck my thumb I was still apprenticed to Thomas Day in North Carolina."

"North Carolina?"

Dinah's hope rose at this volunteered information. Better to keep looking down though. He might decide to clam up again. She tried to pour all her visible concentration into wrapping the injured thumb.

"I just assumed you were born here in Natchez. If I may ask, who is Thomas Day?"

At the mention of this Thomas Day, something seemed to instantly unwind in him as though the simple repeating of the man's name was healing all by itself. Settling his broad back against the wall, he slid his good hand into a pocket of his shirt that lay over his heart.

"Except for Mr. Johnson, I can't think of anyone who has influenced the few good decisions I've made more."

Dinah kept her eyes on the smarting thumb and said nothing. Could Jonathan be speaking of the well-known Negro barber here in Natchez by the name of William Johnson? Oh, surely not. Though his accomplishments as a free black man struck pride in her, she'd also heard he owned slaves. And for Dinah, that cast an impenetrable pall over his other achievements. Jonathan influenced by a slave owner? Of course not.

"At any rate, without Thomas Day, I never would have..."

Confusion clouded Jonathan's eyes as he clamped his mouth shut and pulled back his uninjured hand from over his heart. Immediately, Dinah sensed what he'd searched for: his freedom papers. His jaw muscles worked as he turned away from her. He was never going to let this go, and why should he? The knowledge of freedom must be like having a second skin.

"A relative of yours, this Mr. Day?"

"Oh, certainly not, though he treated me like one. I was just a homeless skinny boy who showed up at the doorstep of his shop in Caswell County, North Carolina one day in '51. When Mr. Day found out what I'd been through just to learn under him, he took me under his wing."

He winced as she tightened the bandage. The big baby. Hadn't he just hefted up that colossal armoire so she could retrieve her thimble without blinking an eye? Funny how men could fight wars and declare duels then turn around and whine all night long over a blister or a toothache.

"There. You're all fixed up." Dinah held her breath as he voluntarily proceeded with his story.

"When Mama died of the yellow fever on a plantation outside Natchez and Papa followed her in a matter of months, I was devastated. I was seven, and had it not been for Mama Tavie, I think, like my father, I would have shriveled up and died from grief."

Dinah detected a hint of bitterness. At least Jonathan had known who his papa was—hadn't had to live with the specter of a loathsome "John" as a parent all his life as she had. She ignored the occasional longing for a father that threatened to overwhelm her.

"Mama Tavie's compassion. Sounds familiar."

"I learned to work hard with her in the fields," continued Jonathan, "and follow my father's pattern of whittling after sundown. When I turned eighteen, my master freed me in appreciation for my parents' hard work."

"That must have catapulted your business."

"In a way. My father had been hired out on the side as a woodworker and had taught me much before he died. He'd told me of a highly-esteemed black cabinetmaker named Thomas Day. But my child's brain had stored it away as unexciting knowledge, not to be remembered until much later. Anyway, once I was freed, I determined I'd find Thomas Day and study under him if it took the rest of my life. As it happened, it took a much shorter time. In a few years, I was back in Natchez bent on keeping my father's name connected to fine woodworking. It wasn't easy at first, but the more the region expanded, the more my skills outstripped the color of my skin. I only wish. . ."

"What? What do you wish?"

He shuttered his eyes, letting her know he had ended his story. He offered a tentative smile.

"Since we'll be working together for a few days, I'd like it if you would call me Jonathan."

Dinah returned the smile wrapped in teasing words. "You sure you don't want to make that Joe-Nathan?"

"Nobody but Mama Tavie has that license, Miss Devereaux." Chortling, he leaned back against the wall once more and looked down at his thumb. "Nice job. May I call you Dinah?"

"Umm, I suppose. And by the way, at supper I hear there's going to be—"

"A batch of hot teacakes waiting?"

"With Joe-Nathan written all over them."

He beamed at her. "She mothers me something fierce, but—"

"Yes, I know. Her cooking is worth it."

They were finishing each other's sentences like they'd known each other for years. Hoping he couldn't hear her hammering heart, Dinah started to lift herself from the floor. He shot to his feet, steadying her with his good hand. There was more strength in one of his hands than both of hers put together.

"Thank you."

Their thanks collided as each of them laughed nervously. He was slow to release her arm, and some foreign bold romantic inside her longed to cling to him. But she pushed this wild new girl back into place. Dinah Devereaux would never go that far.

"Can we start over?" he asked. "I mean as friends."

"Why, yes. I'd like that very much." Dinah couldn't stop smiling. "Well, I suppose if I'm ever going to get this canopy piece finished, I should get back to work."

"Yes. Yes, of course."

Seemingly overcome with shyness, he let go and climbed the ladder back to his post. No matter. For the first time, Dinah was certain he liked her.

Until he remembers those papers again. And what was the chance of that? About ninety-nine in every one hundred. Returning to her work, Dinah sighed in painful resignation.

There wasn't a chance he could ever forget.

"Naw suh. Tonight you eat at the table with everybody else, or you don't eat a'tall."

One look at Mama Tavie's little set jaw and Jonathan knew, with that pitiful scene he and Dinah staged last night, he'd cashed in his last ticket for dining alone. But he had to at least try.

"But Mama Tavie, I feel like an outcast around here."

"And who you blaming for that? Maybe it's time you do something about it. You got a good heart, and I aim to help you show it to somebody else for a change."

How could he make her understand? Dinah's closeness all day long had tilted his very core. It had been all he could do to keep from backing down that ladder and tugging at one of those plaits like a schoolboy in need of attention.

"It's time you enjoyed the company of some folks your age,"

she'd insisted. "Stays too much to yourself in that big old house you bought in town. You can go back to being a hermit once you get back there. But as long as you out here, you gonna act sociable-like whether you want to or not."

LEANING against the wall opposite the one that housed the double fireplace, Jonathan smiled down at a chattering Emerald.

"Mr. Jonathan, you gonna play big-house with me after we eat?"

Ignoring the snorts and giggles coming from around the table led by Eli, he lifted her into his arms and dimpled her cheek with his forefinger. "Never can tell. For a beauty like you, I might be persuaded to build you your own little big-house one of these days."

"Oooo, you mean it? I want me a really, really big-toy big house, Mr. Jonathan." Emerald pointed toward the main house. "Just like that."

"Then you shall have it."

Tension receding from the delight of having Emerald in his arms, Jonathan wondered what her short life had been like so far. Had she ever known her mother? He held this little sweetheart a bit closer. He couldn't wait to replicate Riverwood's stately look in a dollhouse for her. And what would it be like to have a beautiful woman lay out supper in a cozy dining area, while he put a precious little girl like Emerald in her specially crafted chair and waited to offer thanks to the Lord?

Relieved to find something to tamp down these crazy musings, he chuckled as Emerald shimmied down one of his legs as though it were a pole.

"Where're you going, Squirt?"

"I'm going to tell Miss Dinah and Violette 'bout my very own little big house."

Arms feeling surprisingly empty, he watched her skitter

through the door. He took a moment to scan the small space. Someone had had the foresight to build that wall with the double fireplace so that not only the kitchen side of it was always warm, but the place where the house slaves enjoyed a rare chance to wind down was comfortable also.

Still, he was eager to get this eating over with and get to his little cubbyhole upstairs in the matching dependency. He'd talked way too much to the lovely lady from the bayous today. Next thing he knew he'd be telling her every detail of his life story. At least he'd manage to keep his ship's tale from her, the part where the Irishmen had shredded his new freedom papers then started in on shredding him. Subconsciously, he wiggled the sore thumb on his left hand then glanced down at its scarred middle . . .

"And ain't I the merciful one, lad? To leave this little memory in your left 'and rather than yer right?"

Forcing back the memories, he noticed a few house maids trickle in before training his eyes on the men who jostled and joked with each other as they waited for their food. A pang of jealousy struck him. How was it that he always ended up on the outside of life looking in?

"I've got to get out of here." He scanned the room, thankful that no one seemed to hear his unbidden whisper. He'd go without supper if he must, but he wasn't about to allow these muddy emotions to sludge over him right now.

"Good evening, sir."

Jonathan turned around to a pleasant surprise. "Mr. James? How are you, sir?" The butler quirked a brow and Jonathan laughed. "No sarcasm intended."

"None taken. I'm very well, I thank you."

"Didn't expect to see you here tonight. To what do we owe the pleasure of your company?"

Jonathan found himself enjoying the sheepish look on Mr. James's face. Had to have been that little irresistible cyclone named Octavia McMillan that got him here. Everyone knew

James almost always ate alone and much later than everyone else, making sure before he retired for the night every crumb from Riverwood's dining room table was removed, every fire laid or banked according to the dictates of his master or mistress. It simply wasn't like him to leave his post for seemingly no good reason.

"Well, it's owing to you, for one thing. To Miss Dinah, for another."

"Me and Dinah? Why? Has something happened?"

"Not exactly." Mr. James looked discomfited as his voice dropped to a whisper. "It's just that I saw something last evening that bothered me. I don't know if you'll appreciate my mentioning it to you, but I thought since you and she are becoming friends, you might want to hear my assessment of what I observed."

Jonathan's gut rolled. Had bringing the tray last evening to his room lowered Dinah in Mr. James's esteem that much? He shifted his weight to one hip and tugged at his chin.

"Please, go on."

"As you may know, my living quarters are in the basement. Last night, I'd left the main floor to change a pair of trousers. One of the servants had accidentally caused a spill. I was returning to my duties when I happened to see, *harrumph*, Miss Dinah held by our recently acquired gardener, Eli Duggan."

Struggling to mask his feelings, Jonathan simply nodded. After all he had no claim on Dinah. "Continue, sir."

"My intent was to force that rascal to unhand her posthaste. But he loosed her and made for the kitchen before I could get to him."

A blast of heat roared through Jonathan, whistling through his nostrils as he splayed and retracted his fingers. So that was why she was so morose last night. "I can almost assure you, sir, Miss Devereaux was being held against her will. This is my fault. She was bringing up a tray to me."

"No, sir. That is not the case. You have no hand in this goal to conquer Miss Devereaux which that cad Eli has set for himself." He clapped his hand on Jonathan's shoulder. "Pardon my assumption. But in my way of thinking, this calls for a counter plan, one that makes sure she's protected against his trickery."

Jonathan could think of nothing he'd rather do than yank Eli up from that table over there and mix his face with the bricks of the floor. But he had a better idea. He loathed the plight of the slaves, including Mr. James. Might not this be a good time to begin filling that ever-present hole in his heart with something other than guilt? He could begin several things at once: reduce this feeling of isolation from his brothers by at least becoming a part of their conversation; protect Dinah from Eli and any others who might harbor unholy ideas about her; and perhaps seek out any of the men who might be interested in becoming an apprentice. A familiar psalm whispered to his soul.

"Lord, my heart is not haughty, nor mine eyes lofty. . . . Surely I have quieted myself, as a child that is weaned of his mother: my soul is even as a weaned child."

He winked at Mr. James. "Let's go claim a seat."

Ignoring them, Eli proceeded to regale his audience. "Man, that woman so fine-looking she make them japonicas out there in that yard hang their heads in shame."

Jonathan fought to keep from squirming. So now the lecherous Eli was waxing poetic. *Lord, I'm trying to change. Please don't let him be talking about Dinah.*

Jethro, the slave driver Jonathan had seen near the entrance last week chimed in.

"Eli, jes 'cause you 'tend to the yard don't mean you can pick the flowers you want."

What was that weasel doing here this time of evening anyway? Had he come to gaze at Dinah, too?

"The yard still belong to the Massa, if you get my meaning."

"I get your meaning, all right," said Eli, "but everybody

knows Massa only got eyes for the flower he married. Ain't thinking 'bout them in the yard."

Thigh-slapping, guffawing noises filled the room as Jonathan took a moment to size up the young gardener. Reputed to be the favorite among slave women, he flashed a sporty smile of perfect white teeth behind a cocksure smile. Skin glistening like rain on pavement, Eli reeked of dangerous charm. Jonathan winced at the thought. He sure hoped his interpretation of Dinah's reaction to Eli last night had been accurate.

"Evening to everybody." Mama Tavie, Emerald clinging to her skirt, made a bustling entrance. "Let's eat." Violette followed carrying large containers of savory food toward the table.

And bringing up the rear, her beauty enhanced by her shyness—or was it nervousness—was sweet Dinah. She seemed painfully aware of the stares from every man in the room. Especially Eli, and Jethro? Was Jethro making her nervous, too? And if so why?

Eli leapt to his feet as though someone had picked up a hot poker from the fireplace and rammed it into his backside. Jonathan would love for it to have been him. Quickly, he scolded himself. There was no godliness in that kind of thinking. The nimble gardener sailed past Mama Tavie and Emerald, toward the heavy pot Violette gripped.

Violette beamed with surprise, feigning distaste for the gesture. "I swear, Eli, if you drop these neck bones—"

"Here, pretty lady. Lemme help you with that."

Shooting right past Violette, he made straight for Dinah. Even this late in the day, wearing the apron decorated with whatever she'd been learning to cook, Dinah was so much more than Eli's "pretty."

She was breathtaking.

"No thanks. I can manage."

Jonathan blew a breath of relief. The lady seemed repelled.

Obviously chagrined, Violette cut suspicious eyes back and forth between Dinah and Eli. "You better watch where you going, Eli, 'stead of making eyes at her. You make me drop this pot and I'll whip your head into the ground like I done when we was children."

"You ain't never been no child, Vi'let. Always been a big fat pig dressed up like a girl."

The men howled and the housemaids tittered as fuming Violette looked back over her shoulder and glared at Dinah. She slammed a pot on the roughened wood table and took a seat.

Eli winked at Dinah. "Ain't that right, Miss Good-looking?"

"That'll do, Eli." Mr. James's voice was decisive. "Time to pray and eat."

Dinah eased her pot down next to the other food on the bare table. Her hands shook, signaling the return of the panicked girl Jonathan had come upon that first day in the kitchen side of this very building. Something about the way she seemed to effortlessly move between a poised woman one moment and a frightened young girl the next never failed to lower his defenses. But what could have her quite this unraveled, other than that lowdown Eli?

Jonathan tried to stuff down his thoughts. Undoubtedly her sensibilities came from the way she was reared. Part lady, part slave. Whatever it was, it rekindled his desire to smash Eli's face, Jethro's too, if need be, to make sure all the lotharios in the world never looked at her again.

Dinah seated herself next to Violette and Emerald, while Eli plopped down next to her on the opposite side. Mama Tavie moved toward Eli with deliberate speed causing Jonathan to purse his lips to keep from laughing.

"Get up from there, boy. We got us a guest tonight." Ignoring Eli's frown, she tugged him up while smiling innocently at Jonathan. "Come sit right here, Joe-Nathan." Her beckoning fingers signaled mild impatience. "Here, right here. That be fine."

That be fine, huh? thought Jonathan. *Jammed up next to the flawless figure of Dinah Devereaux? That will not be fine and you know it, little lady.*

Unwilling to hurt the one person on earth he knew would do anything for him, Jonathan quietly took the seat he'd been appointed. Dinah smiled down on the empty plate in front of her. Was she smiling at the way Mama Tavie was manipulating him, or was she simply relieved to see Eli's plan foiled? Or could it be she was pleased to be seated next to him?

Jonathan's spirit soared, bringing with it a roaring appetite. Though a bit skimpy in choices, Mama Tavie's menu of winter greens cooked with bacon, slabs of hot cornbread, and pork neck bones stewed with onions made Jonathan want to get up and kiss the cook. The noise of clanking tin forks and plates ruled as the hardworking men and women fell to eating. A fresh stab of guilt pierced Jonathan's soul. He hadn't eaten from this kind of tableware in years.

Mr. James broke the silence. "Miss Dinah? How do you like your new position so far?"

"I . . . well . . . I really do like it a lot, Mr. James. I've always loved creating beautiful things."

"That so?" said the older man. Jonathan watched Mr. James closely. He seemed to be keenly interested. Dinah's lips parted just as an idea lit up Mama Tavie's face.

"You ever done any Christmas stuff, I mean like bows and cedar hangings and all like 'a that?"

"Yes, ma'am, I—"

"Then hurry up and tell us about it, honey. What you waiting for?"

Gently patting her chest and taking several deep breaths, Dinah launched into something that had obviously caught her by surprise. Still, she flashed a wide smile, seemingly energized with the anticipation of the telling. All talk skidded to a halt. Even Violette's.

"Well, when I lived in New Orleans my mistress made me responsible for the Christmas decorations." She stumbled a bit at first, conspicuous in her avoidance of eye contact with the men around the table. "I always started with the pine and cedar brought down from the master's plantation upriver. The smell was heavenly, pungent and invigorating. Using as much of it as I dared, I draped the mantels and staircase and wrapped the newel posts. I always had unused fabric lying about, but if I asked for a little something more to brighten things up, my mistress didn't hesitate to buy it for me. Without children of her own and getting on in years, she relished the compliments from well-wishers who dropped by for holiday calls. So from shiny reds and greens, gold and silver, I made streamers to complement the pines and cedars."

Dinah's eyes took on a sheen that sent Jonathan's heart careening out of rhythm, awareness of her audience falling away like November leaves. He wished he could reach for one of his woodworking tools and fix whatever was causing her to slip into this melancholia.

"When I was twelve, I made my first gifts for Master and Mistress. They were bells and angels made of calico and stuffed with straw. I hid them among the mantel boughs. When my mistress found them, I saw a tear slide down her cheek."

The same wistfulness Jonathan had seen in her the other night in his room had invaded her, causing her to look as though she'd forgotten where she was.

"I waited for the hug I'd wanted all my life. But it never came."

Underneath the table, Jonathan knuckled his fists together. He had all he could manage to keep from reaching over, wrapping Dinah in his arms and making up a thousand times for her mistress's lost opportunity. But he sensed that nothing he had to offer was sufficient to smooth out the wrinkles in her soul.

"I could help you with them hugs," said Eli.

Dinah snapped to attention. Jonathan chafed beneath the pleas of restraint in Mr. James's eyes, gluing him to his seat while

Dinah speared Eli with a look of disgust. Suddenly, she was aware of the rapt silence she'd brought about since she'd begun talking. In that turtle-like fashion Jonathan found so endearing, she tried to bury her head between her shoulders.

"Forgive me. I think I might've said too much. I didn't mean to bore anyone."

Fisting the gardener's shoulder, one of the men grinned mischievously. "Jes think Eli, when you get your freedom and marry this little girl, your house go'n be gussied up prettier than anybody's in Adams County."

The now-familiar wave of laughter ensued as Dinah studied her barely touched meal. Anger and a need to surround her with protection waged war against Jonathan's better judgment. He'd best leave now before he did something he'd regret. He wasn't about to sit here any longer and watch these men lap up Dinah's every movement like starved puppies, then decide to bestow her upon that bigheaded no-account Eli like she was a slave for the buying. Inwardly, Jonathan was yanked back into reality.

What was he thinking? She was a slave.

Jonathan scraped the chair along the floor and pushed back from the table. "If you all will excuse me." He couldn't be sure, but his best guess said Eli was enjoying his discomfort. He knew how starchy he must sound, but at the moment he didn't care.

"Thanks, Mama Tavie. Everything was delicious as always."

James's worried looks bounced between Jonathan and Dinah. "Mr. Mayfield, if you would consider—"

"Where you going, Joe-Nathan? You ain't had none of my 'tater pone yet, let alone teacakes and coffee."

"Yes, ma'am, I know. But I've a long day ahead tomorrow, and it's getting to be past my usual bedtime. I'll have to sample your potato pone another day."

"And I thought it was only us slaves that went to bed with the chickens," muttered Eli.

Shoving aside all reason, Jonathan pulled Eli's chair from the table and spun it around to face him. He caught up Eli's collar.

"Now that I think about it, I might have to take a walk around the grounds before I retire for the evening, to cleanse my lungs of the air in here coming from all the contaminated bad jokes."

Violette jumped up and pried herself between them. "Be careful, Mr. Mayfield. Don't you walk too far. I heard there's some new slave catchers from up North done come to town. Might run into one of 'em out there somewhere." Violette pointed a hefty finger at Dinah. "You don't want to get caught over nobody like her. 'Surely you ain't forgot, Miss Cutie here done burnt up your freedom papers."

Jonathan froze. Of all the devious . . .

Jethro who'd turned conspicuously quiet during supper sat up in his chair. "That so?"

Dinah looked stricken as a collective groan came from around the table. All except Eli who appeared to stop just short of whooping.

"What you say! So the rich free boy done been knocked back down to a slave again just like the rest of us."

Mama Tavie got to her feet, fists resting in the hollow of her petite waist.

"Violette! What's gone wrong with you, girl? Who give you the right to start discussing things you don't know nothing about?" She looked toward the rafters. "Oh, Lord! The little common judgment You give me must be slipping 'cause I thought I knowed this girl better than this."

Violette snatched up Emerald and stomped past Jonathan out the door. But not before spying out Eli, her face an indecipherable mask, and locking gazes with him for a second.

"That's right," yelled Mama Tavie. "Go on up to bed. And I'm gonna be seeking the Lord whether or no I need to ask Missy for some different help in this here kitchen."

Jonathan looked out into the blackness that seemed to swallow Violette whole and the little squirt he'd grown so fond of. He had no intention of leisurely strolling around the estate. Instead, he planned to cross the square and wait in the dark.

Though it was probably against the rules, he was betting on Dinah's risking a turn at stargazing to steal "a bit of fresh air" and clear her head, especially after what just happened. He knew she felt awful about the papers. But now that he'd cooled off, he realized the loss of the papers was just as much his fault as hers. If he hadn't been in such a hurry to get away from her, he'd never have forgotten his proof of freedom. Sooner or later, he'd tell her that. Right now, though, he had to warn her, just as a friend of course, about the ways of the world. He glanced back over his shoulder. Eli was grinning triumphantly. But the look in Jethro's eyes was bloodier than a rooster in a cockfight.

9

Dinah waited until the chatter expired and everyone retired before slipping into the night. She felt exposed and raw from the chafing gazes of the other slaves. Just as she and Jonathan Mayfield had begun to build a fragile friendship, it had been shattered by that girl's clumsy mouth.

Or was that friendly little warning from vexatious Violette really a display of clumsiness?

Something about the way Violette had timed it made Dinah wonder if something hadn't triggered her to deliberately bare Jonathan's Achilles heel.

She sighed heavily and stepped away from the wall, searching the heavens for Andromeda. Wondering what it would be like to be rescued from slavery by her own Perseus. Silly of her to dream so. But wasn't freedom the most precious gift of all, the one for which the Savior had come to earth in the first place? Life-giving memories of the teachings of Jesus flooded her.

The Spirit of the Lord is upon me, because he hath anointed me to preach the gospel to the poor; he hath sent me to heal the brokenhearted, to preach deliverance to the captives . . .

Tears sprang forth as she looked around at the looming shadow of Riverwood.

"Lord, can you give me a clue? I know my attic room in the District wasn't ideal, but why was I uprooted from the only home I've ever known to come here to a daily dose of heartache? Did you not mean those words, about the brokenhearted and the captives, for me and people like me all over this land, too?"

A hint of wood and spices stole into her space. Jonathan. No doubt he'd spotted her and decided to tell her, once and for all, what he thought of her carelessness. Oh, how he must despise her! He must be sorry he ever entered that kitchen and laid eyes on her.

He was headed directly toward her. From the double-barreled fire accidents she'd caused on Friday and the dreamy description of her life in New Orleans in the kitchen tonight, he must already think her the most useless and empty-headed female ever to cross the threshold of a home. But no matter what else he might believe about her, she wouldn't allow her tears to strengthen his idea of a spoiled spineless slave girl who only knew how to make Christmas baubles. She tried to disappear around the opposite corner. But he was too quick for her.

"Dinah, wait. What's the matter?"

Her back still turned, she shook her head without answering. "Oh, Jonathan, how you must despise me. By now every slave at Riverwood knows I've destroyed your papers. It won't be long before everyone in Natchez, even those dreadful types who make a profit of catching free men who've lost their proof, will know what I've done." She tried to stem the flow of tears, but like the words coming from her heart it was impossible. "A-and what about the clientele you've worked so hard to build up? Will they start to desert you once they find out you can no longer prove your status?" Firm but gentle hands pivoted her toward him. "You're crying. Did he . . . did someone . . . do something to hurt you?"

Though it was nearly pitch dark, she could see the concern in his eyes. It melted her defenses just before he pulled her into an embrace. Overcome by the comfort of his body, she pressed her cheek against his chest. My, but his heart was racing. Had Violette upset him that much, or had something else happened in the short while since she'd seen him? Alarmed, she pushed away a bit and looked up at him.

"What's this about, Jonathan? Are you all right? What 'he' are you talking about?"

He backed away and dug his hands into his pockets. "I thought perhaps Eli had . . . well . . . the way he was looking at you, I thought maybe he had harmed you in some way."

And would you care?

"Eli Duggan is a known scoundrel who's reputed to have left several slaves heartbroken and . . . well . . . you know, with children out at the McMillan plantations," said Jonathan.

"Does Jethro know Eli sired the children?"

Jonathan frowned down at her. "Since when did you get on a first name basis with the slave driver?"

"I'm not on a first name basis with him. It's just that I wonder what's to become of the children. Will they be sold?"

His face softened. "It's kind of you to be concerned, Dinah. But that's just the way of plantation slavery. Jethro is a slave driver and a vulture. The whole cycle of things plays right into the straw boss he sees himself as. Ultimately, it's up to the owner as to whom he will sell. But more innocent babies are simply more property for an egotist like Jethro to boss around eventually."

Suddenly chilled, Dinah ran her hands up and down her arms. The recent encounters she'd had with Eli and Jethro and the countless nightmares she'd had as a child about deserted babies encircled her like a ring of starved wolves.

"You can't mean it," she whispered.

"Of course I mean it. Do you think I'd make cavalier remarks to you about something so serious? Do you believe I care nothing for your welfare, Miss Devereaux?"

Dinah lowered her head as her neck heated up. She couldn't

believe she'd just baited him, though unintentionally, into admitting he cared. What kind of woman was she becoming?

"I think I'd better go in before Mama Tavie comes looking for me."

"And takes my head along as a trophy. I can just hear her now. 'Joe-Nathan, I raised you to be a gent'man, and here you is out here sparkin' this po' girl. What's the trouble with you, boy?'"

A tiny giggle escaped Dinah's throat. "Are you sparking me, Mr. Mayfield?"

Another giggle, then another and another. Until she and Jonathan found themselves laughing together. Only a few times had she heard him laugh so easily, viscerally. She was overwhelmed with gratitude for this moment, a moment where she felt truly appreciated, not as an odd pet but as a full person. Without a thought of hesitancy, she lifted on her toes. Her lips grazed the stubble on his cheek.

"Thank you for caring."

Tilting up her chin, he caught her in another embrace, different this time. Deliberate. Electrifying. She had never been kissed before, at least not like this. But when he lowered his head, she felt an undeniable pull. He deepened the kiss—gently, sweetly—before pushing back so forcefully she thought she might lose her balance and hit the ground.

"I apologize. I am completely out of line. I-I forget myself. I only meant to . . . . It won't happen again."

Dinah pressed her fingers to her lip, Cook's words from years ago stabbing her conscience.

"You should have known better than to let Jack Hudson kiss you. You should never let a man kiss your mouth unless you're married to him. To do so is as bad as becoming a woman of the night."

And once again, just like that, the warm side of Jonathan Mayfield was gone, hidden behind a mysterious cloud of mistrust and the hard pounding of his footsteps against the pavers. Dinah stared after his disappearing form. Had she been too forward?

Despite what Cook had said, she'd felt nothing dirty about this kiss. Still, she was crushed, and a little ashamed. Growing up, she'd learned nothing of the rules of courtship. Truth be told, other than Cook's sideways instructions, she didn't even know if there were such rules. Mistress Devereaux had taught her how to be a lady but not how to navigate the attraction between men and women. Chin to chest, she trudged up the darkened stairway. And into a wall of flesh. Violette.

"What are you doing lurking around here?" Dinah brushed past Violette, prompting the girl to almost step on her heels in pursuit.

"There you go with them big words. I don't know what 'lurking' mean, but it seems to me you the one what needs to be answering for yourself."

Dinah winced. Had Violette seen her and Jonathan, and if so who else? Mr. James? Or, God forbid, Mistress McMillan?

"All right, Violette. You've captured my attention."

Violette breathed the scent of onions into Dinah's face. "And don't try to play like you crazy. I seen you out there. You may think you being sparked, but you ain't, not by Jonathan Mayfield."

"I don't know what you mean."

"Well, you go'n soon find out. I got it on good word that somebody on one of Massa's other plantations said that his cousin said that he overheard—"

"For heaven's sakes! Out with it, Violette, or I'm leaving."

"Well, he said Mr. Mayfield ain't gonna never marry up with nobody. Said he heard it from the man's own mouth." Violette pressed a fist into her waist and settled against the wall of the stairwell. Using those fleshy toes of hers, she tapped out a slow agonizing beat. "And if he should marry, it won't be to no slave 'cause he too busy trying to get enough money so he can buy slaves of his own."

Dinah spread her hands against the side of the stairwell to

recapture her balance. She couldn't have been more stunned if Violette had thrown the fresh contents of a slop jar in her face.

"I don't believe you. Jonathan Mayfield would never buy human property."

"You might as well face it, Miss Cutie, your lover boy don't want to have nothin' to do with his own kind. He trying to be like them planters."

Or maybe William Johnson.

"But when some slave catcher find out he ain't got no more papers, he be learning who he really is, a slave like all the rest of us. They go'n cart him off to the slave market quicker than you can say gee or haw. And to my way of thinking, good riddance."

Dinah wanted to grab Violette and shake her senseless. "I'm curious. How do you happen to know so much about slave catchers, and what gives you the right to say such awful things about Mr. Mayfield?" She tilted her head to the side and scrutinized Violette. "You know, I believe you might be sweet on the cabinetmaker. I suspected it all along, but now I'm quite certain of it."

Violette glowered at her. "That's a lie. And you be seeing how much I don't care when he gets sold downriver somewhere."

Without another word, Dinah climbed the rest of the stairs and quietly entered the room, Violette right behind her. She was surprised to find Mama Tavie already releasing a string of soft snores. She pulled the scratchy slave dress over her head and slid into the bed next to the tiny woman who was more and more becoming the mother she'd never had.

Turning onto her side, she tried to clear her head. She simply would not believe Violette's "he-said, she-said" account of neither Jonathan's future nor his heart. Violette didn't really know him. She hadn't witnessed the genuine disquiet in his eyes tonight when he thought Eli had tried to harm her, hadn't felt the beating of his heart as he held her close. True enough, he might be a little ambitious, but she simply did not believe he wanted his own slaves. And what did it matter anyway? Dinah was already someone else's property.

She listened to Violette lower herself onto the mattress next to Emerald and quickly begin her own aria of snoring. Dinah tried to join her roommates in sleep, but each time she closed her eyes she saw Jonathan's muscled frame chained and waiting to be sold. All because of her.

But Violette had managed to plant another image in Dinah's head just as bad. Maybe worse.

Jonathan wanted to buy human beings.

Careful not to disturb Mama Tavie, Dinah shifted onto her other side. Absolutely not. Not her newfound friend. She folded her hands beneath her face and pulled her knees toward her chest. In truth, she had nothing to lose by being friends with Jonathan Mayfield. She had already lost to him the only thing she'd ever owned. Her heart.

10

Jonathan made his way through the servants' hall and up the stairs toward his workplace in the bedroom. He wanted to leap the steps like a hart at the idea of seeing her again. Try as he may these last few days, he hadn't been able to wrestle down the feeling of pure joy each time he thought of her. And that unplanned kiss last night had done nothing to reel in this irrepressible surge of delightful anticipation. Could this be what Papa felt about mama—the reason he didn't want to live without her? Jonathan paused at the landing. No, of course not. Papa had been in love.

Jonathan was definitely not in love.

Dinah Devereaux didn't really mean anything to him—not in that way. She was just a charming intelligent young woman who fascinated him, one he hadn't known for a week yet. He would admit he got a little lonesome sometimes, but this new feeling was simply a matter of friendship and good company come to call. As a craftsman, he was beginning to enjoy working with her, watching her turn fabric into a one-of-a-kind piece of art.

A foot or two from the bedroom door, he drew in a couple of exaggerated breaths and readied himself for another encounter with her. He would just keep to his work today and avoid too much conversation.

"Good morning, Mr. Mayfield."

All reasoning and self-instruction fled his brain as she smiled up at him from the floor. "Good morning, Dinah." He returned the smile. "Do you always work on your knees? And how is it that you manage to beat me here every morning?"

"Oh, just used to it, I guess."

"Working on your knees, or rising before dawn?"

"Both. I've always done my cutting on the floor, and I've always been an early riser."

Jonathan chuckled. "An early riser, huh?"

"And where's the humor in that, sir?"

Though they both knew he had no intention of offending her, he reveled in the affected look of insult she threw at him as she rose from the floor and flexed her fingers against her unbelievably tiny waist.

"Mr. Mayfield, are you questioning my integrity about calling myself an early riser? Do you think me a slugabed?"

Jonathan slapped his hand to his chest. "You injure me, Miss Devereaux. I was only thinking of a time years ago back on the Mayfield plantation when Mama Tavie made me the richest little boy in the world."

"Oh? I didn't know you and she once lived on the same place." Dinah steepled her fingers and brought them to her chin. "Well? Aren't you going to tell me the story of how you became the richest little boy on earth and what that has to do with early rising?" Her face glowed with excitement and a trace of reticence. "By now, you must have guessed that a stargazer like me would love stories, too."

"As a matter of fact, there are leftover sparkles in your eyes from last night."

The observation had simply slipped from Jonathan's mouth, causing Dinah's shyness to take center stage. She lowered her head. "Too much stardust, I guess."

"I guess." Jonathan smiled.

So much for the no-conversation plan.

DINAH CRINGED from the visions of wantonness most likely crowding Jonathan's thoughts about her. She had done it again, been too forward. As if it mattered. She must keep in mind she had nothing to offer the man except friendship. But oh, how she longed to know what Jonathan Mayfield was like as a little boy. In fact, she wanted to know everything there was to know about him.

Suddenly she was woozy with embarrassment. Was she insane? The man had work to do, and so did she. "But if you'd prefer not to—"

"No, no. I rather enjoy telling this story now and again." An impish smile lifted the corner of his mouth. "For one thing, it puts the lie to the idea that you can always expect an honest answer from Octavia McMillan."

"What?" Dinah feigned a gasp. "Mama Tavie? A liar?"

Dinah eased onto the edge of the daybed at the foot of the tester. "Why, I'd sooner believe a July blizzard in Natchez than Mama Tavie's deceiving someone."

Crossing his muscled arms and clasping his biceps in that dizzying way of his, Jonathan leaned sideways against the wall. He smirked, seemingly savoring Dinah's piqued curiosity.

"Well get ready, dear lady. You might be pulling out a snow shovel come summer."

Dinah sat up a bit taller, her hands clasped together over her lap, waiting to be entertained by this man who never ceased to fascinate her.

"On the Mayfield plantation where I grew up a few miles from here, there were only a couple dozen of us slaves. But each Christmas Eve, the master would call us together on the back verandah to give each of us an apple or an orange. And lecture to us with massive words as though we were a congregation of Harvard graduates."

Dinah let herself imagine Jonathan's little body rigid before his master, his sweet face shadowed beneath a mortarboard. She suppressed a laugh, almost afraid to breathe as his deep voice took a playful turn—afraid he'd reenter his shell and leave her to wonder once again what she'd done wrong.

"That must have been interesting."

"In retrospect, yes, though everyone including me heard little of what Master Mayfield said. We were all looking forward to the time when we'd be granted permission to celebrate the rest of Christmas Eve and Christmas Day in whatever way we pleased."

Dinah watched as Jonathan became more and more caught up in a childhood memory, chortling at the end of practically every sentence. A smarter, finer-looking, wittier man she'd never laid eyes on. When occasionally he became a bit pensive, so did she. When he laughed, she laughed too, though thus far, little of what he'd said held any real promise of humor.

"But as far back as I can remember, I'd always gone to the yearly ritual secretly expecting something more. I actually expected the master to give us freedom."

Dinah's mouth formed an O, something her old mistress had taught her never to allow in company. "Freedom? What on earth would cause you to assume that?"

"Hold on there, Miss Devereaux. I'm coming to that." Eyes dancing with mischief, he poked fun at Dinah's social faux pas. "What's the matter? Can't wait to see how I made a fool of myself like I did with the hammer the other day?"

Quickly, she regained her footing. "Forgive me. Continue with your story."

"One Christmas Eve, I was standing next to Mama, Papa, Mama Tavie and her family, waiting for my fruit and my freedom, when suddenly the master's voice boomed so loudly it might have catapulted a tyke like me a few yards if Papa hadn't been holding my hand. 'Early to bed, early to rise, makes a man healthy, wealthy, and wise!'"

"How old were you?"

"Hmmm." Jonathan rubbed his chin. "Can't say exactly. Five, six, perhaps?"

"That young."

"Yes, I'm afraid so, though I'd already started reading lessons with my mistress and had inwardly pronounced myself a learned gentleman. I knew what 'healthy' meant, and as for 'wise,' it sounded like an old-folks word that had no value for me. It was the word wealthy that caught my attention. I asked Mama what it meant. 'It means rich,' she whispered.

"Waves of illogic surfaced in my curious little head. Why, this would explain what happened every Christmas Eve when the master's children became so excited, whispering about how they must go to bed early so they could rise early and receive all the wonderful toys waiting for them. But then I'd created a puzzle for myself. Why would anyone settle for mere playthings when rising early they could receive wealth? Didn't Master's children have sense enough to know wealth could buy all the toys they wanted, all year long?"

"What a smart little boy you were." Dinah was beginning to see where this was heading. This man whom just days ago she'd thought a stuffed shirt was not only a master at cabinetmaking, he knew how to spin a yarn. Obviously embarrassed by her comment on his intelligence, he chose to ignore it.

"Finally, I satisfied myself with the reasoning that since the master's children were already rich, rocking horses, and dolls and wood-carved soldiers must be the next best reward they could get from rising early."

Dinah laughed out loud. "So living sumptuously all came down to how soon one could get out of bed."

"Exactly. With one hand in Papa's and the other in Mama's, I thought the master would never stop his sermonizing. Suddenly, all I needed to become rich was to get up from my pallet for a few days before Mama and Papa rose. I'd start tomorrow, Christmas Day, and soon I'd be rich.

"Now, you must remember I was something of a sluggard, so this early rising didn't bode well for me. How was I going to wake myself up, especially tomorrow since Christmas was the only free day we had all year?"

"You, the future entrepreneur, a sluggard?"

The man actually looked embarrassed. "I'm afraid so. Before my parents' death, I practically worked myself to death each day trying to keep from working." He grinned boyishly, offering a glimpse of what that little slugabed must have looked like. "But that particular night, I was determined to rise before everyone the next day because who knew? It just might be the day I woke up rich. With this thing called wealth I could do so much. Why, I wouldn't have to hope for freedom every Christmas Eve ever again. I could buy it! I could even buy it for Papa, Mama, Mama Tavie and her whole family."

"What a sweet idea. So you too dreamt of freedom at an early age?"

"Oh yes. The more my mistress taught me the more I wanted to join her children in their imaginative play about moats and castles and such."

Jonathan moved to take a seat next to her on the daybed, bringing with him delectable discomfort and setting her heart to thumping.

"As soon as the master gave his customary 'Merry Christmas,' I shot toward our cabin like a newfangled missile. Before my parents reached home and started questioning me, I was on my pallet pretending to be asleep.

"Despite my parents' threats of punishment, for days afterwards I rose early and dug up our little grassless yard, searched every nook in our one-room cabin, and even dug around the outhouse." His eyes twinkled with mischief. "No riches to be found there, I assure you."

Dinah laughed so hard she had to wipe her eyes.

"When I'd exhausted every idea in my head, I confided in Mama Tavie. 'Is that all what's bothering you, child? Just you rise up early on New Year's Day and be at the backdoor of the big-house kitchen before everybody else, and I promise I'm go'n make you the richest little boy on earth.'

"When I got there, Mama Tavie had two hot teacakes and a glass of milk waiting for me, but I spied a virtual mountain of teacakes covered over with a cloth on her worktable. 'Nothin' in the world richer than them teacakes,' she whispered conspiratorially. 'Eat them two I gave you and Massa will never be able to match you in riches.'"

"And did you believe her?"

Jonathan chuckled. "With all my heart. What an easy task that was going to be. When Mama Tavie left to serve breakfast in the big house, I uncovered the stack of teacakes and ate until my stomach felt like a drum skin had been pulled taut across it, all the while believing I was getting richer and richer by the minute. I was sick for two days, even with the ton of calomel my mistress gave me."

Dinah filled the room with unladylike laughter that would have unraveled her former mistress.

Eyes narrowed but sparkling, he returned her earlier mock offense.

"Are you laughing at me, Miss Devereaux?"

"Most certainly, I am, sir. I would never have taken you to be such a . . . a scamp."

"Me? A scamp?"

He joined her in the mirth and they laughed until tears crowded the corner of their eyes. Laughing together was becoming a habit. Dinah trembled as Jonathan cupped her face in his hands and touched his forehead to hers. He slid his hands down the sides of her arms and stilled her hands.

"Do you know how beautiful you are and how wonderful it is that you can make me laugh, something only Mama Tavie has been able to accomplish in years?"

Dinah's breath caught in her throat. No one had ever called her beautiful, a word she'd always thought reserved only for white and octoroon women in New Orleans.

"Ahem." At Mr. James's sedated alarm, Dinah shot to her feet, Jonathan alongside her.

"Miss Dinah, I might be needing assistance from you tonight. Mistress is expecting guests. Also, she said she'd probably come by later to see how the job's coming along, just in case she decides to show off what's been done so far."

"I—uh—I mean, we were . . ."

Their words collided with each other's as James tendered an abbreviated bow. When he raised his gray-streaked head, he was smiling. "Things seem to be coming along real well in here. Real well."

"Thank you," they said in unison before scrambling back to their posts. Barely had Mr. James left and Dinah lifted her basket of sewing sundries when one of Cook's admonitions from her past scurried across her brain like a starved ship rat.

Being out of yer place, that's what got ya compromised. Shouldn't've been near that library in the first place. Don't care what Mi'z Devereaux said. How many times must I tell ya, girlie? A chap the likes of you has no place in them finer parts of the mansion. Yer place is in the attic.

Suddenly, Mr. James's request expanded into full reality.

Tonight. The dining room. Riverwood.

Beads of perspiration gathered against her forehead. "Why, I simply will not do it. I can't."

Like a distant echo, Jonathan's voice reverberated through her mind. "Dinah? Is everything all right?"

"What?" She flinched at the fact that he was backing down the ladder. As much as she'd love to feel the comfort of Jonathan Mayfield's arms around her again, she couldn't risk telling him of her past. "Uh . . . yes. Yes, everything's fine. I-I was just reacting to something silly Violette said this morning."

She managed a steady smile until Jonathan returned to his work. It was one thing for her to ply her trade upstairs in a secluded room. Quite another to mingle—even as an educated slave girl—with the nabobs of Natchez. Cook—no, Jack Hudson —had forced her to learn better.

11

D inah stood perfectly poised next to the elaborately carved sideboard, anticipating the slightest nod from Mr. James. Inside, she was all twists and turns. All her life she'd eaten in the kitchen with the house staff, and when there'd been guests, she was always tucked away in her attic room. So experiencing the theater of Natchez nabobs served in a planter's dining room was excitement mixed with dread of a misstep that would bring shame to this butler of whom she was becoming more and more fond.

"All you got to do is follow James's directions," Mama Tavie had said earlier. "He's the best at what he do. I'd work with him myself this evening. But you know I have to fix the food, and I don't trust Violette yet to behave herself 'mongst Missy's guests." Chortling, she'd lightly tweaked Dinah's nose. "'Sides, you prettier to look at than I am."

But Dinah had been terrified of the idea. What if Cook had been right? What if her very presence among the elite spelled a mishap? She fought to keep from gawking as Mistress McMillan, her widowed friend and her daughter enjoyed quiet conversation at dinner. From the way she and James were subtly disregarded, it was as though they'd become one with the décor. Thank goodness the mistress and her guests couldn't see inside Dinah's head.

Without moving an eyeball, she deposited every magnificent detail of the dining room into her memory bank for safekeeping. From the lofty ceiling, to the pier table, to the rich feel of the carpeted floors, to the wooden Venetian blinds. And suspended over the center of the table was a huge lyre-shaped wooden punkah, patterned after the Greek anthemion style, intricately carved and ready to be swung back and forth by a slave during Mississippi's scorching summers to cool family and guests and to ward off pesky insects. Dinah found no inherent fault in the finer things of life. But shouldn't the poor souls who provided it be offered hope through some kind of compensation?

Shush, girl. No need to agitate herself with such thinking right now. After all, it was 1860, and nothing had happened to repair the breach slavery had created yet.

Towering above all the manmade splendor of this room, however, was Mr. James who in the eyes of Dinah owned the lead role in the unfolding drama before her. A more suave gentleman she'd never seen. After satisfying himself that the fire was laid just so, the candles lit, and the table perfectly placed, he had strode into the drawing room resplendent in his muted gray suit, white collar and cravat, and his meticulously blacked boots, and tendered a bow.

"Dinner is served," he'd announced with perfect aplomb.

When everyone had been seated, Dinah looked on as, from the dumbwaiter, Mr. James uncovered the dishes Mama Tavie had prepared and flawlessly served their contents course after course, passing the used china and serving dishes to Dinah to remove from the dining area. Finally, the meal wound down.

"James?"

The butler deftly moved from his position at the sideboard as the mistress addressed him. "Yes, madam."

"We'll be retiring to the drawing room now." Effortlessly, but with precise dignity and propriety, he assisted the three ladies from their seats.

"Oh, and James?"

"Yes, madam?"

"Offer my compliments to Octavia, will you?"

"Of course, ma'am."

During the entire order of serving dinner, James had never missed a step, never forgot a line. But at the mention of Mama Tavie, it was easy to see that he was hard pressed to smother a prideful smile. Expelling a sigh of relief, Dinah waited until he returned from the drawing room.

"Mr. James?"

"Yes, miss."

Dinah had given up on trying to get him to call her by her given name. "You were marvelous tonight."

"So were you. Just your presence added elegance to the room."

Dinah felt herself beaming. Her footsteps echoed the surefooted butler's as he led her down the servant's hall toward the verandah and ultimately the kitchen. She loved Mama Tavie's kind heart, but something about this man tugged at a different need. What must it feel like to have a man like this for a father?

What must it feel like to have a father, period?

Shame skittered up her spine. She'd die of humiliation if this gentleman's gentleman ever found out her past. *Please, Lord, never let him find out my father was a john.* She startled at the sound of Mr. James's voice.

"A word with you, miss?"

Her stomach somersaulted. Had his kind words just been a means to set her up so that he could point out something she'd done wrong back there? He motioned toward a bench at the end of the servant's hall.

"Please have a seat."

Wordlessly, Dinah obeyed.

"I've not been fortunate to father children, the life of a

butler, in my opinion, being unsuited for family. But if I'd been blessed with a daughter, if I'd been a man able to determine his own choices in life, I would have chosen one just like you."

Tears clogged Dinah's throat. Of all the lovely things to say, especially since she'd been thinking the same thing. "Mr. James, I don't know what to—"

"Don't say anything. Just let me finish." Again he signaled toward the bench. "May I join you?"

"Of course, sir."

Keeping a respectable distance, he eased down next to her. "Well, you see, I was born on a plantation in Maryland, and according to the midwife who helped my mother deliver me, I'd now be around forty years old. When I was a lad of twelve or so, I was sold downriver to Louisiana. I was trained as a footman and eventually sold to my present master. A kind preacher, now deceased, risked teaching me letters and a certain amount of comportment fitting a butler. I've done some things I'm not proud of, but for nearly twenty years, I've tried to serve God and man with the hope that one day I'd be free. I believe that day is soon to come. In the meantime, I've always tried to keep my heart out of my masters' affairs, including his human purchases."

He cleared his throat in that commanding way of his. "But somehow, when young mistress got married a few years back—"

"Oh? The McMillans have a daughter?"

"They do. She now lives in Vicksburg with her husband. Anyhow, on her wedding day, with all the pomp and celebration, I watched with more than my usual interest. All the excitement made me wonder how it would feel to have an upstanding young man ask for my own daughter's hand in marriage. Then you came along. A vision of what life could be like if my people were free to truly celebrate one another. I can't explain it, but from the first time I saw you, you stirred in me what I always imagined a father would feel."

For reasons Dinah couldn't explain, a sense of foreboding

ensued, causing her to squirm underneath James's intense gaze.

"That's why I want to warn you."

"Warn me? About what?"

"Eli Duggan. While Eli is a fine gardener, that's about as far as his qualities go. He cares nothing for preserving the dignity of females, sees them as objects to be conquered and cast aside like so many bales of ruined cotton. He seems to think that collecting females somehow makes him the man he'll never be as a slave."

"Thank you, sir. But truly I have no intention of honoring Eli's advances."

"Shhh. Listen to me now. It's not your intentions that concern me. It's his. I know young men. I've been one myself. And while I'd like to think I was never as callous as Eli, I know how he thinks. You must be watchful and prayerful as you go about your duties here at Riverwood. Though your talents are plain to see, a visibly compromised slave girl doesn't have the option of pleading her case as criminal violation, and her situation might not be tolerated here. She could possibly end up at one of the other plantations."

The butler's meaning was clear. Tingling with embarrassment and a sobering surge of what she'd always feared, Dinah lowered her head. This wonderful gentleman was trying to keep her from the fields. How could he know that was the one thing she couldn't bear? Finally, she got the courage to look at him.

"I never knew my father. Thank Jesus. But I share your sentiments. If I'd known him, I would want him to be just like you. I promise I'll be doubly careful around Eli from now own."

"Good. Mr. Mayfield and I have agreed to do our best to help preserve your honor."

Dinah's heart lurched. Had he just said, "Mr. Mayfield?"

"One more thing. Watch what you say around Violette. I'd guess there's more to that girl than any of us knows."

RELISHING Mr. James and Jonathan's decision to look out for her, Dinah entered the kitchen. Mama Tavie waiting with Emerald in her arms, propelled to the balls of her feet with curiosity.

"Well, how did it go, honey?"

"Oh, Mama Tavie. If I were free to marry and someone like Mr. James asked for my hand, I'd be the happiest girl on earth." Dinah cracked open a sly smile. "What about you, Mama Tavie? Would you ever consider a man like Mr. James?"

Mama Tavie's light-colored skin bloomed into a deep shade of red. "Away with you, girl. I ain't got time to listen to that stuff." She planted a kiss on Emerald's cheek. "Me and Emerald going to bed. Ain't we, sweetheart?"

Dinah allowed a hearty laugh. "Be up in a minute." She'd been duly warned by Mr. James. But the feeling of care and protectiveness she sensed from him were the things she'd choose to think about when she went to bed, savoring them tonight and most likely treasuring them for the rest of her life. She only wished she could feel half as clear about the intentions of Jonathan Mayfield.

OBLIVIOUS TO THE fine dinner being served just yards away, Jonathan paced the small room he'd been given in the dependency. At last he understood. Not only did he understand his papa's pain after losing his mama, he understood his joy all those years before. But had his father's bliss been worth the sorrow that followed? No.

Yes.

"All right. Very well, then. I admit it, Lord. I think I've fallen in love with this girl. Pitifully, irrevocably in love."

He felt like running outside and skipping across the yard the way he used to do when he was headed to Mama Tavie's cabin to play with her youngest son Samuel.

"But it's impossible, Lord. No master would ever let go of a slave as valuable as Dinah Devereaux. And even if he had a mind to, this particular master probably wouldn't, simply because of loyalty to her deceased master. After all, he didn't bring her here because he needed her to make money for him. He brought her to Riverwood in fond remembrance of a friend."

"With Me, all things are possible."

"Yes, Lord, I know but . . ."

Dropping his overly-large frame down onto the torturous mattress, Jonathan let his stubborn rebuttal fade into the darkness as exhausted, he fell into a troubled sleep.

Too lovely to really be his, Jonathan was certain she put to shame all brides ever to come before her and those to follow as she joined him under a live oak by the river. He had always thought nothing could equal a piece of finely-crafted furniture, reluctant even to run his callused hands over it once he'd put the finishing touches on. But watching her come to him, dressed in layers of ethereal pastels, he knew Dinah was the most precious thing he'd ever touched. He reached for her outstretched hand only to watch it slip through his fingers like the rays of the sun, her long delicate fingers fluttering in the river wind, her moist eyes filled with something he couldn't quite fathom.

Like a vise, deep-seated fear and longing squeezed his heart. How could he have forgotten? Sweet Dinah was gone, taken from him by a mysterious ravaging fever, one that must be about to consume him, for quite unexpectedly he'd become hot, so hot—

"No!" Jonathan bolted up from the undersized mattress. His head nearly grazed the low ceiling. His heart thudded like a relentless maul against a timber piece. Had he just had a premonition? Using the tail of his soiled shirt, he wiped the perspiration from his face, neck, chest. He glanced at the multiple scars covering his ribcage and thought of the road that led him there.

"I won't do it. I can't risk that kind of pain. I'll rise early tomorrow, Lord, and put an end to this."

The thought of rising early pricked him with the childhood memory he'd shared with Dinah that morning, a memory he'd always treasure. He lit the lamp and checked his pocket watch. Ten o'clock. Too late to be out, especially without proof of freedom. Dropping back down onto the mattress, he lowered his head into his hands.

Even so, he had to get away from here. Get to the bluffs where he could think exactly what to do.

Trusting the tattlers in the nearby cabins wouldn't reckon it as a sign or suspicion, he decided to leave his lantern burning low. Hopefully, he'd be back safely in bed within a couple of hours, and if he was questioned by someone guarding the estate, he'd say he had to pick up a special tool he'd forgotten in order to do the task he'd set for tomorrow. Whatever it took, he had to get away from Riverwood. Now.

ALMOST THERE. Jonathan flexed that shoulder Dinah had seen him exercising. After the ship incident, it sometimes acted up in cooler weather. He just needed to stop by his home for a minute to get a heavier coat before continuing on to the river. He pushed back against the niggling feeling he was being followed. Just a case of unwarranted nerves over loss of the papers. A few more minutes and he'd be at his special place where he could think rationally, pray heartily.

He turned onto the walk leading to his house. What was that pinned to his front door? He remembered the matches he'd perfunctorily stuck in his pocket as he'd lit the lantern back at the dependency. He struck a flame before tearing the note from its moorings and holding it to the light.

ENJOY THIS WHILE YOU CAN. SOON YOU, YOUR HOUSE, AND YOUR BUSINESS WILL BE AUCTIONED OFF TOGETHER.

Suddenly, the wind whipped up, blowing out the match and sliding the smell of tobacco underneath his nose. An involuntary shudder shook his entire frame.

Or was it the cold wind giving him a chill?

Wham! Weight about the measure of a medium-sized hound assaulted him from behind, enough to ram Jonathan's head into the door. Tiny shoots of light spangled before his eyes as his mind scrambled to catch up with what was happening.

"Bless my soul, I believe we got him at last."

We? How many more were there?

No time to ponder. Pivoting, Jonathan rammed a fist beneath his attacker's jaw, sending him sprawling backwards to the bricked walkway. He reached down and collared him to his feet. He'd give him a good enough thrashing to make him think twice before accosting another man at his front door. Out of nowhere, another attacker caught Jonathan from behind.

Definitely more than one of these thugs. Just as it had been on the ship.

Wobbling like a dying spinning top, Jonathan lunged toward the second assailant. A much larger fellow. Outrage, fueled from the beating he'd taken nine years ago on that ship, kept him on his feet. Images of being scored like a ham on the deck of the ship flooded him. This time he had no papers to worry about. This time he'd fight 'til someone died. He flung the big fellow against a shuttered window and slammed his head . . . and slammed and slammed—

Until sanity grabbed hold.

Even in his fog, Jonathan had sensed this second assailant knew next to nothing about how to defend himself in a brawl, no matter his bulk. Backing well away, Jonathan watched him stumble from the shutter, holding his midsection. The stringy one Jonathan had laid out minutes ago grunted in his effort to rise. Small though he was, he was the scrappiest of the two. He scrambled to his feet and began swinging like a mean angry saloon girl.

"Mr. Mayfield!"

Through the night noises, he heard someone jogging up from Silver Street calling his name. Benjamin.

Thank you, Lord.

"Another one," said the stringy fellow starting toward retreat. "I think we'd best get outta here."

Touching his hand to a cut on his lip and massaging his shoulder, Jonathan heaved in gulps of air. Should he try to stop them, perhaps press charges? He thought better of it. Without proof of freedom, he might end up making matters worse for himself. He turned toward Benjamin whose usually mischievous countenance was wiped clean of anything except concern.

"You all right?"

"Fine, my man. Never been more happy to see you in my life, though. What were you doing coming from under the hill this time of night? And don't say it was to check on a shipment this time."

Uneasiness shrouded Benjamin. "It's not what you think, sir."

Jonathan shrugged and paid for it with a slice of pain beneath his ribs. It really wasn't his place to question Benjamin's business. He was guessing God had a plan for him that didn't include an unsavory life under the hill. Benjamin Catlett was a good man and a good worker. And showing up at precisely the right moment, he'd secured Jonathan's attackers' flight. Jonathan looked over at the piece of paper the wind had kicked against the wall. He knew it was related to the roughing-up he'd just experienced. Still, who were these white men with northern accents, and what did they want with him?

"I think nothing, Benjamin. It's not my affair. As I said, I appreciate your help."

"Yes, sir. Glad I was here, though I think they'd had about

enough of you even before I got here. By the way, I thought you'd still be out at Riverwood."

Jonathan mumbled a terse goodnight. The last thing he wanted to talk about was Riverwood. Too much chance it would lead to a girl named Dinah.

VIOLETTE'S SNORES sounded like a pen of hungry hogs. But for Dinah, sleep was an elusive pearl—perhaps like the ones the merchant man searched for in the Bible. Like Jonathan Mayfield. Elusive and impossible and absolutely enthralling. From the moment she'd laid eyes on him in that sweltering kitchen, she'd felt catapulted into an English novel. His wide-legged stance, his hands clasped behind his back, his sculpted jaw—*Lord, You did an exceptional job with that jaw*—moving in tandem with whatever was occurring in that mysterious mind of his, reminded her of Mr. Darcy in *Pride and Prejudice*.

Enough. Why couldn't she stop applying today's ecstasy to tomorrow's hopes? Determined not to disturb Mama Tavie and Violette, she carefully rearranged the collection of rags she used as a pillow. Jonathan Mayfield could never be interested in a future with a girl like her. And even if by some miracle he happened to see something in her worth wooing, Dinah Devereaux was someone else's property. Nothing could ever change that.

Testing every position possible in the space allotted her next to Mama Tavie on the cornhusk mattress, she finally settled onto her back and stared up at the low ceiling. Mama Tavie stirred, causing Dinah to try to still herself by counting the boards of the ceiling. But the usual light that filtered through the window had been vanquished by a rush of angry clouds. Mama Tavie's whisper startled her.

"You all right, child?"

"Oh, Mama Tavie, I didn't mean to wake you."

Mama Tavie swung around toward the tiny space on the other side of the bed and stretched out her short legs.

"Truth is, so far I ain't slept much tonight."

Dinah circled the foot of the bed and joined her friend on the other side. Hopefully, she'd not committed another perilous act of which she was not aware. "Is something wrong, Mama Tavie? Have I done something to displease you?"

Mama Tavie reached over and lightly patted Dinah's hand. "No, honey. It ain't 'bout you a'tall. I can't rightly put a finger on it. I just got a bad feeling in my spirit, like somethin' terrible trying to get started tonight."

Dinah's breath caught at the sound of hoarseness in Mama Tavie's voice. Terribly wrong? She looked around at the close, sparsely furnished room and thought about how hard this little woman worked every day, from the rising of the sun to the going down of the same. No time off, no pay, no parlor or drawing room to retire to, no privacy to look forward to. And although this room was luxurious compared to the hovels Dinah had heard most slaves were forced to live in, to her way of thinking, enslavement was always "terribly wrong."

"You don't think anything's wrong with Jonathan . . . I mean . . . Mr. Mayfield, do you?"

Mama Tavie smiled and smoothed Dinah's hand once more. "You a discerning little old thing, ain't you? Now how'd you know I was thinking about Joe-Nathan?"

Awash in shamefacedness, Dinah ducked her head to her chest before finally attempting an answer. "Well, I guess I've seen how you look at him at supper, almost the way I'd picture a worried mother examining a son she cherished."

The words hung in the air like the scent of an oncoming storm until Mama Tavie's voice emerged as a line of painful whispers. "You right. I do cherish him. Joe-Nathan was God's ram in the bush for me when I thought I'd never be able to put one foot in front of the other again. Did you know I was once the proud mama of five sons?"

"Mama Tavie! Really?"

Violette's snoring lurched to a halt before she moaned and turned toward the wall.

"Shhhh. Last thing we want is to give Miss Mouth over there a fresh bone to tote around to everybody at Riverwood."

Dinah tittered. "Yes, ma'am. But what happened to your sons? Were . . . were they—"

"Sold? No, they wasn't sold, though they likely would have been had they lived. Such fine strapping boys they was." Mama Tavie's white teeth gleamed in the darkness. "Loved to tease little Joe-Nathan since he was younger than them all. Their papa was rooster-strutting proud of every one of 'em and vowed he'd die first before he saw one of his boys sold. Turned out, he never had to face that test.

"First I thought Sam, that was my youngest, might have just been trying to get out of doing his chores that summer day. All of us had jes come in from the fields when he commenced to complaining of a bad headache. Next thing we knowed the child was vomiting his insides out. Didn't want no supper, nothin'."

Dinah squirmed causing dry scratchy sounds from the mattress. "Mama Tavie, if this is too hard for you—"

"A few days passed and he got a little better." Mama Tavie continued to whisper into the darkness as though Dinah had said nothing. "We thought it was all over, and when the overseer who'd been checking 'most hourly saw him sitting up, he made him go back to the fields. Then his fever shot back up, quick and deadly like. The whites of his little eyes turned the color of a sunflower. His mouth and nose and eyes started to bleed. My baby went plum outta his head. Rambling 'bout things nobody never heard of. Didn't even know who his mama was. And just like that." Mama Tavie made a loud snapping sound with her thumb and middle finger. "Ole Yellow Jack stole little Sam away from us. He was only ten, and he was my baby."

Silence stretched into eternity. "Mama Tavie, I'm so sorry. W-what about the rest of your boys? Your husband?"

"Yellow Jack is a greedy dog, honey. Started with my youngest and he stripped me of everyone I had. And he threw in Joe-Nathan's mother—my best friend—for good measure. After that, the poor little fellow's papa give up. Just laid down and died as though Joe-Nathan didn't count in this world a'tall."

A sense of how selfish she'd been descended upon Dinah with the force of a fallen boulder. She thought her heart would shatter from regret. She'd taken so little time to inquire about the slaves here at Riverwood. From the moment she'd set foot on the grounds, all she'd thought about was herself and how she could keep out of harm's way. Yet for the most part, they'd accepted her as one of their own.

And she'd had the nerve to judge Jonathan's aloofness?

"Joe-Nathan couldn't 'a been no more than seven or eight," continued Mama Tavie. "But with Missy Mayfield's permission, after his papa died, he moved into the cabin with me and called his self taking care of me. In my head, I was in a bad way. Every night I come home from the fields, I wanted to just be left alone to die. But the little rascal kept asking questions and trying to feed me and such. He'd always been a sweet little booger but lazy as I don't know what. But when his mama and papa died, it was like something turned over in him. He brung in kindling for me, kept the cabin clean for me, even tried to cook for me. During the day, he'd do the overseer's bidding in the field 'longside me right close to my skirts. But at night after he'd done all he could to make me comfortable, he'd crawl up in the bed with me and put his little arms 'round me. Trying to comfort both of us, I reckon."

A big fat teardrop plopped onto the back of Dinah's hand. The darkness must have covered for her because Mama Tavie never missed a beat.

"Little by little, he gave me the will to last up and down them rows each day 'til one day I realized I'd gotten my legs back underneath me. He whittled pretty pieces of wood for me. On cold nights when I thought my heart would never thaw out again, he read the Lord's word to me. He became like all my boys rolled up into one. Until one day when he was eighteen, the master up and freed him.

"He dreaded leaving me, but I knowed he needed to go learn to be a real man. And, Praise God, by that time, the Lord had restored me enough to fight my way out of that head fog I'd been in. So Joe-Nathan took out to become the cabinetmaker he already was. He ain't been the same these six years, though, since he come home. Oh, he's made a name for his self, but there's a hollow place in him that needs to be filled with the Lord. And a good woman."

Dinah's heart squeezed. Though she could never be that woman, she understood his pain so much better. But why was Mama Tavie suddenly worried tonight?

"He been clinging to them papers ever since he came back, like they some kind of lifeline. If he was living in a place where nobody knowed him, why, it'd make a lot more sense the way he acts. But it's as though that piece of paper done become who he is."

"Mama Tavie?" Dinah could hear the tentativeness in her own voice. But she had to ask. "Can he get more papers?" Dinah could almost feel Mama Tavie's body tauten on the old shuck mattress. "What is it? What did I say?"

"That's just it. He got more papers. Right here under this bed."

"Then, I don't understand. Why haven't you given them to him?"

"Well, honey, all I can say right now is that's for me and the good Lord to know and for you and everybody else to find out."

12

Something was afoot. Pudgy arms resting upon her ample bosom, Violette possessed an improved smugness this morning that gave Dinah's stomach a tumble. Ignoring her, Dinah hurried through her morning ablutions. My, but the week had flown by. A few more days and she would be saying goodbye to the only man whose touch hadn't made her feel contaminated.

The new sunburst had yet to be attached to the canopy, but Jonathan's woodwork was nearly complete. The room looked splendid. Perhaps today she could steal a few moments to just sit and talk with him about what it was like to be a respected businessman— and dream of what it would be like if that mahogany and rose room belonged to the two of them—before he permanently returned to his house in town.

"You just won't listen, will you?" Violette's voice hit like ice water flung into Dinah's face. "Mr. Mayfield just like all the other rich men 'round here: Hungry for power. Don't say I didn't warn you when he start buying slaves."

"Ha! That shows how little you know about the man."

Having had the time to think clearly, Dinah almost laughed out loud at Violette's silly assumption. Jonathan? Buying other human beings? Not the Jonathan she knew. Not the one that handled her with tenderness she hadn't known existed. Though Dinah's judgment wasn't always flawless, her heart usually gave sound readings about people. And the closeness of the last few days told her that Jonathan Mayfield was at least half as smitten by her as she was by him.

"No, Violette, I won't listen to you because I know you're wrong about Mr. Mayfield. I have proof."

Preparing to leave her disgruntled roommate in the dependency, Dinah groaned at her image in Mama Tavie's shard of a mirror. All her clothing had burned in the New Orleans fire, and the dress she'd worn ever since she'd been here seemed more ill-fitted each day. The color of moss, it was possessed of a nondescript long-sleeved bodice attached to a gathered skirt that made her look like the stuffings of a scarecrow. Standard slave issue clothing so far removed from the designs in her head that it was dizzying to even contemplate. She'd washed the scratchy dress as often as she could. Still, she felt freshness was a thing of days gone by.

If only she had a bit of the lavender scent Mistress Devereaux had given her last Christmas.

Feeling a fresh wave of condemnation at the thought, she had to admit she wanted to smell good today when she saw Jonathan, knowing quite well that if by some magic-wand chance he were to fall on one knee and propose right there in the rose and mahogany bedroom, she'd have to say no. She'd still be owned by someone, making it impossible to consent to join anyone in matrimony. She'd not gotten any feedback from her new mistress about her sewing ability, which could mean the world in terms of her future. But no matter what, this was indeed the day that the Lord had made. And whatever happened, she would rejoice and be glad in it.

Oh, that it was that easy!

JONATHAN HAD SLEPT all night in his clothes. Hadn't even bothered to change before returning to Riverwood. He rested his weight on one hip and looked up at the progress of the molding. Thank goodness his time here was drawing to a close. He'd promised to have the room done by Christmas, and he'd kept his promise. All he had to do was wait until Dinah finished the canopy insert and install it. Man would he be glad when he'd worked his last day with the girl who'd burned his freedom. And stolen his heart.

He touched the swollen cut above his eye and worked to loosen his stiff shoulder—two of the identical spots where he'd been battered so many years ago—then smoothed the rumpled set of clothes he wore.

Admit it. You're strung tighter than a set of fiddle strings.

With good reason. Last night's bizarre experience swept away all doubt that his safety was gone, taking with it his hopes of ever truly being counted as a free man again, re-ushering him into a buried horror that struggled to resurface each day of his life. Too drained to fight the flood of memories, Jonathan felt his shoulders sag as, in broad daylight, he finally gave himself over to a nine-year-old nightmare.

He squinted, trying to see into the foggy Atlantic morning, at least he supposed it was the Atlantic, since he'd overheard the captain say they'd left behind the Gulf of Mexico. And from looking at the heavens earlier before the fog rolled in, clearly the ship had turned northward. He stretched his arms overhead and breathed in a helping of the moist air. Had it only been several weeks ago that Master Mayfield informed him of his freedom? He slid his hand into his thin shabby jacket and patted the papers that declared him free, pinned to his pocketless shirt. Though Papa and Mama had been dead for more than a decade, the master had only recently decided to issue him this priceless document. Unable to contain himself, he spoke his excitement into the cloudy surroundings.

"A few more days and I'll be there in the shop of Thomas Day."

"But yer in the wrong place right now, ain'tcha, lad?"

Jonathan stiffened. The gravelly foreign-sounding voice behind him belonged to the same goon who'd tried to force him from the deck once before. With no choice but to face him, he turned toward the overpowering smell of strong drink.

"Did you hear me, lad? I said explain what yer doing out here where gentlemen belong."

"I told you before, sir. I don't want trouble."

"Hear that, Brady? He don't want trouble."

Another figure, a barrel-chested giant whose shoulders seemed as tall as the mast, appeared out of the fog. Jonathan hadn't known there were two of them. There was a meanness emanating from them—as though to kill him and throw him over the railing would come as naturally as spitting into the ocean. The lapels of his collar closed around Jonathan's neck as the drunken fellow drew him closer, sending his senses reeling from the smell of rancid breath. Jonathan decided to do nothing. Take the path of no resistance. He'd done nothing against them. Surely, they'd come to their senses before harming him.

"By heavens, lad. Don'tcha know you got no right to be out here dirtying up the place where decent men and women be gettin' their air? Yer kind seems to be popping up everywhere these days, taking jobs from the hardworking Irish who've come to this country to try to better the lives of their sons and daughters."

Jonathan felt himself being patted down. His heart struck double time as a hand halted at the sound of the papers.

"Well, well, well. What have we here?"

Yanking the papers from Jonathan's shirt, the man dropped his hold. "Look, Brady. We've got us some papers. I'd wager ones that say this fellow can take jobs we be needing."

Jonathan lunged in the direction of the bow only to be pinned against the rail.

"Whoa, lad. Not so fast. Before we're done here, I want to leave my signature with you, so's you can show it to yer maker, the devil. And ain't I the merciful one, lad? To think of leaving this little memory in yer left 'and rather than yer right?"

The man called Brady held Jonathan against the ship's rail, while the spokesman bragged about something else he planned to do to Jonathan besides leaving the signature in his hand before he threw him overboard. Something ugly. Something unthinkable. So Jonathan chose not to think of it—not to think of anything, for that matter. Except to thank God Mama Tavie would never know of his grave at the ocean's floor.

SURPRISED TO FIND him in the bedroom already bent over his tool box, Dinah stuttered out a greeting. "G-good morning, Jonathan."

"Morning."

Her heart sank. His voice was emptied of every whit of warmth she'd felt the day before. "Is something wrong? Didn't you sleep well?"

"No."

He picked up his hammer and turned to face her. The ever fastidious Jonathan Mayfield looked positively bedraggled—eyes bloodshot, the usually-clean jawline sprouting a beard, and clothes looking as though what little sleep he'd managed had occurred with them in full use.

"You probably miss your own bed."

Grunt.

His movements were stiff. A closer look revealed cuts above one eye and along his face and hands.

"What happened to your eye?"

Silence.

A swirl of panic enveloped Dinah. She needed to feel the warmth of his words flowing into her heart and soul once more.

And from the looks of things this morning, he desperately needed someone to take care of him. Every sign warned her that what she was about to ask was ill-conceived and ill-timed. She was about to run out in front of her Heavenly Father like a reckless child into a heavily trafficked street. But she didn't have much time left to savor Jonathan's nearness, and she was desperate to know. After all, hadn't he leveled the same question to her just a day or so ago? Wasn't turnabout fair play?

"Tell me. Why have you never married?"

FEARING the hopeful glow on her face would melt him into a pitiful puddle of helplessness, Jonathan fought to remind himself of what happened last night. Though he'd gotten the better of the miserable goons, he now knew without a doubt he had to quash his feelings for Dinah Devereaux. He'd not subject her to life with a slave, never knowing when one of them would be sold. He'd already lost his freedom to the carelessness of this girl. And if he didn't put a stop to it now, he'd most likely end up like his father grieving himself to death over a woman.

He steeled his features and forced his back into ramrod stiffness. Jaw, eyes, ribs. All sore and protesting against his resistance to Dinah's charms.

"And what business is that of yours?"

"Well, I-I thought it a fair question. After all, not long ago you did ask the same of me, and we—"

"We what, Miss Devereaux? Hardly know each other?" Her fallen countenance flayed his heart. "But you're right. In a foolish moment I did ask that of you, and your answer was straightforward. I'll do no less for you. My private life is my concern."

Solidly meeting his gaze, she hid her hurt like the lady she'd been raised to be. "Begging your pardon, Mr. Mayfield, but when a gentleman warns a lady against falling into the snare of a roué, regales her with stories of his childhood and presumes to kiss her, I should think that accounts for at least one concerned inquiry about his life."

Inwardly, Jonathan railed against himself for stepping into that last retort. If he didn't come up with something soon, he was going to be worsted, possibly falling on one knee like a besotted dunce. He mustered his thoughts.

Remember Jonathan, if this girl hadn't burned your papers, you wouldn't be a criminal right now. As it is, your business is going to be greatly diminished, possibly closed when you're hauled off to someone's field.

"So you took a few well-meaning gestures as an open door to probe my private life?"

"I beg your pardon. A few well-meaning gestures?"

Again, he gave her his back. "I suspect you're too naïve to even understand what marriage can do to a man."

"Since I'm not a man, I'd hope a sane person wouldn't expect such of me."

Jonathan was relieved she couldn't see the smile forming. My, but she was quick-witted. His back still to her, he went about collecting tools, not knowing or caring if he'd be needing them today or not. If he wasn't so desperate to put a stop to this rising . . . admiration, and God knows what else, toward her, he would have been truly intrigued.

"Well, since I am of the male species, let me tell you. Wedlock destroys a man. That's what it does. Loads him up with responsibility, puts his heart on the line, and then stomps on it."

She stamped her foot on the carpeted floor as though she wished it was his heart. "Oh, admit it. You're too caught up in protecting yourself to understand that not taking risks in life is no life at all. You, you're no African prince," she sputtered. "Ibrahima would never be as boorish as you. You're a mean, stubborn, selfish ogre, just like everybody says you are!"

Shame, confusion, and a little pleasure flooded Jonathan. He turned to face her. "Who is Ibrahima, and whoever said I was a prince?"

"I did, Sir Mayfield, in my naïve stupidity. But I take back every word I said. And . . . and more! Good day," she said, as she ran out the door.

SEATED at the sewing machine Mrs. McMillan had provided, Dinah sneaked a glance at Jonathan over her shoulder as she worked on the drapery to match the tester sunburst. She had thought him a study in contrasts from the moment she'd laid eyes on him. The stylish loose-fitting business trousers, double breasted vest, frockcoat, shirt and cravat tailored to fit a six-foot caramel colored prince had struck her as a bolt of lightning in a snowstorm. But something about the easy way he moved around in those work pants this morning and that collarless shirt, the sleeves rolled up baring his forearms, captured her imagination in a way that left her breath-deprived.

She tried to arrest his gaze to apologize for her harshness yesterday. But it appeared Jonathan was looking for every opportunity to continue to show Dinah his back. Fresh anger spiked in her. Well. She'd show him that most games called for at least two players. She squared her shoulders and set her Howe machine flying at full throttle, hoping the noise would attract him. But she might as well be pressing her foot against a bale of cotton for all the notice he was taking.

Oh, for pity's sake! She felt like tying on one of the kinds of rare tantrums she'd seen Emerald throw when she wanted Dinah to tell her another bedtime story and was too sleepy to hear it. Another minute of this deafening silence and . . . *I declare I shall go mad.*

How was it that in a few short weeks she'd become so hungry for the very sound of this lout capitulating to his bad manners days on end just to be able to hear his voice? Had she always been this starved for company, subconsciously striking an uneasy truce with the looming threat of a lifetime of loneliness in her Garden District attic room?

Crushing that traitorous thought, she decided she didn't want to spend their last hours together with this icy chasm between them. Maybe if she complimented him on his work clothes? Would that be too forward? She stood from her seat at the sewing machine. To steady her hands, she smoothed the skirt of one of the two dresses she'd now been issued at Riverwood.

"Jon—uh—Mr. Mayfield, may I ask who makes your work clothes for you? I mean . . . as work clothes go, they're quite well-made . . . it seems to me."

Dinah stuttered to a halt as Jonathan slowly turned to face her. Instead of the warm smile she'd hoped to see, she found herself staring into a pair of blazing gray orbs.

JONATHAN SIZZLED. Would this girl ever quit? Except for that vague reference to some African prince named Ibrahima, hadn't she'd insulted every speck of confidence he'd tried to build up over the last decade? Now, just because she'd been reared almost as an African princess, the epitome of refinement and the most lovely creature he'd ever beheld, did she have to spell out what a bumpkin he was? Having to earn a living working with his hands rather than behind a desk like real gentlemen did?

"Are you quite finished, Miss Devereaux?"

Without a hint of flirting, she batted her eyes, seemingly totally confused. But he wouldn't be put off by her wiles. In her genteel way, she was informing him of his lack of style as an entrepreneur.

"Forgive me. As a seamstress, I notice these things. I only meant to compliment the artisan."

"You meant to remind me of my boorishness, even in my work clothes."

For a minute, Jonathan thought she might turn tail and leave him alone. Wrong.

"Mr. Mayfield. This is getting to be a most unpleasant habit, sir."

"And how is that, madam?

"Oh, just a simple matter of my continuous well-meaning toward you and your loutish interpretations."

"And do you consider subtle disdain of a man's attire 'well-meaning'?"

Her jaw dropping beneath bucked eyes, she raised her hands into the air and made a complete circle. Jonathan cringed as she shrugged her shoulders and slapped her arms against her sides in a most unladylike fashion.

"Subtle disdain? How did you come to be so pitifully inept that you can't distinguish a pure compliment from subtle disdain? What more do you want from the Lord, anyway? You are a free man with one of the most successful businesses in Natchez. But for some reason, you continue to look for greater feats, choosing to overlook the fact that you have already been blessed to do your day-to-day transactions out of your shop wearing your well-made work clothes."

Her countenance lit up with something new. She cocked her head to the side. Whatever she was about to say was going to hurt him.

"The other day you expressed a wish, one you refused to flesh out, one that's been nagging me all this time. And now I understand. You wish you could be comfortable in your own skin. You don't like yourself, Mr. Mayfield. Why, I've not quite figured out, but I know it's true. So let me tell you something. If you're offended, it's not by my so-called subtle intentions. It's from your own injured confidence."

Goodness! In addition to everything else, the woman was a mind reader.

13

Jonathan was gone forever, hours of painful silence between them finally ended. Her creativity utterly exhausted, Dinah stood on a stool putting the finishing touches on the sunburst gracefully accenting the handsome tester. A combination of light and studied footsteps on the stairs gave way to an unexpected greeting.

"Good afternoon, Dinah."

Dinah? When had the usually formal Mr. James started calling her Dinah?

In full service mode with a touch of uncharacteristic dis-ease, Mr. James stepped into the bedroom and positioned himself next to the door. A gloved hand resting across the small of his back, he extended an arm toward the doorway.

"Mistress McMillan is here to see you."

Mistress McMillan?

Oh glory be! Dinah leapt from the stool, as the mistress of Riverwood stepped across the threshold. Venturing her deepest curtsey, Dinah managed a tremulous greeting.

"Good afternoon, Mistress McMillan. Mr. James."

The mistress lifted a brow before scowling at James. Dinah's breath hitched. Had her reference to the butler as "mister" offended?

"Ahem!" Dinah had never seen Mr. James this disconcerted. "Uh, well. Since Mr. . . . that is, the cabinetmaker, has signed off on the job, the mistress desired to see the finished product."

Mistress McMillan turned to look at Mr. James, her hair pulled back so severely that Dinah wondered if the sides of her miniscule head ached.

"James. If you please. I can speak for myself."

Dinah's heart skipped around like a disoriented grasshopper as the tiny woman allowed herself a slow tortuous gaze about the room.

"Yes. Jonathan Mayfield has certainly lived up to his billing."

Inwardly, Dinah exhaled a breath of relief. *Thank You, Father. She's pleased.* She stood perfectly still as the mistress moved in for a closer look at the sunburst, her face gradually taking on a nondescript stare, her small piercing eyes suddenly black with disbelief.

"But as for this canopy . . ."

In a fraction of a thought, Mistress McMillan had crumbled Dinah's whole world like a morsel of biscuit between thumb and forefinger. A buzz went off in her head, rendering the rest of the woman's comments nothing more than mimed gibberish. This time Dinah would shield herself from the hurt the way she should have that morning standing at the door of Master Devereaux's library.

"I don't have to listen. I don't have to listen," she thought. She'd simply shut her mind down. Besides, why should she listen to what she already knew? She was doomed to fail. First with Jonathan, now with her owners.

Good Lord, was there nothing left for her now except the fields and babies she couldn't afford to love for fear of losing them? And heaven help her, somewhere down the road, a filthy degrading house of ill repute? Prickles of fear danced along her neck and spine, leaving beads of perspiration in its wake. A firm hand squeezed her shoulder.

"My hearty congratulations, miss, er . . . that is . . . Dinah."

Mr. James's voice pulled her back to the present as he pressed a handkerchief into her hand. Unbeknownst to her, tears had mixed with the perspiration coating her face. Thankfully, Mrs. McMillan had moved to examine Dinah's work more closely.

"Congratulations," repeated Mr. James a bit too loudly, "on how much the mistress *loves* your work."

Mistress McMillan looked around from the sunburst. "I do indeed."

Like exotic island sunshine, the butler's words burned off the fog of her mind. She hadn't failed this time. Her mistress actually liked the work. Sarah Susan McMillan *loved* Dinah Devereaux's work. And if it hadn't been for Mr. James's forcing her to listen with a clear head, she would have lost the opportunity for which she'd been praying for weeks.

Mr. James. What a special, special man.

DINAH MANAGED to slip through the servants' hall and out to the other side of the dependency without being detected.

Mrs. McMillan loved her sunburst. And hadn't the lady just guaranteed Dinah many more orders? How long before she might be able to make an offer to purchase her freedom?

So why do I feel totally deserted?

Hot tears coursed down her cheeks. How had she let her heart slip away to a man like Jonathan Mayfield?

Violette had been right all along. Jonathan Mayfield was nothing more than a talented churl who thought of no one's feelings but his own. Whispers of deeply ingrained self-recriminations joined forces to escape her lips.

"No use to blame Jonathan. You're the one who allowed yourself to dream of marriage and family. When will you learn to accept your station in life? No matter what the mistress said in there, you'll never earn enough to buy yourself. You're not good enough. You're not pretty enough. You're nothing but a slave—

"What you crying 'bout, pretty lady?"

Dinah spun around toward whoever was intruding on her private tear-letting.

Eli. Of course.

She couldn't help noticing the wheelbarrow off to the side, filled with holly branches loaded with red berries. Secretly, she'd hoped to be asked to join in the hustle and bustle of decorating. Now even that desire was gone. Would she ever see beauty again, ever rid her mind of these tarnished Jonathan-thoughts?

"Begging your pardon, but I-I wasn't crying. It's the weather that's causing the tears."

"Oh, really now?" He flashed a sinister smile. "I would swear them tears was the real thing." He yanked Dinah so close she could scarcely breathe. "Looks to me like somebody could use a little comfort."

"What do you think you're doing? Let go of me."

"And what you planning to do if I don't?"

"Let me go, I said. And you'd better start explaining what you mean by 'comfort,' or I shall consider myself insulted and report you to the master."

Gripping her waist with one hand, Eli roared and slapped his thigh with the other. "Well, ain't you just the little uppity lady, though." He mellowed into a slow grin as he released her. "Looks like a man be having his work cut out for him if he go'n bring you down a notch."

"Indeed, he would. More than you can imagine, you brute."

Feeling more soiled by the second, Dinah huffed toward the dependency stairs. Midway to the top, Eli's words, shot through with sinister laughing, reached her.

"Hey, Miss Lady. Least I know of one uppity fellow that's already been whittled down a bit, 'specially since them slave catchers done got a whiff of him and whipped him up some.

Next time'll be worse when they haul him down to New Orleans. He's sure gonna bring in a good price down there."

Dinah's heart pitched. Slave catchers? Was that where the bruises had come from? And the rudeness? And the brusque parting? Now more than ever Jonathan would hold her responsible for the loss of his freedom and with good reason.

"Oh, how I wish Mama Tavie would give him that other set of papers," she whispered as she mounted the final steps to their room.

But so far she hadn't. Much as she didn't like questioning her, Dinah was just going to have to ask Mama Tavie why and suffer the consequences.

IT WAS SATURDAY MORNING, and still sore from Wednesday's scuffle, Jonathan gingerly made his way down the stairs of his comfortable two-story brick home on State Street. The pain in his ribs paled next to the ache he'd felt in his heart ever since he turned his back on Dinah yesterday and walked away. Suddenly, his house, a few doors down from the home of the noted mulatto free man and barber, William Johnson, seemed cavernous. Vast and hollow. Though he comforted himself with the knowledge that it wasn't nearly as huge as the Natchez nabobs, what had driven him to build a house this size? The words of a perceptive beauty intercepted his thoughts.

"You don't like yourself."

The memory stung. How could a man who wasn't a man ever truly like himself? Heading for his shop around the back, he paused to think of the scores of black and brown and yellow men in Natchez who'd obtained their freedom, like his assistant Benjamin Catlett, for instance. But although he respected most of them, it was Mr. Johnson, the barber who lived down the street, who had exercised the most influence on Jonathan's realization of his dreams. It was the man's model of possibilities that had shed a distant light upon his path toward financial independence.

Except when it came to owning slaves. That Jonathan could neither stomach nor fathom about the gentleman.

A knock at the door chased away his musings. Who'd be invading his privacy like this on a Saturday morning?

"Who is it!"

"Me, Benjamin."

Go away. "Come in. It's open."

"How're you doing, sir."

The familiar teasing grated on Jonathan more than usual. "What're you doing here, Benjamin?"

"I haven't had a chance to talk to you lately. What was that skirmish all about the other night?"

"If you can answer that, then we'll both be more knowledgeable men." Jonathan pointed toward a seat in the foyer. "Have a seat." He started to pace as Benjamin settled himself onto the settee. "Tell me, Benjamin, have you ever needed to clear your thinking so badly until you'd risk something foolish to get it done?"

"Well, yes, I suppose I have."

"All these years I've had my papers, I never made it a habit to walk the roads around here at night because, though I've been blessed with a good measure of business, there are always a few who don't take kindly to a black man living and working in the middle of town. But Wednesday night, I had to get away from Riverwood."

Benjamin grinned smugly. "And what, may I ask, could have possibly caused that?"

Jonathan knew he'd set that one up, but he would not be baited by a matchmaking zealot like Benjamin Catlett. "Do you or do you not want to hear my theory about the assault?"

Benjamin placed his ankle across one knee and clasped his foot with both hands. Smirking, he leaned forward.

"By all means."

"A week ago, Miss Dinah Devereaux burned my freedom papers in the kitchen fireplace at Riverwood."

Benjamin shot to his feet. "She what?"

"Keep your shirt on. It was an accident. The more important thing here is what happened out there days later—Tuesday night to be exact, in the presence of one Eli Duggan."

Jonathan felt a pang of conscience. Was this really about Eli? Or was he childishly smarting over being avoided at the meal the other night? Benjamin's voice cut through his thoughts.

"Well?"

"Well, what?"

"What about Eli? In case you haven't heard, that fellow's reputation precedes him."

"I have heard. And I'm troubled by it."

"Truly?" Jonathan's matchmaking friend had that impish look about him again. "Troubled for the safety of anyone in particular?"

"All right, if it's Miss Devereaux you're trying so hard to bring into this conversation, yes, I do care about her well-being." Jonathan blew out a weary breath. "Despite the way she drives me to distraction each time I'm around her, it's easy to see she's an innocent."

"Aha! I knew it, saw it the very first day you went to work up there. You're in love with her."

"Whoa! I didn't say I loved her. I said I care about her." Jonathan lifted his hands in frustration. "You're barely twenty. What do you know about love?"

"Frankly, I wonder the same of you."

"Plenty. Much more than I want to." Jonathan felt his body becoming rigid. "I could tell you about how my father would have let a small boy die of neglect had it not been for Mama Tavie. That boy was me. I could tell you about how he claimed he couldn't go on without the love of his life. About how when I awakened in the night and found him staring into the fireplace at the weeks-old ashes, he looked down at me with utter disdain as though I was a bug he'd been left with which he would crush had my mother not extracted a promise from him. Every day he made his feelings clear. 'There's nothing left for me without her,' he rehearsed to me. Every day."

Jonathan dragged his palm down his face. "How did we get on the topic of love and Miss Devereaux, anyway?"

"Sorry. Continue with your theory about why you were attacked."

Trying to decipher if Benjamin had truly settled in to seriousness, Jonathan pinned him with a look before continuing.

"Violette, the other new kitchen worker up there, publicly and deviously I might add, announced the destruction of my papers in front of everybody." Jonathan walked over to a small marble top table in his foyer and picked up a crumpled piece of paper. He handed it to Benjamin. "I wonder if perhaps this, along with the attack the other night, might be the results of some information provided by Eli Duggan, or maybe that arrogant slave driver named Jethro. He was there too. And if it is, what does that mean for the future of my business?"

Benjamin furrowed his brow. "Your business will survive this, man. You're too good at what you do for it not to. But if somehow it doesn't, God will lead you into another calling that you may not yet know is there."

Jonathan looked at his friend. Deep down he knew that what he was about to say was no longer true. But it had been his false truth for so long until he was loath to let it go.

"To be my own man in business is the only calling I have, the only one I want."

"If you love God as you claim, there's always a higher calling than your earthly business, Jonathan."

He'd called Jonathan by his name. Jonathan braced for what was coming.

"I'll leave you to your foul mood then." Pressing down his pant legs, Benjamin stood to his feet and moved to the door. His hand on the doorknob, he turned as if he'd just been enlightened by a mountain mystic. "You know what, Jonathan? You've never really stopped being a slave, to this business, to your stubbornness. To those papers.

Jonathan cringed at the nervousness in his own staccato laughter. "Funny you should say that because all the while I had those papers, I was in fact, still a slave." He dragged his gaze toward his friend's. "The paper Miss Devereaux destroyed, the one I've carried for years, was nothing more than a yellowed lie."

Benjamin released the doorknob and resumed his seat on the settee. "All right Jonathan. It's time to talk. I mean really talk."

"My papers were in good order when I boarded the ship in New Orleans." Jonathan took the chair next to the small table in the foyer. "Still I found the fog cover that morning comforting as I stood next to the icy rail. The wonder of freedom was still fresh on my mind. But free or not, I was aware that several cotton planters on board weren't pleased with the captain's decision to allow me to walk the deck at will. But since I'd paid the captain a good bit of what my father had left me, he'd seen his way clear to encourage the disgruntled planters to let me be."

"What your father left you? I don't understand. I thought he'd died a slave on the old Mayfield plantation."

"He did. But though I was barely above the age of seven when Papa died, I recall his working at night, making all kinds of furniture. He even made rocking chairs."

Jonathan shared with Benjamin how, swallowed by the size of it, he would furiously rock himself in the chair his papa had made for his mother. He explained how Octavia McMillan had taken him in after his parents' death and how he'd learned to labor in the fields alongside the slaves each day of his life. Until one day when he was eighteen and his master called him in.

"Imagine how stunned I was when I was abruptly freed and given the considerable sum my father had been allowed to save."

"Stunned and quite grateful, I would think. Mr. Mayfield must have been a singular master. Most slaveholders would've simply added that sum to their coffers."

"Not so fast, my friend. The man did indeed give me the money. But he dealt a blow to something far more important to a scared young slave who'd never ventured further than Natchez Under-the-Hill. The words my master said to me haven't ceased to sear my soul every day."

Jonathan's insides coiled at the idea of going further. He'd finally opened his personal Pandora's Box, and he knew there was no turning back. Could he get through the telling of this whole nightmare without coming undone? Of course, he could. He was a man. Nothing could undo that.

Or had his manhood already been undone and he just couldn't admit to it?

"'Like your father, you do a fine job with your hands.' That's how my master started the talk, which he'd obviously planned for some time. 'You'll be a good cabinetmaker someday. I'll grant you that.' I stood there, my heart swelling with pride over the only compliment he'd ever given me. Then came the words that have acted as a perpetually-hot branding iron every day of my life since.

"Holding the valise full of money he was about to give me, Ethan Mayfield pointed a crooked finger at my face. 'But don't go getting it into your head that you're going to become some great businessman like the white gentlemen in town. It takes more than giftedness with your hands to build a business. When it comes to figures, Negro males are more of the nature of women. Many women are gifted in running a house. But the lion's share of them are lost when it comes to simple arithmetic. I'm afraid it's not in their blood to wrestle with numbers. And no matter what my willful and idealistic wife has tried to teach you, it's not in yours.'"

Silence rolled over the foyer as outrage emanated from Benjamin. What was this young man's story? Should Jonathan continue, or had his friend had enough? The taut expectant look of Benjamin's frame indicated he would hear more.

"I shriveled beneath this new indictment. My minutes-old hopes drooped like the leaves of a poisoned tree. Could it really be true that I was never to become a man? Wasn't this the same man who'd nearly shouted one Christmas morning, 'Early to bed, early to rise, makes a man healthy, wealthy, and wise? Was I not a man? Or had God written me off as an inferior investment?

"Struggling to appear tall and upright in the presence of this man I and my parents had slaved for all our lives, I couldn't wait to leave that place. Suddenly, I was consumed with the thought of escaping my master's words and the town of Natchez. Though I would miss my beloved Mama Tavie, one day I'd prove myself a real man by purchasing her from Ethan Mayfield with an offer that his constant mismanagement would have to succumb to. And even today I'd make Mr. McMillan an offer for her if I thought there was a chance he'd take it.

"Anyhow, right there on the spot, I determined I was going to find the renowned cabinetmaker named Thomas Day of North Carolina whom my father had spoken so highly of. I reached for the papers, thanked my master, and was gone."

Looking deeply troubled, Benjamin interrupted. "Got any coffee ready?"

Jonathan had been so caught up in his thoughts this morning that he'd forgotten to eat himself, much less offer Benjamin anything.

"Sorry, no. But I can make us some."

Jonathan led the way to the kitchen where he made coffee and retrieved some cold biscuits and jam. Benjamin ate in silence, finally nodding for him to continue.

"You're sure?"

"I asked to hear this, didn't I?"

"All right. Don't say I didn't warn you. After wandering around in New Orleans a few days, I took a small ship up the Atlantic coast. I thought of Mama Tavie every hour of every day, wishing I could have brought her along with me. But the thought of being a free man and finally getting a chance to work with Thomas Day buoyed my spirits enough to press on.

"Then one morning, I was cautiously enjoying the fresh air on the main deck when the same dingy ruffian that had been eying me from the beginning jumped me. Between him and another fellow, they pinned me against the rail but not before they discovered my manumission papers. After promising to carve up my body and pitch me into the Atlantic, the spokesman painstakingly tore my paper into tiny pieces while the other one made me watch. I felt as though they were shredding my future before my eyes. Then slowly they sifted the bits of paper through their fingers into the foggy ocean.

"Something snapped inside me. I realized my short-lived freedom was floating on the brine. Instantly, I'd become a field hand again, no longer equipped to disprove my master's decree against my manhood. My precious right to liberty was gone, and I was again reduced to a six-foot black boy with limitations far worse than those of the white housewife my master had compared me to. Somehow, I managed to wrench myself free. In an instant, I was pounding the lead thug with a fierceness that shocked him and me. But I never had a chance against the both of them. Not in that fog. Not with my lack of experience.

"Then what felt like the heel of a man's boot hit my back as another pummeled my shoulder into the deck boards. I struggled as they beat me senseless, the lead one announcing he was about to make good his promise to leave his signature in my left hand. He turned me over onto my back, and while the giant held me down, he went to work on me, drawing a diagonal line of blood across my palm. But that wasn't all. When he'd finished with my hand, he took another look at his bloody knife and was enlightened with fresh cruelty.

"'Tell you what,' he exclaimed, 'why don't we go ahead and fulfill the second promise—circumcise the lad, so's he'll never forget how important it is to follow the good book.'" Jonathan struggled to find his voice. "That was the last I heard before blessed oblivion overtook me."

"Did they . . . I mean . . . did they?"

Jonathan's body tightened with fresh resolve. All that was left of his dignity was a flat refusal to answer his best friend. Truth was he didn't exactly know what happened himself. Days later, when he'd woken up at a port, he found out they'd stripped him naked and left cuts all over his body, even in unthinkable places. The captain's crew had stopped them just as they were about to pitch him overboard. But Jonathan, affirming the status of being half a man that his master had assigned to him, had lost consciousness through most of it.

Silence hung between them until the usually unflappable Benjamin started to bang his fist into the palm of his hand. "Dogs. Nothing but a couple of mongrels. How did you ever make it to North Carolina?"

"The mercies of God. The captain made arrangements for me to be taken care of at the port of Norfolk, and after a month or so, I was delivered to Thomas Day in Milton, North Carolina who took me in and taught me everything I know. One of his free workers knew how to forge papers. But since Mr. Day had such an honorable reputation in Caswell County, I was never asked to show them around town. Neither did Mr. Day ever find out about the falsified papers. Nevertheless, I pinned them to my shirt over my heart and never went without them, until recently when they were burned."

"And you never told anyone about the counterfeit papers?"

"No one except Mama Tavie, and she would never tell anyone."

Benjamin nodded. "No, I don't believe she would." Eyes moist, he stood to his feet. "I think I finally understand, sir."

This time, the look on Jonathan's friend's face said the "sir" was in earnest.

14

Anxiety pelted Dinah like a hailstorm as she forced herself to sit at the supper table and wait for services to begin. It wasn't that she disliked worship. She'd enjoyed the many religious services the Devereauxs had taken her to. It was just that ever since Eli told her yesterday about what happened to Jonathan, she'd been waiting for a little time alone, just her and the breezes and the glorious revelation of the night skies, so she could pray in solitude for a way to convince Mama Tavie to give him that extra set of freedom papers.

But of all evenings, Mama Tavie had decided the house slaves needed to spend time together "seeking God's face." Not just the usual offering of grace, but a protracted prayer and song service before they began eating the food set before them.

Dinah thrummed her fingers against the table. What was the matter with Mama Tavie? Hadn't she heard what Dinah said last night about the trouble Jonathan was in? *Forgive me, Lord, but I don't understand.* Shame flooded her for that unkind thought against this woman she so admired. Still, she couldn't help but wonder if this worship service wasn't partly driven by her mentor's unease about Jonathan. Dinah fidgeted like a sleepy toddler.

Until the singing started. Never having heard a chorus of her people pour out their souls in song, she was spellbound by the multi-hued notes and chords filling the little room. Suddenly, she was surrounded by music that felt like rich, royal fabrics of brocaded blues and purple silks, all blended together to make strong covers that blanketed her with the presence of her Creator. But the plaintive longing underneath it all, as the men and women she'd come to know stood to the side of the fireplace in rapt expression, was so achingly poignant that Dinah thought her entire being would collapse in a puddle of pent-up desire and despair, released at long last.

Eventually, the afterglow of harmony fading from the room, Mr. James stood at the end of the table. Was he about to preach? Oh, no.

"Most of you know I've not always been a believer. But I take joy in the Lord's parable that upholds the eleventh-hour Christian, for without His limitless grace, I wouldn't be standing here today." He looked directly at Dinah and smiled. "No, Miss. I'm not a preacher, so I'm not going to preach. But God has given the mistress to allow us to worship together now and again. And this evening it falls my lot to lead us."

Mercy! Had she been that transparent? Lightheaded with embarrassment, Dinah steadfastly examined her hands.

"Bitter and rebellious," he continued, "I escaped my master's lash when I was around nineteen. I'd lived a good portion of my life on a plantation in Louisiana. And one day I determined that, for once, I was going to do whatever my flesh desired as hard as I could for as long as I could, even if I died in the midst of it. I set out that very night to fulfill my determination. I got as far as New Orleans where I lied to a free man of color who was a blacksmith, convincing him that I, too, had been freed and was looking for work. He took me on and paid me well. But sadly, I threw away every penny I earned on liquor and women. In the space of three weeks, I'd been recaptured, beaten out of my senses, and sent to the fields. But not without growing in wisdom."

"What was it you learnt, Mr. James?" Violette? Interested in something other than herself and Emerald? Not once raising his voice, the distinguished butler had gained everyone's attention, including Violette's.

"First thing I learned was to become sensitive to the Spirit. I never heard Him audibly, but lying on the pallet in my cabin, sections of my back stripped off like bark from a tree, I discovered that no matter the atrocities committed against me, no one could enslave my spirit except me."

Something eternal ignited in Dinah. She'd never heard it put quite that way before.

"The second thing I learned was that pursuit of fleshly desires—mansions, fine liquors, even bordellos—never meets with its expectations."

Mr. James flushed slightly at the mention of a bordello in his past, but Dinah reeled with the implications of what he'd said. Mr. James? Visiting a bordello, the kind of place where she was born? Then . . . then wouldn't that make him as tainted as she? Or perhaps she as redeemable as he?

"As Brother Paul says in the Holy Scriptures, 'I thank my God' that I discovered a freedom that cannot be stripped away as the flesh from my back was. Though I know that just as God delivered Israel from Pharaoh, so will He deliver us from bondage. Until He does, and make no mistake He will, I boast of a freedom that can never be auctioned off. Let us pray."

Mr. James's prayer was short. Forthright and sincere. But Dinah's thoughts about her past life hovered and fanned over her like the elaborate punkah over the big house dining table. Then the nightmare that never truly went away floated in like pieces of a shipwreck . . . .

Jack Hudson must have heard her crying as he left the library where Master Devereaux had explained her shameful birth.

If only she'd been able to resist hearing the truth.

Tracing the sounds to the drawing room across the hall, he closed the door behind him and took her in his arms. Alarms sounded in her head. But for the first time, she was feeling the strength and comfort of someone's arms. Wasn't that what she'd longed for? Almost twelve years she'd lived in this house and no human touch had ever reached her, at least not since she'd been old enough to recall. Shocked by the revelation of her birth and starved for the warmth of another human being, she leaned into Mr. Hudson's strength until his touch turned intrusive. Frightening. Ugly. She tried pushing back from him.

"I-I need to go. I have work to do."

But he pinned her closer against the French door leading to the gardens, each of his breaths ragged and threatening. "You're destined to be just like your mama, you know—a breeder working the fields before you're sent to a bordello. Might as well get you started."

Spawn of a breeder. Prostitute. Those were the words she'd heard Master Devereaux use to describe her mother. Suddenly, finding the dictionary was no longer necessary. Her very soul rebelled against the ugliness inside those words. Panic rose from her belly, groping at her throat.

"Let me go, Mr. Hudson. Please, let me go."

She fought him—dragging her nails across his stubbly jawline. Blood. Then pain shooting across her face as he slapped her. Over and over and—

"What? Oh, yes sir, Mr. James. I'm fine."

All eyes were upon her, seemingly trying to draw out those vile words that had followed her for so long. She plastered on a smile and blinked away the shame.

"Yes sir, I'm fine. Just fine."

CREATING designs by pushing food around on the tin plate in front of her, Dinah startled when the butler placed his hands on the back of her chair. He censured Eli's objection with a frown and addressed her in his usual poised manner.

"You look like you could use a bit of air, miss."

The statement warmed her, reminding her of Jonathan's use of her verbal habits. He followed her to the door of the kitchen and motioned her toward the steps to the back verandah.

"Is something wrong, miss?"

How is it that Mr. James could read her so well? He was becoming even better than Mama Tavie at detecting her moods. *Lord, what do I do now?*

"Tell him the truth." Dinah jumped, glancing around her to see if someone had spoken to her audibly.

"It was . . . well it was just something you said during your serm, I mean . . . your exhortation. It brought back some things I'd rather not think about."

"From your looks at supper, it seems you have no choice. Tell me, what did I say that upset you so? Surely, you realize I would never knowingly do that."

The older man's sincerity pierced her heart. She couldn't allow him to take on any guilt feelings because of her musings.

"It's just that I was surprised to hear you say you'd visited a— a bordello." Shame covered her at the very utterance of the word.

Mr. James harrumphed. "Actually I've never before mentioned that incident except to Octavia."

Dinah smiled in the dark. She loved the way he insisted on using Mama Tavie's beautiful name.

"And perhaps I shouldn't have said it today, but somehow I believe the Spirit was prodding me. The truth is I loved a woman once."

Dinah's attention moved to another plane. "Truly?"

"We grew up on a plantation together."

"The one in Louisiana?"

"One and the same. We knew, Cecile and I, that our lives were not our own. But there's something in every human being that resists the notion of not being able to plot his own course in life. So, we hoped and prayed from the time we discovered our feelings that someday we'd be together as man and wife." He held his hand over his heart and heaved a breath as though the retelling was physically painful. "It was not to be. When she was fifteen, the overseer chose her as a breeder."

Dinah was certain her blood flow had been stopped. "A breeder?"

"Yes, a breeder. Even as she labored alongside the rest of the field slaves, it seemed she was always . . . well, suffice it to say, three years, three babies. Strong and healthy at the time, I was ordered to be the next one to sire. I refused and was whipped for it. Repeatedly, I was ordered. I refused. I was whipped. Then things turned in a direction neither of us could ever have imagined possible. Cecile became, well, that is, she turned into a lady of the night."

Dinah dropped to the verandah steps. "What? Oh, Mr. James, how could she. And after you'd pledged your love to her!

"Wait." Mr. James gently pressed into her shoulders. "You've not heard the whole story."

Chastened, Dinah quieted herself. How many times had she dived into her attic bed terrified, not reading the rest of the story to see how the fiend or the giant or the monster got his due? Or how about the time, at six years old, when she'd overheard Cook say the milkman would be "making the crossing" real soon. Heartbroken for the poor man, she'd prayed for his soul all day, only to overhear him chatting with Cook the next morning, excited about his upcoming voyage to England and declaring his last day on the job the best he'd ever had. When she'd gasped with understanding, Cook had scolded her about sticking her nose where it didn't belong and jumping to conclusions.

But the wretched habit of not waiting for a story's end had

only grown. Which was part of the reason she'd decided to stay and hear the end of that fateful conversation between Master and Jack Hudson so many years ago.

"I'm sorry, Mr. James. Go ahead."

"My master began selling off his slaves to make up for a poor crop. At length, he sold Cecile. She was eighteen. As I said in there at the supper table, I'd lived a good portion of my life on that plantation. And I had loved a girl. Until my master turned her into a cash crop and then sold her to points unknown."

Dread crept up Dinah's spine. But as on the day of the kitchen fire, she couldn't stop herself from gazing. Only this time, it was into Mr. James's mouth.

"When they took her, the hatred that had been building up in me all my life overflowed its banks, and one moonless autumn night in '39, I escaped, not knowing where to go, simply intent on living life to the fullest if it was only for a day. Then one evening, as I stepped into a two-story brothel in New Orleans that I'd heard was open to black men's money, I spotted Cecile. The madam said she had other plans for her that night and offered me another girl. But when I laid down a week's wages, she relented. My heart broke again when Cecile recognized me. My master had sold her to a bordello. And neither of us could do a thing about it. I recall the building having a name that appealed to my youthful pride." Mr. James scratched his head as a dry laugh escaped his throat. "The place was called 'The Gentleman's Caller.'"

Bits of what he'd said sloshed around in Dinah's head like a surf until understanding set in. *Oh. No.* It simply could not be. The Gentleman's Caller was the name of the brothel Master Devereaux had mentioned to Jack Hudson. Could it be that . . .? No. No way he could have known her mother.

"A rather upscale place after its fashion—"

Dinah's thoughts cut Mr. James's sentence in half. The autumn of '39. Dinah had been born in June of 1840. She knew this to be true because of what Mr. Devereaux said to Jack

Hudson that day and the many other times Mistress had told her. Trembling fingers pressed to her lips, she jumped to her feet and started to back her way toward the steps of the dependency. Mr. James followed closely, a pained look distorting his usually placid countenance as he sought her eyes.

"What's the trouble, miss? You look about to faint. "

This couldn't be. It simply could not be. There were only two people in the world she despised, could never forgive. Jack Hudson and her imagined father. And Mr. James didn't fit that second slot, not at all. Feeling lightheaded, Dinah turned her back to the perplexed older man. Without a word of explanation, she fled up the steps to her room not knowing if she wanted to throw back her head and shout for joy or scream her lungs out.

Mr. James, who day by day was becoming the model of the father she'd always dreamed of, could quite possibly already be the real father she'd loathed all her life.

THE NIGHT WAS CLOUDED OVER, as Jonathan turtled down into his coat and dropped to his knees at his favorite spot near the bluff's edge. He steepled his hands as Mama Tavie had taught him as a child.

"Father, I need you to light my way, and I need it quickly."

Instinct flared, causing him to pivot on his knees. But he'd waited too late. Before he could set himself, a wiry attacker smelling of stale tobacco and cheap rot was upon him. Attempting to lift himself from a kneeling position, he pushed hard at the man's midsection. Only to find himself stumbling backwards over the edge, hurtling toward the Mighty Mississippi.

Father God, have mercy on my soul. And please take care of Mama Tavie. And Dinah.

THE WIND PICKED UP. Chest ablaze, hands gripping a skinny branch, Jonathan hung suspended from a tree located on the interminable drop-off from the bluffs. Somehow he knew the tree was *his* tree. The tree that had for years been a non-judgmental audience as he'd stood in the same spot along the bluffs and levied many and varied complaints. The tree that seemed hard pressed each year to handle the weight of its own foliage let alone Jonathan's substantial frame.

What the dickens had he gotten himself into now!

Steadying his nerves against the mounting possibility of crashing into the Mississippi at any moment, he strained to hear the argument just above his head.

"You bumbling fool! Now look what you've done, probably cost us upwards of fifteen hundred dollars. We've come all the way from Ohio and have only bought and sold two slaves, just enough to keep us from starving, and we've already used up the money we made."

"I reckon it was you, Mr. Boss Man, who used up all the money. Gambling.

"Don't start talking about that again."

"Well, then, don't you call me no fool no more."

"You're working for me. I'll call you whatever I please. Whenever I please."

A quick round of grunts and scuffles assailed Jonathan's ears before it sounded as if the boss had subdued his opponent.

"Don't ever jump me like that again. Too bad I can't think of a word stronger than fool that would do justice to your stupidity. This Mayfield fellow could've been our prize catch here in Natchez, set us up in business until we could establish a reputation. Now he'll most likely serve nobody's interests except the fish in that overrated muddy river down there."

Jonathan's arms throbbed like a giant toothache—every muscle, it seemed, separated into shreds. Dangling from the branch, his six-foot frame must resemble a scalded hog strung up and ready for dressing. Anxiety pounded his chest. Every nerve in his body was primed to collapse. He tried and failed to steady his feet against the ridged embankment. In a moment, when he was no longer threatened by the bullet of a gun, he'd try again. *Please, Lord. Grant me the strength to hold on until they move away from the edge*—that is, if a steamboat didn't sight him first swinging from the side of the bluff. No, not likely, since God had thankfully snuffed out the stars Dinah loved so well. If only he could scale the few yards up and catch his attackers off guard, perhaps he could take both of them down at once.

And then what? Jail? Sale? Of course. Probably both actions but not for the men who assaulted him. Jail time and selling would be for Jonathan himself. Without his papers . . . he willed his mind back to the present crisis. Was that a small boat he saw down there? No matter. In seconds he was going to plunge into the Mississippi River anyhow. Right now, he needed to keep his focus.

"But you said to apprehend him."

"Apprehend him, yes—with the gun in your belt, numskull! Not by pushing him over the edge."

"I didn't mean to push him. I couldn't see how close he was to the edge. I reached for him and he lost his balance. D-ya ya think he's dead?"

"How would I know? I didn't hear him cry out. What with the wind up and the noise of that steamer that just passed, I couldn't tell. Probably struck his head on something on the way down." The boss sounded almost wistful. "All I know is he appeared stronger than a mule, and that alone would have brought in a sweet sum. Plus, he had the extra selling point of knowing how to make fancy furniture."

"I could've caught him a half hour back down the road if you'd let me."

"Sure. And alarm all these folks around here that's so fond of his work? No, our safest plan was to catch him and quietly take him to the New Orleans market. We were supposed to become the Franklin and Armfield of the lower South, remember?"

Franklin and Armfield again. Who *were* these men?

"Well, you can't blame me for that. I tried to get you to go back to Alexandria so's we could work for them men what took up the old Franklin and Armfield business on Duke Street."

"That's your problem. You always think too small. My plan was solid. Why sell cheap to a middle-man in a slave trading firm when we could scour the area down here ourselves and sell straight to New Orleans? But you've ruined one of our best catches now, the chance that could have set us up for the long haul."

Slave catchers from up North? But why would they target Jonathan? How would they have known to? Unless someone informed them he no longer had proof of freedom. His mind reeling with questions and confusion, Jonathan felt himself teetering.

Crack!

Somewhere between consciousness and despair, he heard footsteps running away from the bluff's edge as the limb of his fragile old friend snapped in two, releasing him into the churning depths of the Mighty Mississippi. Dark as the hell that lay beneath it.

"Do again."

Dinah repositioned her weight a bit and giggled at Emerald's terse but sweet order. She'd needed something to send Mr. James's revelation into hiding. And rehearsing fairytales to this most lovable child was the perfect chaser.

Sitting on the edge of the mattress combing through the waves of the thick untwined braids she always covered with a rag, Violette looked up and smiled.

"This the last time, Emerald, you hear? You already just as wore out as you can be."

Pleased that Violette's iciness toward her seemed to be thawing a bit, Dinah smoothed the side of Emerald's face as she settled the sleepy child against her breast. Having sat on the floor of their quarters for over a half hour, Dinah's long legs needed to be stretched. But it was so soothing, obeying this third command to retell the story of *The Three Billy Goats Gruff*.

"'Trip-trap, trip-trap,' went the first little billy goat as he carefully made his way across the mean old troll's bridge."

Emerald's soft even breathing signaled that the newly-converted story lover had finally fallen into what Dinah hoped was her own dream world of fairytales. Violette crossed the small space, stooped over and lifted the child.

"No!" Knuckle-rubbing her eyes, Emerald whined and struggled to return to Dinah. "I wanna hear 'bout the gruff-goats."

Violette looked at Dinah—a what-now plea in her eyes? Dinah stood to her feet and reassumed Emerald's slight weight. She carried the child to the mattress and sat down with her on her lap. She reached for Mama Tavie's Bible and opened it to the Psalms.

"You see this?"

"Yes'm."

"This is a book and inside are words." She fanned the pages of the Bible. "The ones on these pieces of paper are the best ones in the whole world because they show you how to live to please the Almighty God who made everything on earth. But there are many, many more books like *The Three Billy Goats Gruff* that have words that can take you all over the world."

Emerald bolted straight up. "All over the world? Even to New Orleans?"

Dinah chortled. "That's right, even as far as New Orleans. But first you have to learn something called the alphabet so that you can tell what the words are saying. How about if I teach you the alphabet so you can learn how to please God and travel everywhere in the world?"

"You will?"

"Yes, I will. But only if you eat well and go to bed on time and do whatever else your sister tells you."

"Thank you, Miss Dinah." Emerald threw her arms around Dinah's neck. "I can't wait to go to New Orleans."

The child turned her little back to the events of today and quickly fell asleep. When Dinah turned around, Violette's eyes were shining. "That was a mighty nice thing you done there. I want to thank you for it."

Dinah's heart swelled at the idea of finally pleasing this enigmatic girl. "You are so very welcome."

"W OULD YOU BE WANTIN' me to call for a doctor, lad?"

"W-what? Wh-who are you?" The still-familiar brogue from the men who robbed him of his freedom so many years ago set Jonathan's gut afire until he remembered where he was. Shivering uncontrollably, he recognized he'd been put into his own bed. "T-thanks, but that w-won't be necessary." Something hot and a good night's sleep was all he needed. He couldn't believe he was alive—that he'd fallen close enough to that boat to get this man's attention. But thankfully, he explained to himself, his fall had been broken by foliage, ridges, and other debris before he tumbled into the water. Still, when he finished reasoning it all out, Jonathan knew, except for the grace of God, he would be dead.

The water's surface had shocked him, seemingly splitting every bone he had. Despairing of his ability to gain the landing, he'd seen a man jump from a boat. Somehow, his lungs nearly shattered, Jonathan had managed to hang on until the Irishman swam to him and brought him up the hill to his home. Now his muscles ached from hanging from that double-crossing tree, and his teeth rattled uncontrollably from the frigid water that nearly finished taking his life.

"Y-you s-saved my life, and th-that's enough."

"You took a mighty dangerous fall there, but all glory to the Creator you fell in such a way that saved yer neck. As it 'tis, you're still banged up pretty badly, seems to me. A cup of somethin' warm might go a long ways. I'll go down and see what I can find."

Jonathan grunted his thanks. He couldn't help but make the comparison between this Irishman who'd jumped from the boat and dragged him to safety and those devils years ago who'd shredded his papers, tied him up, beat him to a pulp, sliced his left hand like it was a melon, then scored him inside and out for life. Just because they could. Bitterness rose to his scratchy throat just before a saying from his mother's repertoire imposed itself upon his brain.

"There's good and bad in people all over the world. As much as you can, keep your eyes on the good."

Suddenly, he was drowning again. This time in shame. Here was a man who, even after learning Jonathan's color, had gone out of his way to help him. He'd obviously wrapped him in a blanket, hired a wagon from someone under the hill, found Jonathan's home, and started a fire much like the Good Samaritan in the Bible. And Jonathan had been looking at him askance because of the way he talked? He reached for the steaming cup extended to him. The swallow of hot tea felt like life poured into his bones.

"May I ask your n-name?"

"'Tis O'Bannon, sir. Sean O'Bannon."

"I will be forever grateful, Mr. O'Bannon for wh-what you've done for me tonight." Jonathan tried to lift himself from his bed, but his legs failed him. "Would you be k-kind enough to hand me the leather pouch in the drawer of that desk?" Jonathan reached inside and extended a goodly sum toward his rescuer.

The man jumped back as though Jonathan had thrown a

moccasin at him. "Oh, no sir. 'Tis not fittin' in God's sight that I should take yer money. Yer safety is my reward." He stood smiling for a minute. "I'll be sayin' goodnight to you then."

Jonathan barely answered, for though his body remained partly upright, his mind was fast being overcome by sleep.

15

Dinah treasured this rare time alone with Mama Tavie. Although she now spent most of her days turning beautiful fabric into signature works, she was also becoming more and more adept in the kitchen. And since her talk with Mr. James had left her nerves as frayed as the edges of unfinished silk, she was especially savoring these moments washing dishes with this wonderful little woman. Mama Tavie reached for the gigantic iron pot Dinah handed off to her.

"You done a good job with that beef today. You sure is catching on quick, now that you ain't so nervous 'bout going to the fields no more."

Dinah beamed at the compliment. She had begun to feel a kind of sixth sense in the kitchen—the art of seasoning, timing, flavoring all somehow coming together to make something pleasing to the eye as well as the palate. Images of Jonathan standing over her shoulder, inhaling a savory pot as he slid muscled forearms arms around her waist, sent her senses reeling.

"Did ya hear me, honey?"

Dinah's face warmed at her obvious inattentiveness. "Oh, yes, ma'am. Thank you, Mama Tavie. You can't know what that means to me."

"I meant what I said. You gettin' real good which is why I let Violette play with Emerald for a while this evening. Violette got her way, but she really do love her little sister. Don't know why they sort of claimed me as granny to the child, but I know there's a story in there somewhere." Mama Tavie placed the huge pot on a hanger. She crossed over and gave Dinah a big hug. "Your cooking coming 'long even better than Violette's."

Dinah threw her arms around Mama Tavie. Unfamiliar words rushed from some deep closed off well inside her, words she'd never been told. Words she'd never repeated.

"M-Mama Tavie. I love you. You saved me from the fields. I-I don't think I could have borne that."

Mama Tavie eased Dinah back until she could see her eyes. "Why is that, honey? I of all people know it feel like God-forsaken work in them fields. But I'm sensing somethin' more'n hard work got you running scared, 'cause you one of the hardest working girls I ever seen."

Dinah searched the older woman's face. There was absolutely no guile there. She knew it in her heart and soul. It was time this burden that had bowed her spirit since she was a child be shared with another of God's children. She slumped into one of the kitchen chairs and expelled a long weary breath.

"I was told my mother was an exceptionally beautiful field worker from Louisiana who doubled as a breeder. After her master used her body to increase his property, he sold her—her beauty still intact—to a bordello in New Orleans. She conceived by one of her 'clients.' But by the time the madam discovered it, it was too late to use her usual means to rid my mother of the child. The madam ordered her to get rid of the child once it was born. That child was me."

Forehead creased with concern, Mama Tavie walked Dinah to the table on the other side of the dividing wall. She pulled up a chair next to her, listening without interruption as Dinah told the rest of the story of how Horace Devereaux found her on the street and gave her a home, only to find out days later that her mother had died from exposure.

"I've always felt if I ended up in the fields, I'd follow my mother's path, ending up having a lot of babies that I'd have to see wrenched away from me as though they were puppies, then sold off to, to—"

"All right, sugar. Hush now. You don't have to talk about it no more if you don't want to."

Dinah nestled into the embrace of this woman who'd treated her like family. Feeling a long overdue measure of relief, her rush of tears flowed into the evenness of Mama Tavie's heartbeat. Finally, Dinah found the strength to pull away.

"M-Mama Tavie, if there's ever anything I can do for you. I mean anything . . ."

Streaks of crimson crept from the older woman's chest toward her neck. She struggled to look Dinah in the eye. "Well, yes, there is. That is, if you've a mind to."

Dinah bolted up straight. "What? Do you want a new dress? A shawl? I'm going to have lots of fabric scraps soon. I'll do anything."

"Then teach me to read. I'd kinda like to study with, well, you know who I mean."

Dinah felt herself beaming, quickly drying the tears that had seemed unstoppable moments ago. "Oh, Mama Tavie. I'd be so happy to."

"Thank the Lord something done made you perk up. But I expect it's mostly 'cause you done got all that other stuff out. You be feeling better from now on."

Suddenly, Dinah felt her spirits shift. Trouble was, she hadn't quite got it all out. There was still the haunting thought of what happened with Jack Hudson to contend with every single day.

And now to add to it there was Mr. James.

SILENCE HELD sway between them as Dinah and Mama Tavie walked across the grounds to join the rest of the slaves near their cabins.

"Christmas is almost on us, but this here day is like a child of springtime," said Mama Tavie.

Dinah bobbed her head in agreement, her ears pricking up as the sounds of playing children floated on the unseasonably warm air caressing the late afternoon with whispers of distant hope, while parents sat in the doors of their cabins savoring stolen glimpses of that elusive specter called rest.

Suddenly, a small boy emerged from behind one of the cabins brandishing a long flimsy twig. Squealing delight, he shook it in the air as though he'd struck gold, scattering the other children in every direction, their faces lit up with excitement tinged with fear. Suddenly, that old companion of isolation fell in step beside Dinah. What must it have been like to play games as a child?

"What are they playing, Mama Tavie?"

"Hidin' the Switch. Don't tell me you ain't never heard tell of it."

No, ma'am. I'm afraid not. It looks mysterious."

Mama Tavie laughed. "Ain't nothing hard about it. Somebody hides a whipping switch and whoever finds it first gets to chase the other young'uns with it like he or she 'bout to give them a licking. The game's been around for a while. The children have fun with it, but I can't help wondering if it didn't get started with the little ones seeing some things happening that they shouldn't oughta seen in the first place."

"Like what?"

"Like they own mamas and papas gettin' their backs whipped, not with a little ole switch, but one of them mean pieces of leather like Jethro uses."

"Hmmm." The more Dinah learned of Jethro, the more she determined to keep a healthy distance between herself and him. Laughing at the children swirling around the grassless yard, she spotted Emerald her face aglow with excitement.

"Hey, Mama Tavie, Miss Dinah, guess what!"

Dinah stooped to receive the child's warmth just as Jonathan had done a few days ago. Oh, for heaven's sakes. Dinah scolded herself inwardly as she plastered on a smile. Was there nothing she could do anymore without thinking of him?

"Well, I simply cannot wait a second longer. What wonderful thing have you done?"

"I said my al-fuh-bets for Violette. And I didn't make no miss-takes."

"Any mistakes. You didn't make any mistakes." Dinah repositioned herself to her knees. She loved the way Emerald slowed at the unfamiliar words, making sure her enunciation was correct. "You really didn't, you know. I've heard you lots of times, and you never make any mistakes."

"Shhhh!" Violette lumbered toward her little sister. "Emerald, how many times I got to tell you this our secret? Mine and yours and Miss Dinah's."

Following Violette's lead, Dinah tamped her voice down to a whisper as she gently rocked Emerald from side to side. "Why, you smart thing. What am I going to do with you?"

Instantly Dinah's glimpse of joy was smudged by the sight of Eli Duggan.

"Y'all best shut her up, if you know what's good for you."

Though Mama Tavie had called the warm day a child of springtime, Eli's smirk chilled Dinah's blood. "Massa 'nem find out you showing that little girl how to read and you might find your pretty self in a heap o' trouble."

"Go on way from here," said Mama Tavie. Violette joined right in.

"You just keep to your yard work, Eli, and stop always trying to speak for Massa." Fear and something else Dinah couldn't put her finger on marred Violette's expression. "Don't you be worrying none about Emerald."

"Now listen, all o' you. We didn't come out here for no ruckus," said Mama Tavie who had lifted the confused child into her arms. "Everybody settle down or me and Emerald going back to the kitchen. We don't want to hear no ugly talking, do we honey?"

"No'm."

"Miss Tavie! I need to speak with you."

Along with everyone else, Dinah turned to find Jonathan's right hand man sprinting toward the cabins. Deep foreboding erased the sun from the spring-like day.

"Benjamin? What is it? Is it Joe-Nathan?"

His chest ebbing and swelling, Benjamin held everyone's attention captive as his lungs demanded air before he spoke again. "Yes, ma'am. He's really in a bad way. Needs you to come quickly."

"Oh!" Mama Tavie staggered a bit before Mr. James stepped forward and gentled a hand to her elbow. He took Emerald and passed her to Violette.

"Easy now. Be easy." He turned to Benjamin. "What happened, son?"

"Well sir, after that scuffle the other night with those two northerners, I thought I'd best check on him."

Dinah glanced at Eli. His face was as inscrutable as a poker player.

"I found him in bed about an hour ago practically out of his head with fever. Kept talking about two white men who pushed him into the river. Something about the likes of Franklin and Armfield coming to Natchez."

Franklin and Armfield. Infamous slave traders from Virginia to New Orleans. Dinah pressed her fingertips to her temples. Her head droned so loudly she was tempted to ask if anyone else heard it, and her mouth felt as dry as a ball of lint.

"Get your things, Octavia," said Mr. James. I'll see if the mistress will write a pass."

A sudden longing to be by Jonathan's side pierced Dinah's heart. "Mr. James, please, may I come too? Please."

The older man looked at her, frustration etched in every

nuance of his distinguished face. Deep regret pooled in his cinnamon gaze. "I'm sorry, Miss. But the most we can hope for right now is a pass for Octavia."

His words spoke volumes. Something awful had happened to the strong wonderful mysterious cabinetmaker she'd come to love, and nobody standing in this circle was free to do a thing about it. She nodded and swallowed down a new bitterness she'd never quite sampled in New Orleans. She too was completely powerless to go to him.

Even worse, whatever had happened to him was all Dinah's fault.

DURING THE NIGHT, rain had come and the weather had turned cold. Peering through the smoky window pane, Dinah was surprised to see upside down spikes of ice lining the edges of the eaves. She dragged herself from the mattress and splashed cold water on her face. She glanced over at Violette who was honking like a flock of geese. Oddly, concern had ridden hard across Violette's brow last night after Benjamin's shocking report, before she'd finally joined Emerald in a restless sleep.

But for Dinah, sleep in any form had failed to show up.

Throughout the storm, she'd offered up snippets of prayer, frequently interrupted by images of what Mama Tavie's face would look like when she returned with the news of Jonathan's death. She dropped to her knees and prayed once more, her forehead pressed against clasped hands. Though her prayer was silent, she could hardly contain the choking sobs threatening to awaken Violette and Emerald.

Dear God. Lately, I know I haven't been diligent about seeking your face. I've been so focused on my own fears that I've stumbled into hurting others. I know it's not an excuse, but I didn't mean to. Except for Mama Tavie and Emerald, I've never had feelings this strong for another human being before. Dinah ignored the twinge of conscience nudging her to include Violette on the list of people she cared about even if her heart wasn't quite there yet. *But I think I'm starting to love Jonathan Mayfield—aloof, arrogant, wonderful, kind oaf that he is. And now I might have killed him.* She pushed her fists against her mouth hoping to contain the burgeoning sounds.

God, I can't stand it if I've killed him. Nobody's ever made me feel that special, and I'd rather go to the fields, bend my back to the whip than have Mama Tavie tell me he's gone. So if you've made plans already to take him home, well, I can understand that, but I'm asking you to take me with him. I hope I'm not being too selfish, but seeing my mother and being with Jonathan seems the most heavenly thing I can think of right now. One more thing. Please show me how to feel about Mr. James. He's not the evil man I've always drawn him to be in my mind, and now I don't know how to let go of that picture. Help me. I pray this in the name of Your Son, Jesus. Amen.

She rose from her posture of prayer and washed her face again. Emptying her heart to the Lord had offered relief. Though she'd not got an answer, she'd found a measure of peace. And now she must try to fix breakfast for everyone in the big house. She slid into her scratchy dress. Using the same pins she'd brought from New Orleans, she crisscrossed her braids against her neck. She crossed over and gave Violette, who cradled her little sister, a gentle shake.

"Time to get up, you two. Mama Tavie is depending on us."

She straightened and squared her shoulders. She could do this. She had to, for Mama Tavie and for dear, dear Jonathan.

DINAH SHOT furtive glances toward the several slave cabins on the far side of the dependencies. Without Mama Tavie, things had been so hectic in the kitchen this morning that she'd sent Violette to take Emerald to one of the cabins to be looked after so Violette could concentrate on helping Dinah get dinner started. But the girl had yet to return.

Hoping she'd not be summoned by the big house, Dinah took a chance on a ten-minute respite upstairs before time to start preparing the noon meal. At the top of the stairs, she exhaled a rush of air and smiled.

She'd made and served breakfast, and Mr. James had said it was delicious.

Hardly able to look at the man she believed to be her father, she had nevertheless been grateful for the compliment, and she was quite sure he took her reticence as worry about Jonathan. Mind flying every which way, she opened the door to the cramped bedroom.

Violette knelt on the floor, her backside facing Dinah most unceremoniously.

"Violette? What're you doing down there?"

Violette yanked her hand from beneath the mattress and jerked around toward Dinah. She'd been so intent on whatever it was she'd set out to do that she'd not heard Dinah approaching. The old Violette, the one Dinah had met weeks ago when she came to Riverwood, snarled like a cornered animal.

"None o' your business. You ain't my mama."

"As far as I can tell, very few of us on this estate have the blessing of a natural mother to lean on. That doesn't mean we don't look out for one another. So what are you doing plundering the underside of Mama Tavie's bed?"

Violette hefted herself to her feet and lifted her chin. "Ain't plundering. Just looking for one little thing is all."

"And that would be?"

"No concern o' yours."

"Very well, then. Have it your way. Since Mama Tavie is away trying to save Mr. Mayfield's life, I'll just go and get Mr. James. I'm sure you'll be much more comfortable explaining to him why you're violating the poor woman's privacy."

"No! Wait." Mama Tavie had said Violette was around

seventeen. Right now, wringing her hands and studying her bare toes, she looked all of ten. "Please?"

Dinah's heart moved a little toward Violette. Who was this girl, really? One minute rabid in her self-defense. The next, utterly desperate. She looked so lost right now. Still, Dinah had been left in charge, and she wouldn't let Violette off with rifling beneath Mama Tavie's mattress without some kind of explanation.

"I'm listening."

"I-I just had to make sure, that's all."

"Sure of what?"

Violette continued to wring her hands as though somehow she could squeeze an acceptable answer from them. "Well, I'm not so sure I know how to say it."

Tapping her toe, Dinah jammed her fists into her side. Could anybody be more exasperating than this girl? Dinah's patience was leaking faster than a rundown roof. "Out with it, Violette!"

"Aw right, aw right." Violette exhaled a long sigh before sinking onto the bed. "I'll tell you, but you got to promise not to tell Mama Tavie."

"I will make no such promise."

Violette leveled a long gaze at Dinah before finally giving in. "Okay, well you see, when Eli gets his mind set on a woman, he'll do anything to get her. It's like a game to him, and right now you the prize."

Dinah bit back a gasp. She didn't like the direction this was going. But since she was the one who'd pushed the girl to talk, she had no choice but to listen.

"Anyhow, when Eli heard me say what I did about those papers that night, he decided that next time Jethro stopped by he was gonna tell him and see if, being as he's a driver and all, he knowed any slave catchers he could sick on Mr. Mayfield."

"But why? Why would Eli do that to Jonathan?"

"I just told you, girl. Didn't I? Eli wants you, and he knows Mr. Mayfield do too."

Moments like these made Dinah love the skin she was in even more than she did already. Otherwise, right now she'd be every shade of red in the spectrum.

"But first," continued Violette, "he cornered me to make sure what I'd said about them burnt papers was true. Said he'd send Emerald to Jethro if I'd lied to him, if some kind of way Mr. Mayfield come up with some papers."

Dinah's concern for Violette resurfaced. The girl's breathing had become so labored that it seemed she needed every drop of oxygen in the room just to survive. Dinah moved softly toward the edge of the bed where Violette sat.

"All right now, take it easy, Violette. You're going to make yourself sick."

"I can't lose my Emerald. She all I got in the world. That's . . . that's when I decided to tell him what I'd overheard y'all talking about, you and Mama Tavie."

Dinah scanned her brain for what conversation between her and Mama Tavie could have been of interest to Eli. "What are you talking about? What did you hear, what did we say?"

"Don't you remember—that night when y'all thought I was sleep and Mama Tavie said she had more papers?"

Dinah froze. "What? Y-you betrayed Mama Tavie when you really didn't have to? How could you, Violette? Eli didn't even know about those papers."

"You don't understand, Dinah, what it's like to be desperate. I had to make sure 'cause of Emerald." Violette trembled as tears spilled over and down her baby-faced cheeks. "You . . . you one of them play-actin' slaves from the city what don't know how it feels to try to claw your way outta the fields to the kitchen, just for the sake of your—"

"You're right. I don't understand how you could do this to someone who's been nothing but kind to you and your little sister."

Violette leapt to her feet, her words pitched to the ceiling.

"But don't you see? That's just it. Emerald ain't my sister. She my baby, mine and Eli Duggan's."

Dinah felt like all the air had just been let out of her lungs. That sweet-tempered child belonged to Violette? And Eli? Two of the most selfish, mean-spirited people she'd ever known. How could they have produced an angel like Emerald?

"The same way I produced you. Neither you nor Emerald is an extension of your parents but precious souls unto yourselves, My jewels, my treasure."

Dinah turned her back to the girl to try to clear her head of the words that had just washed over her.

"Don't hate me, Dinah. Please don't hate me. When I learned I'd be sent to town, I begged and bargained with that lowdown Jethro to put in a word for me so's I could bring my baby with me. I promised to put her under Mama Tavie's care to feed her good and build her up if I could have her near me for a while. He got the overseer to let me keep her 'til she gits a li'l older and stronger. Then they go'n take her back to the fields. Or try to sell her."

"You promised to get that baby ready for the fields?"

"I'd have promised anything to get a few more years or even months with her."

Merciful Father.

Dinah shivered, wondering what this poor girl had had to do to strike this kind of sick bargain with that slimy driver called Jethro. She didn't want to know. Flashes of what had happened with Jack, how when she was even younger than Violette she stupidly leaned on him, blinded her with guilt. How could she judge this poor girl after the mistake she'd made? Taking a seat on Mama Tavie's bed, she motioned to Violette.

"Sit down, Violette. I don't hate you. I just need you to tell me everything."

Violette obeyed like a scolded puppy. "I was fourteen when Eli decided he wanted me. I was skinny then, and Eli told me I was right cute. My mama hadn't told me about men like Eli, and what he said kinda went to my head. Or maybe I should say I lost my head and ended up in the family way.

"About a month later, the overseer sold away my Papa and all my other brothers and sisters. Since I was the youngest, he decided to keep me and train me for the big house. He kept Mama too 'cause she could pick as much as three hundred pounds of cotton a day. Next thing I know, my mama telling all the other women she in family way. With Papa gone and me being the last time she'd bore a child, it proved too much of a shock to her. She sort of went off in her head.

"I didn't have the heart to tell her I was in family way, too. It just so happened I was one of those womens who gained weight but not in my stomach. I didn't tell a soul, not even Eli. Somehow I knowed he wouldn't care no how. Once he'd tamed me, he soon found little use for me anymore. When my mama passed out in the field one day, they brung her to the cabin. The old granny dug every herb she knowed out of her bag to try to save her, but mama was plumb wore out what with having nine more babies before this one. She and my li'l brother died the next day. And when I went into labor that very night, the granny told me just to pretend Emerald be my mama's baby, my baby sister. Said it would go better for me that way.

"Like my mama, I was a hard worker, so when Riverwood sent word they needed someone to help Mama Tavie, they picked me. I wanted to bring Emerald, but Jethro said I didn't have sense enough to take care of her. She always was such a weak little thing." Violette picked at her stubby nails. "But afterwards, I mean, after we come to an understanding, he said he'd see if Mama Tavie would take her 'til she was old enough to be sent to the fields or sold." Violette sniffled and lowered her eyes." Truth be told, I'm a good housekeeper, but I don't know much more about cooking than you do."

Dinah stared out the window. She couldn't begin to fathom what this girl had been through these last few years, but she was beginning to see what lay beneath the constant bitterness. Still, she was having difficulty accepting Violette's betrayal of Mama Tavie. And why did the girl dislike Dinah so?

As if she'd read Dinah's thoughts, Violette picked up the story as though she'd never stopped. "In spite of how no-good he is, Eli is still Emerald's papa. And I reckon somewhere deep down, I hope he'll come to his senses one day. When he do, I'll be waiting, even though I tried to steal the papers underneath that there mattress to make sure Mr. Mayfield could get sold and Eli would have a chance with you."

Half-laughing, half-crying, Violette ran her sleeve across her eyes. "You don't have to say it. I already know it don't make no sense. But sometimes love and crazy mean the same thang. Don't you think?"

Thinking of how desperately she wanted to get to town to see a man that, if he lived would hate her, Dinah could only nod in assent.

"Anyhow, when they moved me and Emerald to Riverwood where Eli had been moved a few months earlier, I thought my dreams had come true. He'd started looking at me again, even started to play with Emerald sometimes. Then you came, and not only have I lived every day scared that Mama Tavie would prefer you and send me back to the plantation, from the first time Eli laid eyes on you, he flung me and Emerald to the side like two dirty dishrags."

Dinah burned with hurt for this girl. And shame, so much shame for the pain she had unwittingly caused her. "Oh, Violette, honey, why didn't you say something?"

"Wasn't nothin' to say. In my heart, I always knowed it wasn't your fault." Rising from her mattress, Violette scrunched her shoulders and moved to where Dinah sat. "C-could you maybe think about forgiving me sometime down the road?"

Dinah sprang to her feet. "No." She smiled as Violette's shoulders sank in defeat.

"No. I won't forgive you down the road. I forgive you right now, that is, if you can forgive my blundering lack of sensitivity."

Violette's head fell onto Dinah's shoulder as Dinah felt her heart completely open up to this misguided girl. Joy flooded her as she took her in her arms and thought to herself she might be gaining the sibling she never had.

"Ladies."

Loosening themselves from their hug, they turned to find Mr. James standing in the doorway. The usually collected butler looked like he'd just pulled the only bad-news straw in the whole can and was still struggling with the idea of being named "it."

16

Dinah held on to Violette and waited for the horrible news that never came. Jonathan was not dead. Instead she was being ordered to see after Jonathan Mayfield. Alone.

"I can't do it, Mr. James—not by myself."

"You can, Miss, and you must. I've already secured the pass for you, and the mistress has even allowed one of the yard men to take you in a wagon." A gasp caught midways Dinah's throat. Mr. James shook his head furiously. "Not Eli. The mistress doesn't trust him any more than I do."

Unbidden, Mr. James's words from days before came to rest in Dinah's heart. *If I'd been a man able to determine his own choices in life, I would have chosen a daughter just like you.* There standing before her, resplendent on the outside, wise and loving on the inside, was the father she'd always wanted. Suddenly, Dinah felt the urge to climb into this man's lap, pull up her knees and lean her head onto his shoulder. Not even suspecting who he was to her, he was obviously drawn to her and wanted to protect her in a paternal way from Eli. She creaked out a response.

"Th-thank you for that."

"The master is coming home tomorrow night, and he's bringing important guests with him. Granted, you've done well in the kitchen, but it will take Octavia to handle a group like this. He reached over and steadied her wringing hands. "You mustn't fear, now. God is with you."

Suddenly, she knew Mr. James spoke the truth. As he'd done ever since she'd been at Riverwood, God was offering guidance. Somewhere she'd find the strength to take care of Jonathan Mayfield whether he wanted her to or not. And wasn't that what she'd been praying for the last twenty-four hours?

"I'll get my things."

DINAH'S short nervous breaths set forth a rapid line of clouds in the air. Using the brass knocker, she called at Jonathan's front door. She heard the faintest creak of the stairs as someone slowly descended. "Come on in, honey. I left the door open for you."

Dropping her sack and throwing off the coat she'd brought up with her from New Orleans, Dinah rushed to embrace Mama Tavie. Never had she seen her look so drawn, so small.

So defeated.

Huge drops of water slid past the few fine wrinkles in her yellow skin. "I'm afraid I done made a terrible mistake with my boy."

Dinah's heart shifted inside her chest. Spotting a settee in the foyer, she bade Mama Tavie sit next to her. "That's not true, Mama Tavie. Nobody could ever look out for that boy the way you do. You've spoiled him something awful. Why, we would never get teacakes at Riverwood if Mr. Mayfield wasn't in the picture."

Mama Tavie sniffed and tried to smile a bit. "But if he dies up there in that lonesome room of his, he'll never taste another one of my teacakes. And it'll all rest on these here shoulders."

Gently Dinah rested her hands on those shoulders. "Now you listen to me, Mama Octavia. I just can't allow a grand lady like you to say such a thing about herself. If anyone is to blame for what's happened to Jonathan, it's me. My clumsiness is what destroyed his freedom."

"But that's just my point, has been all these years. Papers don't really bring freedom. They bring opportunity—a chance to do some things you want to do. Only Jesus can give us freedom. That's why come I kept them papers hoping he'd learn to lean on God before anyone or anything else."

Dinah ached to offer consolation, but she sensed it was best to listen. Mama Tavie started to weep again. "All these years with them papers, Joe-Nathan ain't never been freed yet. He believes in God, but he don't trust Him. Something happened to him that stole his trust. Even before he left to go to Carolina. To tell you the truth, it was right after he got them papers that he started to change for the worse. Started doubting his self about every little thing he done. And when he come back from Carolina, he was even worse."

Dinah smoothed the hair peeking from the edges of the ever-present blue-checkered triangular rag Mama Tavie wore around her head. If she lived to be a hundred, she'd never understand why slaves seemed ashamed of their hair. But that discussion was for another day.

"True enough, God had done give him a gift and the opportunity to polish it, and he'd learned to use it well. But it was never enough. Not only did he get to be kind of sulkified once he went into business for his self, he went into a hissy fit if he even thought he'd left them papers anywhere."

Sulkified? Dinah smiled inside, thinking of how Jonathan always accused Mama Tavie of making up words.

"Right away, I saw what them papers was doing to him, taking the place of his confidence as a man and his trust in the Almighty. So I decided I'd hide that second set what Massa Mayfield had gave me in case somethin' happened to the first set. But I was also trying what I thought could work—praying he'd come to see what a fine brave man he is and not spend his whole life letting fear take away every ounce of the joy the Lord seen fit to bestow on him."

A deep groan broke the silence.

Jonathan.

Mama Tavie struck out toward the stairs, Dinah at her heels.

FOR THE FIRST time in eons, Jonathan felt cool and dry. The so-called Father of Waters he'd left behind didn't touch the river flowing before him. Glassy, with just the slightest ripple, it was so clean and inviting Jonathan thought he could gaze into it for eternity. He sat down on an exquisitely carved bench finished with a citrus-smelling lacquer, the likes of which he'd never even imagined, let alone seen.

"Peace be unto you."

A gentleman with an indescribable, fathomless smile casually joined him on the bench as though it was the most natural thing in the world. His voice was the trills of a thousand water brooks, his presence more welcome than anyone's Jonathan had ever felt.

Immediately, he knew it was the Lord. Just as the disciples of the New Testament had intuited so many times after the Resurrection, Jonathan knew it was the Savior. He was in heaven. And he knew without a doubt the answers to all the questions that had plagued him for years was finally within a hairsbreadth.

"When are You going to free my people? Why did You place this burden of half-freedom, paper freedom, upon me? Why did You choose to free me and not Papa or Mama or Mama Tavie or any of the other hundreds of thousands of slaves? This guilt I feel each time I see a small slave child running naked or a child-laden woman bent in the fields—I don't know how much more I can take."

"And my handmaiden, Dinah? Did you not have a question about her?"

Jonathan was as tongue-tied as a thirteen-year-old. He could only watch as the Lord's smile relaxed into something just short of teasing, His eyes flashing green and brown, blue and gray before turning into a deep colorless well of concern.

"Did you know that Frederick Douglass was free long before he escaped the evils of slavery?"

Frederick Douglass. Jonathan had heard that name somewhere. Yes, this was the bold black abolitionist orator that was causing such whispers of shocked loathing in dining rooms and parlors all over the south.

"Before his bodily escape," continued the Lord, "Frederick had learned whom he was inside, giving him the Divine strength to fight for his brethren." The unfathomable smile opened up again. "You know, of course, that he whom the Son sets free is free indeed."

The Lord locked gazes with him, His eyes lighting up with what Jonathan could only call hope. Except the word "hope" fell pitifully short. But he knew that the term his brain searched for was not in the endless, yet finite, earthly scroll of human languages.

"Never mind asking about Dinah," said the Lord. "When you return, you'll know what to do." As much as he longed to stay, Jonathan had already sensed his time here was temporary.

Then came the question Jonathan had asked himself hundreds of times. Only this time it was the Lord Himself doing the inquiring. "Have you ever been truly free, my son, Jonathan?"

As though rolling over a hundred-mile canyon, the question echoed so loudly that Jonathan wanted to press his palms to his ears. But as he opened his hands, he realized he had just one more question. He stretched his scarred left palm before the Lord.

"Why?"

The Lord unfurled both His hands, the myriad of scars there thinning the lone mark in Jonathan's palm into a single thread. "I have inscribed you and all my children in the palms of my hands. Your many scars, Jonathan, are only proof that you are mine."

Many scars? Of course, He would know about the numerous other scars Jonathan's body bore that he'd managed to keep private.

Aware that he was much more scarred on the inside than out, Jonathan tried to hide his inferior scarred hand behind his back. But he couldn't seem to lift his arms. So very heavy. Sweltering heat re-enveloped him. From what seemed like the far end of a narrow tunnel, he thought he recognized a familiar lovely voice.

"What's wrong with him, Mama Tavie?"

Dinah? It couldn't be. He must have slipped into another of these half-dreams he was having.

"Don't know, honey. He got a fever. No question 'bout that. Been burning up like you see him there ever since I been here. I can't say how long he was in that river, but it's no telling what he caught in there. Thank God, though, it ain't ole Yellow Jack. I'd know him anywhere."

Noisy quiet took over. Soft steps moved about the room. It sounded like Mama Tavie was showing Dinah or whoever it was how to do something. Was she about to leave him?

"I'm still just so sorry for what I done. I ain't never been free, but I imagine it's hard to let it go, honey. 'Specially when you have a stout heart like Joe-Nathan's."

Jonathan knew he was no longer in heaven. Still, he could speak to neither Mama Tavie nor the young woman. His gut clenched at the sound of the woman's cry.

"And to think I told him he didn't like himself."

Dinah. So it was she. Unbidden the Lord's smile returned, and immediately Jonathan was impelled to seek her forgiveness for the awful arrogant things he'd said to her. He fought desperately to push the words out, but they wouldn't come. If he could just . . .

"He's gettin' fidgety again. Dip that rag there into that bowl of water. Wring it out and place it on his head."

D-Dinah, my love. Before he returned to heaven, which in this sudden state of agitation he wondered if he must be about to do, he had to speak to her, tell her that he loved her more than life. In the dark suspension in which Jonathan reentered, he whispered her name inside himself, until finally he was pulled back down into a restless sleep.

"Go."

Dinah kissed both Mama Tavie's cheeks.

"The wagon is waiting for you. Jonathan will be just fine. And so will I"

Against Mama Tavie's protests, Dinah wrapped the coat she'd brought from New Orleans around the older woman's shoulders and nudged her out the door before closing it. Having watched from a first-floor window until the wagon faded around a corner, she checked several times to be sure the door was securely locked then hurried back up the stairs.

Thump. Thump.

She strained to locate the sudden sound from below. Halting on the landing, she wondered if she'd heard something, or had her imagination jumped ahead already now that she had sole responsibility for Jonathan?

She placed her hand over her galloping heart. What had possessed her to offer Mama Tavie all those empty assurances moments ago? Looking upward toward the rest of the wooden stairs, Dinah trembled at the possibility before her. She knew nothing of nursing. What if Mama Tavie's beloved Jonathan, and hers, died while in her care? The magnitude of the responsibility hit her with hurricane force, and she realized she was more afraid than she'd ever been in her life. Except maybe the time with Jack Hudson.

Startled by the sound of the front-door knocker, Dinah nearly slipped as she spun around and descended the stairs.

"Yes? Who is it?"

"It's me, Benjamin. Mama Tavie? That you?"

Relief deflated Dinah's chest. She fumbled with the lock until she got it open. "Benjamin, I'm so glad you're here."

"What's the matter? Has Jonathan—"

"No, no. He's the same. Please come in out of the cold."

Holding a small sack in one hand, Benjamin lifted a heavier sack from the edge of the threshold, obviously the source of the earlier noise, and hefted it into the vestibule.

"I brought more medicines and a few things Mama Tavie requested from the mercantile."

"Good. I need to check on Jon—Mr. Mayfield. Would you like to join me?"

"Yes. I'd love to." Concern morphed into a smile of relief. "I don't want to get in the way, but Mama Tavie has been allowing me to sit with him for short whiles over the last day or two."

Dinah gazed at the simplicity of Jonathan's bedchambers. Rather than the elaborate hand carvings she'd observed in the room he'd suited out at Riverwood, all the lines were elegantly understated. The perfect place to retire after a day's work.

Almost unaware that Benjamin was behind her, she gently touched the back of her hand to his forehead. Still hot. His sleek black brows folded toward each other in complaint. No bewitching smile, no sudden bewildering arrogance. No regaling her with antics from his childhood, no impulsive embrace.

"He doesn't. It's himself he finds distasteful."

Remembering similar words she'd hurled at Jonathan a few days ago, she turned to face his friend. "Why do you say that?"

Benjamin looked at her the way Dinah imagined a concerned brother would. "Will you sit for a minute? There're some things I think you should know."

JONATHAN TRIED to lift his head from the pillow. Pure lead. He fought to stop Benjamin from what he was about to tell Dinah. She must never know about his weakness on the ship, the uncertainty of his manhood. *Mama Tavie, are you there? Help me to stop him.* Calls for the woman who had mothered him for the last twenty years were a futile echo inside his head. Voices of his best friend and the woman he loved became distant as he felt himself shut out of a conversation that could change his life.

DINAH WAS DISTRACTED by Jonathan's sudden thrashing. Jumping up from the chair she'd just taken next to Benjamin, she straightened the covers that he'd managed to push down. Embarrassed by his bare chest, she averted her eyes and sucked in a breath of air before her head snapped back and she gasped outright. Short scars of all shapes covered his chest, shoulders and forearms. Dinah's hand flew to her mouth. What on earth could have happened to leave such a congested field of mutilations?

Glancing over at Benjamin, his lips compressed into a downward curve, she wondered what else she might do to sooth Jonathan. Mama Tavie had saturated her mind with instructions, but right now none of them seemed fitting. As carefully as she knew how, she bathed his scorching forehead until he calmed again.

Loath to supply an audience for Benjamin's story, she reluctantly resumed her seat. "All right. What is it I should know?"

"Until his master freed him, Jonathan was raised by Mama Tavie."

Dinah folded her hands and tried to hasten him on by nodding prior knowledge of what he'd just said.

"But until a few days ago, he never told anybody all of what happened to him weeks after he became a so-called free man."

The usually clean-cut jocular young man she'd met at Riverwood seemed to age before Dinah's eyes, as though the retelling of what he was about to say was already layering on wrinkles of anger and bitterness to his soul. A chill swept over Dinah causing her to glance toward the fireplace. But the flames Mama Tavie had kindled before she left danced confidently, promising heat for quite a while.

Dinah should stop Benjamin's story right now. But something prevented her. As sure as the famous Mississippi ran just yards away, she knew the mystery of the man who lay sleeping feet away was finally about to be unraveled. And she needed to hear it once and for all.

"After the death of his wife, Jonathan's father disdainfully neglected him, practically turning him over to Mama Tavie, until he willed himself to follow his wife to the grave. Jonathan swore he'd' never marry—never subject himself to the love of a woman."

A flicker of understanding lit up Dinah's heart. The way he ran from her the first day they met, the way he'd seemingly recoiled from what had seemed a magical first kiss—

"Last week wasn't the first time his papers were destroyed. His first parting with his newfound freedom took place on the deck of a northbound ship in the Atlantic."

Twisting in his seat like a restless schoolboy, Benjamin spat out how Jonathan's master pronounced "his kind" incapable of running a business, even before the innocent eighteen-year-old could get his hands on his proof of manumission. The intensity of Benjamin words sped up Dinah's heartbeat as he explained how the young newly-freed slave watched his papers being shred and thrown into the drink.

But nothing compared to Benjamin's barely concealed rage, as in vivid detail he recounted the "signature" etched into Jonathan's left hand by a couple of planters' goons before they stripped him of his clothes aboard that ship and meticulously etched meaningless markers all over his body—including places improper to mention in a lady's presence.

"Besides nearly losing his life, for the last nine years Jonathan has lived with the question of his manhood, not only concerning what old Mayfield said to him, but what those devils on that ship did to him. All because he stood on a deck trying to replenish himself with God's own air."

The rest of the story of how Jonathan got back to Natchez came in faint spurts as Dinah could precisely process nothing else except what this beautiful man had suffered on that ship. She stood dismissively, not really knowing whether Benjamin was finished with his story. Inside and out, she stretched to her full height.

"I appreciate your telling me this, but Jonathan Mayfield will be just fine."

Somehow, she would fight for this man's life with every ounce of her being. And with God's help she would win.

17

Dinah knelt on the padded stool Mama Tavie had drawn up next to Jonathan's bed, watching the ebb and flow of his breaths, his beloved papers conspicuously absent from his broad chest. The doctor had left minutes ago. And though he'd congratulated Dinah on how well she'd tended him so far—praising her for getting several spoonsful of broth into the semiconscious patient—he'd spoken sternly against getting her hopes up too soon.

"We've ruled out yellow fever. Something toxic is in his bloodstream, but we have no way of knowing exactly what he ingested from that river water, especially being in such close proximity to the landing where all kinds of refuse is dumped. If the fever doesn't break within the next twenty-four hours, I'm afraid Jonathan will die."

Admiring the strength of Jonathan's brow and the sleek dark eyebrows reminiscent of a panther's coat, she ran her thumbs over his eyelids. Lying there with his majestic head slightly elevated on a pillow, he looked so fiercely handsome, yet so completely at rest. Every whit the African prince with just the right touch of boyish innocence to set her heart on a wild goose chase, running after another heart she could never capture, wasn't worthy of capturing. Feeling a little foolish, Dinah looked around before brushing her lips to his forehead and whispering near his ear.

"That's right, Mr. Cabinetmaker. Get plenty of rest now because you're going to need it to complete all the orders that will be lined up after the Natchez elite sees that room at Riverwood."

Her lighthearted attempt took flight, and the horror of never having a chance to talk to him again nearly overwhelmed her.

"Jonathan, please come back," she whispered.

Eyes blurred, throat clogged, she dragged herself away from the high bed to the window to take in the view of the Mississippi River. Twilight had set in and the lights on the riverboats blinked as though they were paltry practicing understudies for the celestial stars above them. What would it be like to stand at this window every night relishing Jonathan's nearness, watching the river lights utterly routed by the splendor of God's Creation? Just when she thought she was totally cried out, fresh tears rushed down the side of her face.

It's not fair, Lord, this so-called system of slavery—not fair to me and not fair to Jonathan. If not for the sham of freedom papers that's kept him living a life of uncertainty, he wouldn't be lying here fighting for his life. When, Lord, when are you going to help us?

"Soon."

What? Dinah's eyes frantically searched the room. Had the Almighty just condescended to speak to her? Chills shimmied down her back, prompting her toward praise and worship for the awesome God that would deign to answer someone like her. "Soon," He'd said. But when she turned back toward the river, doubt slammed into her like a runaway train. The word had not been audible. Still, it rang in her head as sound and true as the chime of a church bell.

"Mama Tavie? You here?"

Jonathan.

His voice couldn't have been more clear. Dinah flew to his side. "Jonathan, you're awake. How are you feeling?"

Offering a lopsided smile, he winced as he tried to heave himself to his elbows while smothering a cough. "Dinah—my love."

Now, she *knew* she was hearing things. Never had anyone used those words to her. Lord, please let him say it again. Love. Love.

"Dinah, I-I think I went to heaven."

Soon. Love. And now heaven. All in the space of seconds. Her hearing was definitely amiss. He couldn't have said he'd gone to heaven. Master Devereaux had always been adamant about that kind of mystical talk, calling it "undiluted nonsense." Then that must mean either she or her poor darling was hallucinating, which is why if he had said the word love, she needed to hurry and put it aside.

Wondering if the fever had worsened, she reached her hand toward his forehead before quickly withdrawing. She shook so furiously that she wondered if she might not poke him in the eye or do some other stupid thing. After all if it hadn't been for her, he wouldn't be in this position. Finally, she leaned over and touched his head.

Cool as an autumn rain.

He reached for her again. "It was so beautiful there. I didn't want to come back. But I knew I must. I had to see you."

"You just lie still now." She smoothed the thick stubble on his jaw. "Do you know what a scare you've given everyone? How did you ever get back home from the river?"

He furrowed his brow, obviously not ready to talk about the particulars of what had occurred. "What day is it?"

"It's Wednesday. You've been asleep for four days."

"Four days! Where's Mama Tavie? I thought she'd been here. And Benjamin, I need to speak with him. I-I have to get back to work." He tried again to lift himself before collapsing onto the pillow with a frustrated sigh.

"Shh. This fretting won't help your healing. Mama Tavie didn't want to leave, but the McMillans sent for her. As for Benjamin, he's been hovering like a mama bear. Just got rid of him about an hour ago. But you're not to concern yourself with these things, you hear me?"

Jonathan's eyes shone with an unusual brilliance. But his speech quickly faded into exhaustion. "Heaven was beyond beautiful. B-but I knew I had to return. I have t-to talk to you." Dinah couldn't help smiling as his eyelids shuttered his view. It brought to mind Emerald's lost battles to sleep as he succumbed to peaceful repose.

With all the excitement of having Jonathan back, Dinah, overcome with exhausted relief, had almost forgotten that one word, "soon," spoken to her so clearly just before Jonathan came back to her. Had the Lord of the universe truly answered her question? Too tired to ponder it, she pulled up a rocker she was sure Jonathan had made and drifted off into her own sweet rest

Thursday, December 20

SUNLIGHT PEEKED from behind the heavy draperies of the darkened bedroom. Dinah had sat by his bed all night jumping to his every whimper, watching in grateful wonder as his fever, which had spiked only once more, settled into a comfortable temperature.

Her stomach pitched between fear and hope as he opened his eyes and drew in a leisurely breath. He tried to shift his large frame to the side toward her.

"Wait. I'll help."

"So you haven't deserted the incorrigible ogre yet, huh?"

Dinah was terribly discomfited by the sight of his uncovered chest. She helped him get comfortable, thinking now that the fever had passed she needed to help him into a proper **shirt.**

With a contented sigh, he captured her gaze. "Can we talk now?"

Dinah felt an urgent need to busy herself. She retrieved a shirt from the armoire. "Let's get you dressed."

For days, she'd subsisted on little food or drink, praying fervently for Jonathan's recovery, and the simple brush of his hand ever since he'd awakened yesterday sent her pulse hammering out of control with joy. So why was she terrified to hear what he had to say?

She knew why.

And Jack Hudson was his name.

Perhaps she was wrong about that look in his eye last night when he'd said he wanted to talk to her. But whatever else could be said about Jonathan Mayfield, he was a man of integrity. And if, by some impossible chance, he was about to declare his love, she could not accept it, would not subject him to a tainted woman with a sordid legacy. She got to her feet and wiped her hands against her apron before silencing him with a finger to his lips. With remarkably renewed strength, he caught her wrist and kissed the palm of her hand.

"Dear, Dinah. I've missed you so."

She wriggled her hand free. "I-I've missed you too, we all have. But right now you need to get dressed like a proper gentleman. You need sustenance, and you need to rest. I have chicken and vegetable broth that will have you with a wood gouger back in your hands in no time."

"Ugh. Chicken broth. I was thinking more of—"

"Teacakes?" Dinah chuckled as she moved to uncover the fresh batch of broth simmering on a makeshift trammel in the fireplace. "'Fraid not, my good man. It's a bit too soon for that. Besides, I have something else for you, but first you must get this broth down. Mama Tavie's orders."

One spoonful and he'd seemingly forgotten the teacakes. "Umm. Best soup Mama Tavie ever made." He consumed about half a bowl before stopping to catch his breath.

"That's enough for right now," said Dinah, "and I'll have you know I made that broth."

He winked at her. The scoundrel. "Don't tell Mama Tavie, but she's come up with a formidable competitor." He took several more gulps. "By the way, have you ever heard of a pair by the name of Franklin and Armfield?"

Dinah held his shirt as he gingerly slipped his arm into a sleeve. Helping him get dressed was the most disturbingly comfortable sensation she'd ever experienced. "Why yes, as a matter of fact, I have. Growing up in New Orleans, I read about them once or twice in the *Picayune*."

"So who are they?"

"More like who were they. It's my understanding that their partnership is long since dissolved and their so-called business is now being perpetuated by other slave traders."

"Slave traders?"

"Yes. I remember being struck even as a child by the coldness of it. If memory serves me, a few decades ago, two men in Alexandria, Virginia by the names of Franklin and Armfield founded a major domestic slave trade, setting up offices for all the world to see, advertising to buy black men, women, and children of the upper south to be sold down to New Orleans and Natchez at a whopping profit." Dinah fidgeted with the counterpane to offset the very idea. "I believe Franklin even stationed himself in Natchez for a time to handle the business of selling humans down here."

A groan escaped Jonathan's lips. He deliberately cracked his knuckles as some unbidden comprehension seemed to darken his brow. "Isaac Franklin. From that cursed Forks-of-the-Road slave market located not quite a mile from here. I was too young to remember much about it. But I do recall that his very name struck terror in every adult slave on the Mayfield plantation. My papa said he was one of the most serpent-hearted slave traders Natchez had ever seen." Jonathan's voice had declined into a defeated whisper. "That explains it then. The two ruffians who attacked me at my home and ultimately pushed me into the river had obviously worked for Franklin and Armfield's successors and are now trying to start their own business of capturing and selling enslaved men.

"But from what I overheard, one of them had gambled away most of their earnings. They must've gotten a little desperate since coming to Natchez, hoping to find some unsuspecting slaves and sell them in order to get back some semblance of financial stability. Evidently, I fit the bill perfectly. Someone must have tipped them off about my loss of papers, and they decided they could reinvigorate their business by selling me as both field hand and skilled craftsman at the port of New Orleans. And I'd bet my boots I know who it was who sold me out."

Knowing it was most likely Jethro via Eli, Dinah scrambled for an answer. Should she tell him? How would it impact Violette's stay here at Riverwood—and Emerald's—if she did? She'd been relieved to divert Jonathan's mind for a while from whatever it was he wanted to say. But now it seemed she'd wriggled from a bear's paw into a lion's mouth. Quickly, she went to her bag and removed a folded garment.

Please, Lord, don't let him see this as a condemnation of his wardrobe but as a promise kept.

"Are you ready for the surprise I brought you?"

"Not quite as nice as the one I burned up, but I hope you like it."

Jonathan's jaw dropped as Dinah shook out a deep gray frockcoat more exquisitely tailored than anything he'd ever purchased. She dipped her head and lifted her shoulders as though she expected him to scold her. And why not? Hadn't he made a habit of belittling most everything she'd said or done since the first day he saw her in the kitchen? His Adam's apple rose and lowered. Somehow this sweet woman had perfectly matched the garment to his taste.

"May I touch it?"

"Oh, yes." Dinah handed over what she'd obviously put her all into. "Yes, of course."

Thinking his roughened hands might somehow mar it, Jonathan gently fingered the gabardine coat. Unbelievable. Where had she gotten the materials?

Starting with the stylishly notched lapels of medium width, he let his eyes caress the knee-length coat, featuring expertly covered buttons that ended just below the seamed waist. Sleeves, hinting of the comfort found in the sack coat, finished the look of an expert tailor. He tried to speak but nothing came.

"Jonathan? Don't you like it?"

"Y-yes, yes I do like it. Tell me, how did you know my size so precisely?"

She studied her feet again. "Have you forgotten how much time we've spent together lately?"

Jonathan feigned hurt feelings. "Here I'd been hoping when I'd caught you looking my way, you were drawn to my good looks, when in fact you'd been sizing me up for a frockcoat." Turning it over more than once, he was touched beyond expression by the skill that had gone into it. "How did you ever find the fabric and the time?"

"Well, I did beat you arriving at work a few times, remember?"

"That you did."

"And as for the fabric, I found bolts of it in a chest in our room." Dinah gasped. "Oh! I didn't mean our room. What I meant was—"

Jonathan cleared his throat. The moment he'd been waiting for was getting away from him, and he couldn't let that happen for fear he'd never get up the nerve again to say what he must.

"Dinah, do you know how incredible you are? I've never met a woman like you. Look how you just solved the mystery of

Franklin and Armfield for me. How did you ever amass such knowledge as a slave?"

"Other than learn to sew, I had little else to do except read, and when it wasn't in use, my master and mistress gave me full access to his library, both at our old place and in the new home in the Garden District."

Jonathan paused to try to collect himself. He'd wanted to say this for what seemed an eternity. But in truth, he had only gotten the nerve and unction since he'd returned from that experience with the Lord. Feeling exhausted from so much excitement, he'd begun to crave sleep again, but he sensed this might be his only chance. He had to get this right. If the pained look on Dinah's face was any indication, his attempt so far was still ages away from its target. He dragged his fingers through his thick coarse curls and circled back to what he needed to say.

"I must, that is, I am apologizing to you for the boorish inexcusable way I've treated you since the day I met you. You see, it was because . . . How can I explain it? I'd never before met a slave, at once, so refined, so utterly pure and innocent, yet so well-read and sophisticated." Not to mention, so achingly lovely. "Someone who put the shackles of slavery to the lie by a simple entrance into a room."

"Jonathan, please don't. You need your rest."

"I understand you must be put off by me. Truth is, I wouldn't blame you if you never wanted to see me again. I know Mama Tavie probably finagled you into coming here, and I shall always be grateful to her for that. Yet, I also know you'll be leaving soon. You don't have the option of staying here much longer. That's just the way of it in slavery. But before you leave me, that is, before they send for you to return to Riverwood, I have to let you know that I . . . well, I have feelings for you that I can no longer deny. And when I'm well, I . . ."

"Oh, Jonathan. I almost forgot." Dinah sprang to her feet, accidentally knocking the frockcoat onto the floor. "The doctor said to let him know if there was a change in your fever, and here it is the next day and I've said nothing about your recovery." She laughed nervously. "What kind of nurse would I make? Do you think you'll be all right while I go fetch the doctor?"

"But Dinah, I'm feeling fine. I need to—"

Amidst his feeble protests, she ran down the stairs and out the door. Like Job, the thing that Jonathan had feared all along had come upon him. She wanted and deserved a real man, not a scarred-up fake like him.

Allowing his head to flop back onto his pillow, he valiantly fought his body's need for rest until he conceded to a dreamless sleep.

HE'D BEEN ABOUT to say that word.

Love.

Clutching her pass, Dinah hurried through town toward the doctor's office, snippets of Jonathan's other words relentlessly pounding her brain.

"Pure and innocent, pure and innocent."

She hadn't been altogether truthful back there. The doctor's exact words had been to let him know if the fever continued to spike. But she'd had to get away from Jonathan Mayfield and the powerful draw he levied upon her. She hoped the noise of the street would drown out her guilty thoughts.

"Father God, please forgive my deceit. I'm afraid this dear man has developed feelings for someone who doesn't exist."

At full stride, she turned a corner and ran squarely into a rock-solid frame. "Oh, please pardon me, sir." Dinah looked up into the scowl of Benjamin Catlett.

"What's the matter, Benjamin?"

"Haven't you heard? There're rumors flying all over the place that South Carolina is pulling out from the Union. I can't think what that will mean for the slave population in this country."

"Soon." Once again, the Lord's promise shook her to the core, causing her to almost lose her balance.

"Miss Devereaux?" Benjamin held on to her shoulders to keep her on her feet. "Where are you off to in such a hurry?"

"I-I was just on my way to the doctor's office."

"Is it Jonathan? Has he taken a turn for the worse?"

"No, no. I'm sorry. It's nothing like that. As a matter of fact, he seems out of danger. I was just headed to let the doctor know."

He touched her elbow and steered her back around in the direction from which she'd come. "Why don't you let me take care of informing the doctor later? I've just come from Riverwood, and the mistress has sent me to pick you up."

Oh, praise God. Immediately, guilt washed over Dinah. "Do you know what the problem is? Why do they need me?"

"According to the butler, they're expecting a number of guests for the Christmas season, and she wants everyone and everything in order."

"But who'll see after Jonathan?"

Benjamin looked half-amazed, half-scornful. "You really are an innocent, aren't you? Slaves can't concern themselves with those kinds of choices."

Dinah felt her anger rise. If she heard the word "innocent" just once more today.

"I am quite aware of that, Mr. Catlett. It's just that . . ." That what? Everything he said was true. Whether she wanted to or not—and a part of her desperately needed to—she had to return to Riverwood. They walked in silence until they reached Jonathan's front door.

"I'll just get my things and wait here in the foyer for the wagon."

Benjamin started for the street before pivoting. "Miss Devereaux. Jonathan thinks an awful lot of you. If he thought I'd offended you—"

"Certainly not. It was stupid of me to question the order to return to Riverwood. I understand and agree."

Dinah watched Benjamin disappear into the crowd to where he'd parked the wagon. What with the rumors of secession and Jonathan's health, she couldn't help but notice the concern beneath his cool demeanor. In any case, her job here in town was finished. She looked around at the sparse yet well-appointed surroundings. She would probably never step over the Mayfield threshold again. And that was just as well, for she couldn't say how she'd react if the fascinating owner of this home came that near to proposing again.

18

Dinah sat down to the kitchen table with the paper and pencil Violette had somehow "found," in order for Dinah to continue teaching Emerald how to form the alphabets.

Friday, December 21, 1860

Dearest Mr. Mayfield,

> *I trust you are continuing to heal from the horrible experience you suffered last week. For fear of marring the deep sincerity with which I make this assertion, I dare not try to say how grateful to the Lord and how enormously relieved I was when first you opened your eyes and began to speak to me.*
>
> *I should say immediately, however—though I pray not too abruptly—how overwhelmed I was by your heavenly experience as well as what seemed to be a change of heart where I am concerned. How can I ever offer a decent enough apology for the way I ran out on you without a proper goodbye? The truth, sir, is that I was frightened beyond what I could ever explain to you or what you would appreciate hearing.*

Please know that I only wish the very best for you and your business. A reply from you would show graciousness far beyond what I deserve, but it would also soothe the grating of my offended conscience, which will not permit me peace until I am forgiven.

Sincerely,
Dinah Devereaux

Saturday, December 22

"Either you deliver it, or I will do it myself."

Jonathan hefted himself from the bed where he'd penned the brief response. He had read Dinah's missive so many times over the last twenty-four hours that when he'd turned over in the bed at night, he'd repeated it to himself, flawlessly.

Struggling to get to his feet, he refused to grab the bedpost. And though his head spun, he hoped his palm in Benjamin's face was enough to indicate he would accept no help.

"You are the most pigheaded man I have ever known," said Benjamin.

Jonathan offered a crooked smile. "Truly? I'd always reserved that dubious honor for you."

"Why don't we just skip the pitiful humor right now, hmm? That note is so . . . so untruthful, and you know it."

Jonathan lifted a brow. "You calling me a liar, Benjamin?"

"Use the label that suits you."

"Not important. I put her on the spot with all that flowery talk, and now she's feeling guilty. I don't blame her for not wanting to see me again, but I know how hard she can be on herself. I won't have her pitying me."

"But how do you know it's pity that's driving her? You're throwing away a special lady, man!"

Jonathan scooped up Dinah's note from the bureau and thrust it at Benjamin. "Read between the lines. She calls herself 'overwhelmed' and 'frightened.' Since you seem to have developed an acute case of dimwittedness, shall I translate that for you? She's trying to tell me she's not interested in someone like me, but she's too much of a lady to say it. Besides she's still McMillan's property."

Benjamin waved him off. "I've read that note thoroughly and there's nothing there beyond what it says. You're simply trying to find a way to return to that shell of yours. And as to her slave status, how will you ever know Mr. McMillan won't sell her unless you try? After all, he didn't take her in because he needed another slave. He took her in as a favor to a friend. You need to at least try to approach him about it."

"And how do you suppose I do that, since I have nothing to prove I'm a free man anymore, and it seems everyone in Natchez knows that now."

"How many times do I have to tell you? What happened to you, at your doorstep and at the bluffs, was an aberration. After those two worthless drifters found out how respected you are in this town, they left and nobody seems to know where they've gone."

Jonathan knew much of what his friend said was true. Still, the practice of slavery was the fearless dictator that drove the South—so clearly demonstrated in this frenzy toward secession. Who knew when Mississippi would join the ranks of South Carolina? Then what good would the papers do either him or Dinah? At any rate, right now without proof of manumission, a black man in Mississippi was a slave. He wouldn't put Theodore McMillan in the posture of having to deny him.

Gaining his footing next to his bed, Jonathan splayed his hands below his waist. He was tired of this conversation, tired of pretending to be the man he'd never be. He simply wanted to let Dinah Devereaux off the hook and hopefully never see her again.

"I need an answer. Will you deliver my response or not."

"I'll deliver it but not willingly, only to keep you from killing your foolish self. Sir."

DESPITE THE WHISPERS ABOUT SECESSION, Riverwood had been operating in high gear all week. So much polishing and carpet cleaning and mattress airing taking place until Violette had been called to the big house, leaving only Dinah and Mama Tavie to man the kitchen.

While Dinah greased the pan for the apple dumplings, Mama Tavie, who had been thoroughly rejuvenated by the news of Jonathan, moved around the kitchen as fluidly as a deer.

"That moping 'round you been doing lately don't become you, honey." Mama Tavie placed the last of the folded apple dumplings into the pan and placed it on a sideboard. She went to the door and slapped the flour from her hands. "You ain't said more than a handful of words since you come back from Joe-Nathan's. With the good news you brung, a body would 'a thought you'd be dancing like King David."

"I know, Mama Tavie. I'll try to do better."

"Aw, honey. Mama Tavie don't want you to just do better. I want you to feel better."

"Yes, ma'am. It's just that I know how much you love Jonathan, and my being with him, well it really didn't help matters at all."

Mama Tavie stopped and looked across the kitchen at Dinah. Her eyes were shining. "You done got to be my girl much as Joe-Nathan is my boy. Don't you know that?" She smiled, her yellow skin aglow with the lantern light. "Now I want you to listen, honey child. Surely, you already know how hard it is being the property of another man or woman. It's one of the worst things the devil ever dreamt up. And if you let yourself think about it too much, you'll think yourself right on out of your senses.

"But every now and then—when that same ole devil done

about made you believe there ain't no God nowhere and things ain't go'n ever get better—the Lord will show up with something that makes you want to go a little further. Last month when you showed up, a real lady, pretty and proper, sweet and wide-eyed, and oh so scared, we slaves here at Riverwood—even Violette, though in the wrong way—had us something new and wonderful to talk about and to get up in the morning for. Our lives won't never be the same 'cause God gave us Dinah."

"Oh, Mama Tavie. If you only knew who I really am."

"From what you already told me, I thought I did. But looks like you needs a fresh emptying of yourself. So I want you to sit down right here and tell me who you think you is."

Mama Tavie's unhurried manner encouraged Dinah to tell the story of Jack Hudson, a narrative so muddled and murky she hardly knew how to begin.

"A hundred times, I'd heard the cook say it to her little boy. A hundred more, my mistress to her cat. 'I. Love. You.' Then came the day when I learned that the likelihood of someone saying those words to me had died on the day I was born.

"A book to read, that's all I wanted when I heard my master telling a young lawyer in his firm named Jack Hudson about my birth. I'd seen Mr. Hudson a few times and marveled at his impeccable looks. But truth be told, I'd always been a little frightened of him, too. Something about the way he looked at me, as though my gowns were transparent, always left me feeling damaged.

"I suppose I already had the body of a woman, quite tall for eleven, though I was as innocent as a six-year-old. But I'd heard enough from the servants over the years to guess at things between men and women. And the German cook, whose words I took almost as gospel, warned me never to let a man kiss my mouth unless I was married to him. To do so, she'd said, was 'near as bad as becoming a woman of the night. Sometimes' she said, 'it leads to bringing into this world an unwanted child.'

"When I heard my master describe my mother to Jack

Hudson, I instantly reasoned my chances for becoming like her were very high, especially after how easy Cook had said it was to fall into sin. I ran across the hall into the drawing room and hid, trying my utmost to muffle the sounds accompanying my tears. I'd hoped to stay there until Jack Hudson, whom I'd heard announce he was about to let himself out, cleared the front entrance and I could search Master's dictionary for the meanings of some of the words he'd used. But it was not to be. Mr. Hudson must've heard my sniffling because the next thing I knew I was crying my eyes out in his arms.

"For a moment, it was like I'd found the older brother or father I'd never had. Finally, someone was holding me, comforting me. In my innocence, I wondered if he might say those coveted words, 'I love you,' the way cook did to her little boy. Then maybe, just maybe, I'd feel whole for once in my life.

"Then it happened. The thing Cook had warned me against. Jack Hudson started kissing me, a brutal disgusting assault upon my mouth that left me feeling confused, soiled and ashamed. I tried to get away, but he pressed in tighter, exploring places he had no right and threatening me with being sent to one of Master Horace's plantations in the river parishes if I spoke of what he was about to do. 'You're destined to become your mama, you know. I noticed you yesterday, asking for it, flouncing around like you had some ownership in this household. Your master might see you as almost a member of his family, but I know better,' he said. 'I know what you really are. A prostitute in the making, and now I know where you got it from.'"

"Dirty lowdown . . ." Mama Tavie's jaw flexed in barely controlled anger. She smoothed Dinah's dampened hair and gathered her closer to her chest. "It's all right, honey. Everything'll be all right."

Finally, a string of dying sobs shook Dinah as Mama Tavie continued patting her shoulder. Disgust and anger emanated from the older woman as thick as the kitchen's moisture. "You want to get the rest of it out now, or do you feel like you need to wait a while?"

"I haven't felt clean a day since that happened. And had it not been for Cook calling after me, forcing Jack Hudson to escape through the side doors that led to the garden, only God knows what else would have happened."

Mama Tavie gently pushed her back and looked into Dinah's eyes, her face a mixture of confusion and hope. "Wait a minute, honey. Is that all? Is you trying to tell me nothin' else happened 'sides that nasty kiss? That buzzard didn't get a chance to have his way with you?"

The tiniest bit of insult feathered Dinah's brain. Was Mama Tavie making light of the ordeal she'd been through? She sat up straight and wiped her eyes with her sleeves. "All? What do you call what I just described if it's not having one's way?"

Mama Tavie clapped her hands and laughed out loud. "I call it the Lord saving you from much worse. That's what I call it." She placed her hands on Dinah's shoulders. "Now you listen to me, and don't you say a word 'til I finish. First off, let me tell you somethin' about your mama and all the other brave souls like her in these here United States. Them fields what she worked in didn't make her no less of a lady. You might think you came to be a lady watching your mistress in New Orleans. But not so. You was born a lady because of the field hand what bore you. No matter what the meanness of men have tried to make them, fields have been temporary dwelling places for some of the noblest people in the world. If you don't believe me, just take a minute and think about how God blessed Ruth to glean for food in the field of one of the Savior's ancestors. And then He went on to sanctify the fields where the shepherds witnessed a show from heaven like no play-actors could ever put on when the Savior was born.

"Yes, 'tis true what happens to our people out in the fields every day is a 'bomination. But just like in the case of your mama, God can take a cotton field and a whore house and produce eternal music in them just like he did with you and all the brothers and sisters you never saw. Like King Solomon, born of a union sullied by murder, your birth, Dinah Devereaux, was music in the Lord's ears.

Then in painstaking gentleness, Mama Tavie explained to Dinah her own innocence, things about God's way for married men and women that, if Dinah had just been honest with herself about it, she'd figured out long ago. She'd just needed someone like Mama Tavie to say the words to her aloud.

A burden the size of the St. Louis Cathedral lifted from her. She walked over and looked out the door toward the twin dependency where Jonathan had resided for nearly a week. What an absolute willful fool she'd been. Knowing what she now did, could there yet be a chance for her and Jonathan? And what about Mr. James?

"While I'm blabbing my life's story, there's something else I need to get out."

Mama Tavie picked up a wooden stirring spoon and began to test one of her pots. "What's that, honey?"

Wondering if she was about to overstep, Dinah took a moment to breathe deeply. But looking at the way Mama Tavie had now suspended her spoon in the air, Dinah knew it was too late to back out.

"I have reason to believe Mr. James might be my father."

"Say what?" Mama Tavie dropped the spoon and joined Dinah at the door. "James? My James?"

Footsteps crunched on the path leading to the kitchen. Dinah wondered if it might be Mr. James. If he'd overheard her. Her insides clinched when she recognized Jonathan's friend.

"Benjamin? What are you doing out here?"

"Is everything all right with Joe-Nathan?" asked Mama Tavie.

Benjamin pursed his lips and crossed over the threshold. "Yes, ma'am. As far as his healing is concerned, Jonathan is doing fine. It's his stubbornness—well, anyhow, he sent me here to deliver this note."

Mama Tavie frowned and reached for it. "Much as I'd love to be able to, that boy know I can't read a lick."

Benjamin pulled the note toward his chest before rerouting it to Dinah. "I'm afraid I wasn't clear, Miss Tavie. The note is for Miss Devereaux."

Finally.

Dinah's hand shook so violently she wondered if she'd be able to hold the note steady enough to read it. Ever since she'd reluctantly approached Mr. James yesterday, asking him if he might be able to get a note to Jonathan, every pulse of her heart had beat out a fresh hope that Jonathan would decipher the real meaning behind everything she said and declare his love for her.

Silently, she read from the paper that carried Jonathan's spicy masculine scent.

Miss Devereaux,

Thank you for your concern. However, I consider myself much improved, given the circumstances, and quite able to see after myself.

I apologize if I embarrassed you with my bedside ramblings. I would only ask that you put it to the account of my over exuberance from the realization of the misfortune I'd undergone, accompanied by the relief that I had indeed survived. Allow me to assume that many humans might commit a similar faux pas under like conditions.

I will forever be indebted if you would weigh any and all statements I tendered against the sensible man you know me to be, as I humbly lay the cause of my erratic behavior at the feet of a near-death experience.

My fondest greetings to Mama Tavie and Emerald.

Regards,

Jonathan Mayfield

Wordlessly, Dinah folded the note and slipped it into her apron pocket. There'd be no more crying, no more running to Mama Tavie. She'd gotten her answer. She was done with Jonathan Mayfield. And clearly he was done with her. From now on, it was up to her how she would face the rest of her life. But one thing was sure. It wouldn't be with the heartless cabinetmaker.

"Anything you'd like me to tell him?" asked Benjamin who'd not bothered to take a seat. "Or perhaps you'd like to send a reply?"

"No thank you. No reply. Only that his request is forever granted."

IT COST Jonathan every bit of strength he had plus an entire ten minutes to get to his front door where the banging refused to cease. He opened the door to the fiercest look he'd ever seen.

"Good heavens, woman! You trying to finish killing me?"

"No. Just knowed you'd be bullheaded enough to survive the stairs. If I can't help Dinah see the light, maybe I can help you."

Octavia McMillan looked up at Jonathan from across his threshold, the remnants of sunlight from across the river leaving her face in shadow. A package clamped to her sides, she brushed past him into his foyer. "Shut the door." She rammed the package at him and took a seat without being asked.

Jonathan looked down at the package wrapped in one of her head rags. "What is this?"

"Don't you worry 'bout it just now. I'll let you know when it's time to deal with what's in that package." She tapped her foot on his polished wood floor. "You is the foolishest boy I ever seen in my life."

Jonathan chortled. The Mama Tavie he knew and loved in full verbal regalia.

"Well, now. Being called names among people that I most care about seems to be running rampant these days. Just this morning Benjamin topped his extensive list of epithets with 'pigheaded.' Anything else you'd like to call me before I offer you that seat you've already taken?"

"Just you listen. I know you got it in your head that it was Violette what got you in all this trouble."

"Mama Tavie, I think I have a pretty good handle on—"

"But it ain't. Oh, Violette had a little somethin' to do with it, but it was that lowdown Eli what told Jethro and that lowdown Jethro what told them slave catchers how valuable you was and how you couldn't no longer prove you was free." Her voice took on a hoarseness. "And your Mama Tavie had a little something to do with it, too."

Before Jonathan could respond, Mama Tavie was in his face with the package he'd placed on a table. "Open it. Quick."

Jonathan offered a wobbly bow and untied the handkerchief. "Yes, ma'am." He took a seat and opened the musty document.

February 21, 1851

> *Know all men that I, Ethan Mayfield, of Adams County,*
> *Mississippi do free my slave, Jonathan . . .*

Humor and sarcasm fled Jonathan like a fog at high noon, his mouth suddenly so dry he could hardly speak. "W-where—when —did you get this?"

Mama Tavie didn't blink an eye. "I got 'em the same time you did, from the same Massa, Ethan Mayfield."

From Master Mayfield? She'd had a legal set of his papers for nine years and had said nothing about it? Betrayal slammed his gut making him near nauseated. All the teacakes in the world would never be able to erase this. Jonathan got to his feet. He stood over Mama Tavie and tried to steady himself. This felt more painful than the cruel beating on that ship all those years ago. Why? Why would the woman who'd held him through nightmares after his parents' death deceive him like this? Other than Benjamin who'd just recently learned about it, she was the only one who knew the papers he'd carried all these years were counterfeit. So why would she keep the authentic ones from him?

"Now no matter how hard you tearing up your brain right now trying to figure me out, I want you to stop and do something for me. Then after you've done it, if you feel the same way, I'll leave you be and pray someday you be ready to see me again."

Right now, as much as he loved her, never seeing her again sounded like a workable plan to Jonathan.

"I want you to place them papers right next to your chest—go on, do it."

Foolishness, but he owed her that much before he opened the door and ushered her out of his life forever.

"Now I want you to search your heart while you hold your freedom papers next to it and see if there's any peace there a'tall."

He would accommodate her this last time before completely severing ties with her. The very thought pierced him like an awl.

"Well? Do you feel free?"

How long it took the question to infuse him, Jonathan couldn't say. But now a searing heat was spreading through him not unlike the fever he'd recently experienced, only hotter. He felt as though he was in a crucible, and the dross of imitating the fine houses and business achievements, plush carriages and stylish clothes of the Natchez nabobs, was falling off all around him.

He sat back down across from her, waves of regret threatening to level him as he thought about the last decade of his life. He continued to clasp the old paper next to his heart, but something new and clean on the inside was pushing back. It was as though the absence of his false freedom had somehow taken the fear along with it.

Deep within, he knew he'd never truly been free. He had allowed Master Mayfield's words to bind him to his own deep-seated feelings of inferiority, and now he realized no piece of paper would've ever been enough to set him free. The Lord's words blew onto his soul like a gentle breeze.

"Frederick Douglass was free long before he escaped the evils of slavery. Have you not heard that he whom the Son sets free is free indeed?"

Slowly, he loosened his fingers, the crumpled papers quietly slipping from over his heart to the floor. He struggled to kneel next to the woman whom the Lord made his surrogate mother and bowed his head. Mama Tavie, still as limber as a twenty-five year old, slipped to her knees to join him.

"Dear Lord, I am so ashamed of myself. For these nine years, I've been so busy protecting my heart against further hurt that I have sucked all the joy from my so-called freedom." Jonathan felt the tears trickle down through a day's worth of beard to meet beneath his chin. "Freely You have offered me an abundance of earthly gifts. The gift of parents who, though in the end not themselves perfect, modeled for me a near-perfect devotion to each other. The gift of a curious mind and hands that crave creativity. And the gift of outward freedom from this heinous condition called slavery.

"Yet, I have repaid you by spurning the greatest gift of all, the unfathomable gift of love. Love between my parents, love from this angel that kneels next to me called Octavia McMillan." Jonathan's heart turned over at the sound of Mama Tavie's weeping. "And love, I hope, from the sweetest woman on earth, Miss Dinah Devereaux.

"But most of all, it's been Your abiding, eternal and all-encompassing love that has sustained me. I praise You, Lord, for taking the time to speak to me of true freedom. Yet, for days after, I've followed the road of my own willfulness. You reached down from heaven and lifted me above a sorrowful deadly illness to a place of indescribable peace. Still, when I returned, I chose my own treacherous path. For these transgressions and countless more, I am ashamed. Please forgive me."

Rest suffused his soul. Jonathan paused in silent reverence.

"But I have much to be grateful for, too, dear Savior. You have guided me and protected me all the days of my life, allowing me to sit in heavenly places with You, the One True God, and learn of You. And now, I am ready to do your bidding, great or small, for no matter the circumstances, I shall never be a slave again. Amen.

"Oh, and Lord? If Dinah Devereaux is the one for me as my heart insists she is, I'll be listening for Your instructions. For no matter what scars I have, soul and body, I shall be trying with all my might to convince her to accept me. Amen again."

Together, they laughed and they cried and they reminisced, Jonathan and his Mama Tavie, until she went to the door and beckoned for Mr. James. Surprised the two most dependable slaves at Riverwood were able to get away at the same time, Jonathan posed the question.

"How did the two of you ever manage to pull this off?"

James smiled cryptically before revealing a written pass suspiciously similar to his master's hand. "With God and innovation, all things are possible. And besides, I happen to be one of two butlers at Riverwood. As for Miss Octavia, here, she's finding quite the culinary competitor in one Miss Dinah Devereaux." He laughed outright. "Don't worry. God's left enough daylight for us to get to Riverwood and back in our places in plenty of time."

Mama Tavie turned from the door. "Joe-Nathan? Why come I feel like there's something else you ain't telling me?"

"Because there is, and I don't intend to. When the time comes, God will give me what to say."

Mr. James stepped forward. "Far be it from me to try to take

the Lord's place, but if you should ever need to talk to someone .
. ."

Jonathan looked at Mr. James. Though a kinder man he'd
never met, the butler wasn't a novice. Perhaps.

"You're a strong man, sir." Mr. James removed the hat he'd
just placed on his head. "And I know I asked your help in
protecting Dinah. But right now I'm offering an ear to you, man
to man, if you ever need it."

He trusted this man. And though Jonathan had already told
Benjamin about how the men on the ship had threatened to
emasculate him, talking to Mr. James about his concerns might
protect Dinah from a life she neither wanted nor deserved.

"Mama Tavie, would you excuse us for a moment?"

Jonathan was about to tell the butler about one of the tiny
scars on his body that, along with Ethan Mayfield's words, had
haunted him for nearly ten years, making him wonder if he was
less than the man God intended him to be.

19

Sunday, December 23

J onathan stopped to pray for guidance one last time before heading for the back steps of Riverwood. Waiting to approach Dinah had required more patience than any piece of woodwork he'd ever created. Granted, Mr. James's advice to take some time to pray about the best way to win her back—and the older man's insistence that Jonathan give his worry about his scars to the Lord—had been a stroke of godly wisdom. But had it not been for the work he'd done with his hands last night, Jonathan might have lost his senses. Now finally, his thinking had crystallized.

Last night, he'd carved some special things for Dinah, and just today he'd decided to ask a woman in one of the local shops tomorrow about helping him choose a few store-bought things for her. But now he'd come up with a real plan to go along with the presentation. He was about to put a stop to this torture, or at least try. He smiled inside. Only an hour before, the Lord had confirmed that the only way to do that was for Jonathan to talk to Theodore McMillan and then let his heart go free.

Having left his carriage behind a stand of trees, Jonathan

bowed his head and closed his eyes near the beginning of the long curvy driveway. It wasn't everyday an ex-slave walked up to a planter's house unannounced and asked for an audience.

"Lord, I know I've disappointed You many times with my arrogant antics. But if You'll prompt Mr. McMillan's heart to see me tonight and accept my offer, I promise to spend the rest of my life trying to make it up to You, and *her.* You, O God, are the only true Master. Please let Dinah's earthly master say yes. Amen."

He opened his eyes to two silhouetted figures near the stables so closely embraced that he could hardly make out who they were. They were kissing. Or were they? It almost seemed the female was trying to wrench loose. The man half-growled, half laughed as he suspended his open hand above her. He was about to hit her.

Dinah? The woman seemed a bit too rounded, but who else could it be?

"Since when you get it in your head to pull away from ole Eli??"

Eli.

Fury seized Jonathan, squeezing his faculties dry of any reason. He winced as he picked up his pace toward the stables. He'd finally be the man to teach Eli Duggan a lesson he wasn't apt to forget any time soon, a lesson that would put him in hell where he belonged. Jonathan felt a warped sense of privilege laid out in front of him. He would kill Eli Duggan. Rid the world of him once and for all. He was a decided man. Until he saw another man emerge from the stables beating Jonathan to the cause.

"Unhand her, right now, or I will kill you!"

Mr. James. With a pitchfork raised above his shoulder. He poked Eli right down to the ground. Jonathan stopped and slapped his hands together. He wanted to jump in the air and cheer. Instead he eased his sore frame behind a magnolia tree and kneaded his brow for several minutes as the Holy Spirit spoke comfort to him.

She's safe. Let James handle it.

He turned and headed for the big house. Mr. James didn't need his help, and Jonathan didn't need to be distracted from his mission. He'd give this one over to the older wiser man, but one day soon he'd have to create something special for the gentleman.

"WHAT YOU DOING OUT HERE? You ain't well enough to be out in this night air. And why you got that chappish grin on yo' face?"

"Still making up words, huh, Mama Tavie?" Jonathan reached for a teacake. "What's a 'chappish' grin anyway?"

"Don't try to get around answering me. You been up to somethin' I see it in your face."

It never ceased to astonish him how insightful this woman was. "I'm just surprised at how easily the inner man can succumb to flesh. Immediately after a heartfelt prayer, I almost killed Eli tonight."

Mama Tavie's countenance went slack. "Joe-Nathan, no. The Lord just raised you from the sickbed. Please don't tell me—"

"I think I went a little insane, Mama Tavie, when I thought Eli was about to hit Dinah."

"What? Eli hit Dinah?"

"No, no. All is well. First of all, by the time I closed in on him, Mr. James had him pinned to the ground with a pitchfork."

"James?"

"Yes, ma'am. Seems Mr. James had walked over to the stables for some reason."

"Yep. Believe it or not, James sometimes goes out there and prays with the horses. Says something about their sounds soothing him. Guess going out there finally paid off in a big way."

Jonathan chortled. "Just seeing him in his shirtsleeves was shocking enough, but I think that pitchfork scared Eli more than anything I could have done." Jonathan locked gazes with Mama Tavie.

"Second of all, it was Violette, not Dinah, Eli was roughing up."

"Aw naw. He after Violette, too? Where's that poor child now? Did he hurt her?"

"I don't know where she is. I don't think she even saw me before she ran off, but she didn't seem hurt."

"So you never touched Eli."

"Fortunately—or perhaps, unfortunately—no."

Tears slid down Mama Tavie's face. She wiped her eyes with her apron." You can't follow your feelings all the time, son. I don't even want to think about what could 'a happened if you'd got your hands on Eli tonight. You might 'a kil't him, but in your condition, it might 'a been the other way around."

He pulled her tiny body into his embrace then gingerly lifted her into the air and twirled her a few rounds. "True, Octavia McMillan. Following my feelings hasn't always worked for me. But a few minutes ago, inside the mansion there, I believe I followed the heart of the Lord, and I think you're going to be pleased with what I've done."

Laughing harder than he had in years, Jonathan barely felt Mama Tavie's small fists beating against his back. "Put me down, boy," she protested, "or I'll, I'll, well, I don't exactly know what I'm go'n do with you!"

An hour later

DINAH CLIMBED the back steps to the verandah. She'd been summoned again, not by Mistress McMillan this time but to the master's library where she prayed she wasn't about to be banished from Riverwood.

At least this time her master awaited her. Not like years ago when she'd stumbled upon that painful knowledge no little girl should ever hear.

She paused at the door to the servants' hall. What could Theodore McMillan possibly want with her? Had someone finally informed him of Eli's antics toward her? Then again, maybe it was the problem of profit loss that seemed to be inherent in cotton farming. Had she become too much of a liability to Riverwood and its sister locations?

She moved from the servants' area into the sweeping hallway. The house was resplendent with holly and cedar, candles and pinecones. Days ago Dinah had ached to be a part of the ongoing decorations. But now as she stepped over the threshold into her first audience with the man who'd saved her from the streets, she was numb to the usual draw of holiday preparations.

"Close the door behind you."

Instantly, Dinah was back in the drawing room of the Devereaux mansion, Jack Hudson's eyes probing her like a poisoned dagger. After all she'd been through, had it come down to this again? Dread filled her chest. Her knees rattled beneath her shift. But she mustn't grab hold to the back of a chair without asking permission. Suddenly the man smiled, his face displaying a hint of the same kind of concern she'd grown accustomed to receiving from Mr. James. Or was it simply her hopeful imagination? Dinah remembered to lower her eyes before the man who owned her, hopefully not too late.

Please, Lord Jesus, don't let this be another Jack Hudson situation.

If this was about what happened in the kitchen while Master McMillan was away, she could explain just as she'd done with the mistress. If only he'd give her a chance.

If only she could find her voice.

"I've heard that Eli has taken an interest in you."

So this *was* about Eli? Dinah squeaked out a, "Yes, sir but if I may—"

He shot her a warning glance, stilling her tongue. "You should know, Dinah, that while Eli is an excellent groundskeeper, he has a sullied reputation among slave women. If Horace Devereaux even suspected you had feelings for a cad like Eli, he'd turn over in his grave after all he invested in you."

Invested? True, she'd lived an unusual life for a slave girl, but she'd earned her keep. No telling how much money she'd added to the Devereaux coffers since she'd turned professional in her seamstress work. Standing with bowed head before her earthly master, she could no longer see what was in his eyes. But she sensed he was about to deliver life-changing news. Her heart pounded against her chest wall as she again besought her Heavenly Master. *Lord, give Your servant strength to bear it.* Dinah barely heard Theodore McMillan's next words as a familiar proverb washed over her.

"The fear of man bringeth a snare, but whoso putteth his trust in the Lord shall be safe. . . ."

"Anyway, enough about Eli. Excellent gardener, but I'm hearing things lately that make me think I might've made a mistake bringing him here. Let James know if you're ever troubled by him."

"Yes, sir. Thank you."

Mr. McMillan tapped an empty pipe on his desk. "Horace, man of integrity that he was, has left you under my supervision, which is why that rascal, Jack Hudson, was trying to steal you on the night of the fire."

Jack Hudson tried to steal her? Dinah's breath caught in a maelstrom of confusion, fear, and disbelief.

"S-sir?"

"He knew of and meant to get the earnings, of course, before he sold you."

What earnings?

"And he would have succeeded had it not been for a neighbor in the District who happens to be another friend of mine and stepped in until I could be notified." He shifted in his chair. "But back to Horace. It seems he's left everything you earned in trust for you to dispose of as you please at his and his wife's death. A nice sum, I might add. He also augmented the accumulation with funds of his own."

Without thinking of the consequences, Dinah gripped the chair in front of her. Her master nodded. "The door is closed. You may sit."

Easing onto the chair, her heart slowed. Her spirit soared. True, she'd lost the one thing she wanted most on this earth, Jonathan's love. But she'd just gained the means to obtain the next two best things in line. A sewing-designing business of her own and her freedom. She knew she couldn't have them both, not right away. But there was no question which one she wanted most. Knowing she risked a breach of protocol, she sat up tall as her new master continued.

"Now. Is there anything you'd like to say?"

"Sir, I have but one request. And for its fulfillment, I relinquish every dime I own."

Part concern, part surprise seemed to lift her master's brows. "And that would be?"

"My freedom, sir. Only my freedom."

He smoothed his hand over his mouth. Having come from the North, he spoke with a rapid and curt accent, but his eyes were warm. "You ask for the one thing I cannot give you, and I'll brook no inquiries as to my reasons."

Dinah stared in disbelief. That made absolutely no sense. What was she to do with the money if she couldn't spend it as she wished? Her body shook with wanting to ask, but she'd pushed this man as far as she dared.

"I see," was all she could manage. Once more, in a matter of minutes, her world had changed from wonderful to woe.

Monday, December 24

DINAH HELD a lantern at her feet to fend off the darkness of the recently-worn path. The McMillans had ordered her to go to a temporary gazebo set up behind the mansion for the enjoyment of the house guests and decorate a small tree, waiting for her in the lovely octagonal retreat. The trimmings would be there also.

But why this time of evening? All afternoon she'd been virtually idle, in a vortex of despair about her new unheard-of status as a wealthy slave—hanging around Mama Tavie's kitchen offering help that wasn't needed and stuffing herself with sweets while Mama Tavie couldn't stop grinning about something.

And why her? When clearly her master and mistress had preferred others to decorate the house? Furthermore, she'd never decorated a tree in her life, so why had she been chosen?

She startled as the open-sided structure suddenly lit up with lanterns hung from the outer edges of the circled ceiling. Someone saw her coming. From the distance, she could make out the form of a man, perhaps one of the cabin slaves sent to assist her. Eli?

No. The man was too tall to be Eli. Besides the master had been very clear about Eli not coming anywhere near her. Then who? Needles of fear poked at her before she squared her shoulders and proceeded. Surely, her master wouldn't send her to a place this far from the big house to work with a stranger. In the dark. Would he?

Mounting the two steps, she lifted her skirt with one hand and the lantern with the other to get a better view of the man who obviously awaited her.

Jonathan.

"What are you doing here? Please leave."

He smiled at her, almost in—amusement? Surely, not. Not

even the world's most conceited cabinetmaker could make sport of what he'd said to her in that letter days ago.

"Mr. McMillan directed me to look out for your safety out here. One never can tell what might emerge from these woods, like that haughty lustful rascal Eli, for example."

Haughty? How could Mr. Jonathan "Prideful" Mayfield let that accusation proceed from his mouth? Dinah was so angry her very toes seemed to tremble. She let her lantern down and shook her finger in his face.

"Haughty? Why you're the biggest chunk of haughtiness ever to sully God's green earth. And not only that, Mr. Mayfield, you're a fickle clod of arrogance, at that. At least Eli has never wavered in his interest in me. His lechery is consistent."

Dinah knew she was sputtering, her redundant words unable to match the pace of her incensed thoughts. "Don't you dare deign to my safety. I don't need your protection, and I certainly won't bear your presence while doing this job." She picked up her lantern and stomped off toward the house. "Let me know when you're done skulking around out here, and I'll resume my assignment. Until then, I shall be in the dependency."

"No, wait!" Was that a strain of desperation in Jonathan's voice? "Your master insists that I be with you. Direct orders."

Her back still turned, Dinah dug in her heels. "I won't do it."

"But you must. Have you forgotten? You have no choice. Though your work is unsurpassed by any I've seen, you're still a slave." His voiced dipped to a hoarse plea. "Please, Dinah. That didn't come out right. I promise not to nettle you while you're doing your job." Turning slowly back toward the gazebo, she watched him move away to the farthest edge, as far as possible from the small perfectly-shaped cedar waiting to be trimmed. Absent his usual wide-legged stance, he continued his plea.

"I promise I won't say a word until or unless you do."

Dinah knew she'd been outdone. Not only were his pleas beginning to tug at her heartstrings, what he said about her being a slave was true. Once again, she had no choice but to do as she was told. But she didn't have to like it, and she would never say a word to Jonathan Mayfield again, not tonight, not ever. With a protracted sigh, she climbed the steps to the gazebo. She knelt before the wooden box of decorations and opened the lid. Her hand flew to her chest as she caught herself about to squeal out her delight.

Oh, mercy! Her decorations from New Orleans.

But she didn't utter a sound. She didn't dare open up conversation with this—this cad, rake, roué! There were three miniature wooden Christmas ornaments that matched the kinds she'd created in the Garden District. A bell. A wreath. An angel. So beautiful. Meticulously created by . . . unmistakably Jonathan. But how could he have known—except . . .

Except for the night she'd described them at Mama Tavie's supper table, the night he'd kissed her.

Calico pouches were filled with hard candies. Silver tinsel, colorful streamers, white snowflakes embroidered with red, all the things she'd described crowded the large nondescript wooden box. Who'd had time to purchase all this?

Bubbles of joy threatened to burst forth from her soul. Somebody cared enough to do this for her? She could feel the anticipation from Jonathan, feel his waiting for her to ask who. But she would not. She would not let him touch her heart again. On and on, she pulled out the lovely pieces that seemed to be waiting for the right spot on the bare cedar top next to her.

And then she saw it. A smaller finely carved wooden box in the shape of a star, the name DINAH etched into its center. No one but Jonathan could have done this so elegantly. This time she couldn't stop herself. She gasped aloud. "What is this?"

"A star for the stargazer."

"You know what I mean. What's inside?"

"You won't know until you open it, now will you?" She turned to look at him. He was obviously still in pain. But hope mixed with a touch of angst glistened in his eyes.

Hands shaking like leaves in an autumn breeze, she opened it to find two pieces of delicate parchment rolled and tied with a narrow string of gold ribbon. She asked again. "What is it?"

"Open it."

At length, she managed to pull the ribbon loose. The glow of her lantern turned the fine parchment into a soft yellow.

December 24, 1860

> *In exchange for furniture making and installation, Jonathan Mayfield has entered into an agreement with and purchased from Theodore McMillan, Dinah Devereaux, formerly of New Orleans, Louisiana, presently a slave at Riverwood Plantation . .*
>
> .

Dinah leapt to her feet, images of the sale of her mother racing through her head like a brush fire. Violette's prediction had come true. Mama Tavie's Christmas treats tried to make their way up her throat as her mind reeled with the awful declaration she held in her hands. Jonathan had never wanted to marry her. All along he'd only wanted to begin his repertoire of slaves so he could be the next William Johnson, the black prestigious barber and slave owner whom he called his hero.

"You—you *bought* me?"

He had the gall to look confused. "I thought you'd be pleased."

"Pleased. Pleased? Tell me, Massa, what do you expect to do with me, use me up and then sell me to an under-the-hill bordello like a common tramp?"

"Where on earth . . . Dinah, you've got this all wrong. I—"

"After the way you led me on at your house and then asked for forgiveness for your 'ramblings' as though you'd casually mentioned the wrong calendar date instead of declaring your love for me, now you sashay back into my life and announce that you own me?" Dropping the paper as though it were a scorpion, she backed away from him into the rail. "How could you do this to me, Jonathan? How could you?"

With two strides he was at her side. "Dinah, please. Let me explain. I don't know what you mean by all this, but you have to hear me out."

But everything in her brain blossomed red. Making a wide arc around him, she stumbled away from the rail and flew down the steps she'd hesitated to climb minutes ago.

"Violette was right all along. You do think yourself better than the rest of us slaves. I hate you, Jonathan Mayfield, and I intend never to see you again. Though I'm your property now, *Massa*, you'll have to drag me to you lair!"

20

Mid-January, 1861

Jonathan gulped down a cup of bad coffee recalling for the thousandth time how a few weeks ago he'd made his way—stunned—through the front entrance of Riverwood and out onto the dark road. How absurd it all seemed now, especially since Mississippi had now joined South Carolina in secession from the Union.

"Lord, how could I have entirely misread you so?"

He opened the door of his shop where Benjamin and Henry had already begun sorting pieces and slipped into his work apron. Though Mississippi had essentially declared itself a slave state forever, Jonathan's business had taken off like the bullet of a sharpshooter since the Riverwood job. He appreciated that McMillan's accountant had generously spread the word about their business dealings, and Mr. McMillan himself had sent him a message over a week ago to stop by at his convenience to discuss "the status of Dinah." But after the disaster on Christmas Eve, Jonathan could hardly bring himself to pass the gates of Riverwood, let alone enter them.

Glancing out at the gazebo he'd relegated to a corner, he

thought of the queenly way Dinah had thrown her shoulders back when she'd become angry and the way she always bit the side of her lip when she was fearful.

Heavenly Father, please help me to know what to do. I miss seeing her to the point of physical pain.

But she'd said she hated him, and he was determined to give her space to do that if it brought her some sense of justice. Each day he caught Benjamin watching him, looking he imagined, for some kind of sign of hope. But under the hollow threat of firing him, Jonathan had forbade his good friend to mention Dinah's name. So far, Benjamin had honored it.

Dreading his workers' daily attempt at lighthearted back-and-forth to lift his mood, he groaned at the sound of Henry's first question of the day.

"Mr. Jonathan, you ever heard tell of a black man what come to live in Natchez named E-bra-hema?" The young slave apprentice took pains to pronounce Ibrahima's name.

Jonathan bristled. No doubt in his mind Benjamin had put Henry up to this. Benjamin clapped the boy on the shoulder and chortled. "Good job Henry, with the pronunciation, that is." He turned to Jonathan. "Sir, would you like to tell Henry what you know about the legend of Ibrahima?"

Somehow Benjamin must've found out that Jonathan had swallowed his pride and asked every older slave he'd come in contact with these last few weeks about the story of the African prince. "No. I have too much work to do this morning to tell tales." He speared both his workers with a commanding stare. "And so do you, by the way."

"Aw, come on, sir. Be a sport and tell us what you know about the African prince."

"Did I not just say—"

"Please, sir?" Henry's look of innocent anticipation caught him off guard. Glancing at Benjamin, he resignedly expelled a breath of air through his nostrils.

"Oh, all right then. Five minutes, that's it, while we continue to work. Seems somewhere during the last ten years or so of the 1700s a true African prince from a people called the Fulbe was defeated in a war and enslaved and brought to Natchez. He claimed to have originated from a place called Futa and to have studied at a place called Timbuktu."

"Tim-buck what?"

"Timbuktu, a place in West Africa." Jonathan couldn't help but smile. Henry's thirst for knowledge about his history was palpable. "Legend has it that though Ibrahima did what he was forced to do, throughout the decades he was enslaved he never lost his regal presence and was actually referred to by some as 'Prince,' right here in Natchez."

"What you mean by regal presence, Mr. Mayfield?"

"He carried himself with the stamp of the royal blood that ran through his veins, Henry, all the while maintaining unusual loyalty, integrity, and dignity."

"Sounds like you, sir. Did he have children? Could you maybe be one of his kin?"

The young man had just touched Jonathan with a compliment he'd never forget. "Thank you, Henry. That's one of the finest things anyone had ever said to me. And yes, he did have children, and toward the end of his life, a white man whose life his father had saved back in Africa found Ibrahima and helped him back to the land of his fathers."

Jonathan found himself enjoying the flow of the tale until he looked over at Benjamin who'd crossed his arms and assumed a meddling smirk.

"Hey, Jonathan, you still haven't mentioned what or *who* got you interested in Ibrahima in the first place. Hmmm?"

"No. And—"

"Was it Miss Dinah?" asked Henry. "Benjamin said he'd heard her talking 'bout him one time."

Dinah. It was the first time he'd heard her name spoken aloud in weeks. The beauty of it pierced his soul and set his heart aching.

"Dinah." He repeated her name, the taste of it settling on his tongue like summer berries.

"I beg your pardon, sir?"

"Oh uh, yes. Yes, it was Miss Devereaux who brought it up some time back."

Jonathan saw Benjamin gesture ever so subtly toward Henry who jumped to attention. "Ahem! Hadn't heard you mention her in a while, sir. I reckon you was pretty sweet on her back there at Riverwood."

He was going to kill Benjamin when he got him alone. Right now, though, he felt like a trapped rabbit. "Don't know where you got that idea from, Henry, but it's totally false. Now let's get back to work, shall we?"

But the damage was done. He'd heard her name, and he knew that at the least he had to go to Riverwood to make sure she was all right, that neither Eli nor anyone else had touched her beauty. And since Mr. McMillan had already sent for him, he had just the excuse he needed to do it.

DINAH GLANCED OUT THE WINDOW. It was proving to be a spectacular dawn as she pressed the circle of dough with the heel of her hands before pinching off measured hunks and rounding them into biscuits. The bustle of the holiday was long since passed, and she couldn't be more relieved. Relieved to see the elaborate decorations reminding her of her old life removed. Relieved to see the last of the demanding holiday guests return to their own mansions. Relieved to reenter the numbing routine of sewing and cooking. Relieved, and heartbroken, to see Jonathan's gazebo quietly disappear by the hands of Benjamin and Henry.

Jonathan, the man who owned her, the man she thought of every hour of every day in spite of his betrayal, hadn't set foot in Riverwood's kitchen in nearly three weeks.

Lightly dusting with flour the fat biscuits she'd placed in a greased pan, she checked with Mama Tavie before putting them into the oven.

"These look all right, Mama Tavie?"

"Humph." Mama Tavie assumed a mock frown. "I'm go'n have to keep an eye on you. Bless my soul if James ain't starting to crow about your biscuits more than mine."

Dinah studied her feet, pleasure from the compliment warming her to the tips of her toes. "Aw now, Mama Tavie. You and I both know that's not true."

"Not true, my foot. That man dotes on you worse than a mama bear with a cub."

Mama Tavie was prone to exaggerate. But Mr. James *had* taken it upon himself to appeal to his master to sell Dinah's freedom to her. Theodore McMillan had refused, however, offering the rather nebulous answer that he could not sell what he no longer owned and adding that he was willing to keep her on until Jonathan decided what to do with her.

Mama Tavie put the finishing touches on the white gravy and poured it into a cornflower blue Wedgewood gravy boat.

"Honey, I been meaning to talk to you about James. If James is your papa—and from what you told me, I don't doubt that he is—he would want to know so's he could do right by you. Truth is, seeing y'all together lately, it ain't much of a stretch to imagine the same blood running through your veins. James would pleasure in trying to look out for a daughter like you, I mean as much as a slave is able to."

"But don't you see? That's exactly why he must never know. The one thing I want most now is my freedom so I can help others learn to design and sew, kind of like Jonathan does at his shop. Anyway, if Mr. James knew, he'd feel duty bound to try to act like a father, and even if it came from the heart, what could he do to help me gain my freedom? He's a slave like all the rest of us."

He could love you. Dinah startled at the soft answer that floated into her head.

Love.

That word again that had clearly captured her attention when Jonathan had woken up from his illness. Dinah sensed it was the Spirit talking to her. But in the flesh she was too weakened, too battle-scarred, to listen. So much had happened within the last month. She'd tried this thing called love. She'd offered it up only to have it soundly refused. She couldn't bear another rejection. Not this soon.

Soon. Another of the precious words that had covered her heart at Jonathan's home. The Lord had said He would deliver her and her people from slavery soon. Mississippi had just seceded and there was talk of war. What if—what if in her lifetime she was able to call James her father as a free woman? What if James, as a free man, was able to own her as his daughter? And what if Jonathan—

"You don't know James like I do." Suddenly, Mama Tavie seemed a bit shy. "What I'm trying to say is when James cares he cares hard. You can believe me. He cares about you in a way I've not seen him care about anybody in a long time."

"Yes, ma'am. I want to believe that, and a part of me does. But I heard it from Mr. James's own lips. After the pain of losing my mother, he's never considered a marriage and a family because he doesn't think an enslaved butler would make a good family man."

It took only a suspended moment for Dinah to realize what she'd said. She clapped her hand to her mouth as Mama Tavie struggled against deflating before her very eyes. "Oh, Mama Tavie. I couldn't be more sorry for what I just said."

"Oh, that's all right, honey. I've pretty much always knowed what my chances were with James anyhow. And that boils down to no chance at all, unless the Lord says different."

"*Soon.*"

Joy unspeakable rose up in Dinah. If the Lord said soon, then

He would know what He was talking about. And if soon meant soon, Mr. James—a godly man if she'd ever seen one—deserved to know and plan for and love his daughter while he waited for soon to come.

"Yes, ma'am, Mama Tavie. Unless the Lord says different."

"Mr. James?" Dinah knocked softly at the basement room beneath the verandah. "It's me, Dinah. May I come in?"

Sounds of scrambling and knocking things over, so uncharacteristic of the suave butler, came from the other side of the door before it swung open.

"Miss? Is anything wrong? Are you all right?" His facial features hidden by the darkness, Mr. James radiated alarm. "Did Eli—"

"Oh, no sir. Eli's been sent away. Don't you remember?"

"Of course. I'm overreacting. I don't know what came over me." He smoothed his tousled hair. "Forgive me, won't you come in?"

Dinah stood aside as he lit a lamp to a spotless room of relative comfort. Beautiful pencil sketches of landscapes, animals, and houses punctuated the spotless walls. But none of people. He motioned toward a new overstuffed chair cozied up to a small polished table. No doubt in her mind the table was Jonathan's work. On it sat spectacles and a large bible.

"Please. Sit down. Can I offer you a cup of tea?"

"No, sir."

In hindsight Dinah wondered if this was such a good idea. Mr. James's life was the epitome of order. Why would he want to know about a daughter born of a prostitute? What if he rejected her flat out?

"Mr. James, perhaps I should have waited, but I know how busy you are all day. And I didn't think I could wait another day without talking to you."

He smiled, showing his usual confidence before bringing a cane-seat ladder back chair over next to her. "I assure you it's more than all right. So please, tell me what's on your mind."

"Well, uh, I know you can read, Mr. James. So I was wondering if you'd had a chance to peruse anything in the big house concerning all this talk about—"

"War? Rumors are flying everywhere about the impasse between the North and South."

"Do you believe, I mean, it seems most of the other slaves are totally oblivious to the possibilities."

"Trust me, they're not oblivious. Treated like so much wallpaper, slaves gather enough information on a daily basis to start their own newspaper."

"Then what do you think?"

Mr. James lit up with hope. "I'm trying to do more praying than thinking, but I'm failing miserably at that. All I can tell you is if this rift keeps widening, this country is never going to be the same. And for you and me that could be the greatest blessing we've seen in our lifetimes." Mr. James tilted his head to the side. "Now what's the real reason you're here?"

"I think . . . that is . . . I need to know if I might be your daughter."

Dinah leapt to her feet before he could catch her eye and began pacing the small quarters. Mercy. This wasn't how she'd imagined it at all. But once she'd blurted it out, the rest came gushing forth. She knew her mouth was running like a train trying to make up time, but she had to get it out before he could respond. If she gave him time to refute her, to say he was sure he'd never had a daughter and never wanted to, she would never be able to speak to him of it again.

"My mother was a prostitute at the Gentleman's Caller. I, that is, my master found me, not more than a day old, on the streets of New Orleans in June of 1840. When you said that you'd been with well, you know, a woman in the fall of '39 at the Gentleman's Caller, it was too much to overlook. Besides I—"

Was that mirth she heard? Tumbles of laughter like a happy waterfall fell from Mr. James's lips. He clapped his hands and lilted a step as though he were on a ballroom floor.

"I've prayed so long for something to remember her by." He hugged Dinah so tight she thought her bones might be injured. "I suspected it from the minute I saw you. You're just as lovely as she was and so much the image of her." He eased her back to arm's length. "Just think of what this means, dear girl. We've so much to catch up on. So much to live for." He released her and plundered a drawer inside the table holding the Bible. He lifted a crude-looking book bound with homespun cloth. He leafed through it in a frenzy of anticipation. Finally he turned to her, his face aglow. Wordlessly, he handed her a yellowed sheet of paper.

Dinah gasped. "It's like staring into a looking glass."

"I sketched it on the last night we were together in the Gentleman Caller. It was my first and last sketch of a human being. I loved her more than life and vowed I could never find a human face as interesting." He hesitated, a catch in his throat. "I loved her, but no more than I love you."

He loved her. Finally, somebody loved her.

DINAH WHISTLED a tune as she lay out the sweet potatoes for the noonday meal. Never before had she felt this kind of contentment. She'd found her father last evening, and he loved her. No longer were those words reserved for others. He loved *her*. He said so and meant it. For the first time since coming to Riverwood, she felt safe. Mr. James—Papa—would somehow keep her from the fields. And one day, God willing, she'd be free to become the designer she was born to be.

Thankfully, the threat of Eli was gone too. He'd been fired. Fired? Dinah shook her head at her own silly word choice. How could a slave be fired when he or she was never hired in the first place? She had to get a handle on her way of thinking. Except for Jonathan, she'd seen nobody around here doing contracted work like the men in the Garden District sometimes did.

But whatever the term, good riddance to that lustful rascal who'd been shipped across the river to another plantation. She glanced over her shoulder at the mother of his child. If only Violette felt the same way.

Ever since Eli's deportation, the poor girl had been awfully subdued, probably more afraid than ever of the gaping uncertainty that came along with being a slave. Her very movements spoke defeat, her loss of appetite for life and food apparent in her near-submissive manner, and her rapid weight loss. The only topic of discussion that sparked interest in Violette these days was Emerald who was chattering to herself and her ragdoll just outside the door.

"Lucy, you is my bestest friend. You know that? But you don't ever comb your hair. Why come is that?"

Dinah and Violette laughed out loud.

"Violette, I couldn't be more pleased by yours and Emerald's reading progress, and Mama Tavie is scheduled to join us soon." Dinah looked up from peeling sweet potatoes to a weak smile. "Thanks, Dinah. It's a blessing to both of us. Somethin' I been wanting all my life."

"You're welcome, and you may be sure your secret will always be safe with—"

"Mr. Jonathan!" Both their heads jerked toward the squeals erupting from Emerald. "You comed, I mean, you came, to see me again."

The paring knife Dinah held clanked to the brick floor as she imagined Emerald dancing around Jonathan until he picked her up.

"And who else would I be coming to see, Squirt?"

"Who indeed?" piped the familiar sarcasm of Benjamin Catlett.

Dinah, as mesmerized as she'd been before the kitchen fire

weeks ago, watched as Violette moved toward the door. "Y'all come on in. 'Fraid Mama Tavie's a little under the weather, today. Just me and Dinah in the kitchen."

Holding Emerald, Jonathan entered the kitchen.

"Hello, Dinah." His baritone voice ignited every nerve in her body, turning it into a mixture of fire and ice.

Dinah managed to nod. The way he said her name, all the resentment she'd worked so hard to accumulate these last weeks threatened to go up in a cloud of vapor.

"You're looking well," he said.

"Thank you. You appear quite improved yourself."

In truth, he looked . . . well . . . magnificent.

Awkwardness seemed just about to suffocate everyone except Emerald, until Violette spoke up. "Uh, would y'all be wanting to sit down?" She pointed toward Benjamin who bore a large crate. "That there must be kind of heavy."

Benjamin placed the crate on the worktable while Jonathan shook his head and smiled. He looked at Emerald who still sat on his forearm. "Thanks, but the little squirt here is enjoying the height I think. And I'm certainly enjoying her."

"Yes, I believe I will sit," said Benjamin, placing the crate on the floor and straddling the only chair in the kitchen. "Unless, of course, you ladies would like to."

"No." Both answered at once. "We still have work to do," said Dinah glancing at the crate.

Following Violette's every move, Benjamin rested his chin on the chair's back. "What have you done to yourself, Violette?" He flashed his rakish signature grin. "You look different somehow, lovelier, if I may be so bold."

Seeing Violette's mortification, Dinah stepped in to ease the awkwardness. "What brings you all out here today?"

Benjamin's grin broadened. "Actually, we were summoned. Isn't that right, sir?"

Dinah barely got her voice to cooperate. "Oh? A-another job?"

Jonathan seared Benjamin with a scowl. "Truth is, uh, we . . ."

Emerald wriggled loose from Jonathan's arms. She skipped across the small space and plopped into Benjamin's lap. "Wanna hear me say my al-fuh-bets?"

"Emerald! Where your manners? You get off Mr. Benjamin's lap and beg his pardon. Right now."

Finger in her mouth, the child drew up a bit. "But me and Lucy . . ." She cut a glance toward Dinah. "I mean, Lucy and I want to see what's in that box."

Dinah stifled a giggle. Emerald, who seemed suddenly taken with Benjamin, was having none of Violette's newfound manners, and neither was Benjamin. Rather, he seemed delighted by the child's open interest.

"So you're tired of that stiff gentleman over there too, huh? Can't say I blame you, but don't mind him. He's just old. By the way, that beautiful baby doll I saw out there when I came in, by any chance was that Lucy?"

"Uh-huh. Her name Lucy. Her won't comb her hair."

"Tell you what, then. Why don't we go out and join her for a while, see if we can talk her into a little grooming." Winking at the captivated child, he handed her over to Violette and reclaimed the crate. "Come on. We'll see what Mr. Jonathan put in this crate, too. Maybe your sister would like to join us?" Violette looked to Dinah.

"Go ahead. It's fine."

Arms stretched out, Jonathan feigned hurt feelings. "Have I been replaced here? Doesn't anyone care about poor old me anymore?"

Emerald looked torn as she glanced between the two men. She ran toward Jonathan who stooped to embrace her. She threw her arms around his neck. "I love you, Mr. Jonathan, but you done already heard my al-fuh-bets. And I want to see what's in that box."

Laughter rang out as Jonathan shooed them out of the kitchen. Dinah rinsed her paring knife and commenced to peeling the rest of the potatoes as Jonathan clasped his hands behind him and moved closer.

"I hear you've become quite the cook."

"I've become better, but not great. Making sweet potato pone is not exactly a highly touted culinary art, you know."

"Oh, I don't know about that. I visited a cabin once over in the next county, and the young wife offered supper. I swear the potato pone she served was the color of summertime grass, though not nearly as vibrant and inviting."

Dinah giggled. "Oh, go on with you. No one makes green potato pone. Not even the Dinah of three months ago." She placed her paring knife on the table and wiped her hands on the apron. "Excuse me, but I have to finish this before Mama Tavie comes down. I don't want her worried."

He relaxed his clasped hands and strode in her direction. Without touching her, he grounded her to the spot, his imposing frame scented of spice pinning her against the same worktable from which he'd rescued her back in December. Before she could even think to stop him, he trailed a knuckled hand along her cheek.

"Dinah, I've missed you so."

"Jonathan, please."

Every muscle in his finely-chiseled body seemed to tense with desire for her. "Walk with me?"

Dinah had to end this quickly. Something inside was melting fast—like the spring thaws in the mountains she'd read about. She'd already set her mind to forgetting Jonathan Mayfield, and though her heart cried otherwise, she couldn't let go of the pain of betrayal. He'd purchased her against her will, and she'd never forgive him for that.

"I-I'm sorry. I simply have too much to do. As I said, Mama Tavie . . ."

"I know." He stepped back a few feet. For a moment, the hoarseness in his voice and the pleading in his eyes belied the rigid stance he'd resumed. Then he righted himself, his eyes drained of any residual passion. "It's all for Mama Tavie. Well, then. I suppose I'll be going."

Feeling utterly addlepated, she was suddenly desperate to hold on to him. To drink a bit longer of that majesty he didn't even know he possessed.

"But didn't you want to say hello to her?"

"Thank you. Some other time, perhaps."

And he was out the door. Again. Shortly after, she heard another squeal from Emerald. Evidently Benjamin had waited after all for Jonathan to open the crate.

"Mr. Jonathan, you made my big house!"

Dinah sank her elbows into the worktable. With everything he must have had to do to keep his business afloat after the loss of his papers and with a body that must still be healing, he'd remembered his promise to a little slave girl. Then how could a man of this kind of compassion have purchased Dinah as though she were wood for the little big house?

21

Spring, 1861

The stars over Riverwood melted into the lavender of the early morning sky, leaving Dinah to wonder if there was anything in the world more beautiful than the dawning of a new day. Weary of all the talk of war, the McMillans were on a short holiday in New Orleans, so she felt free to visit the sweeping front verandah with its four imposing Doric sentinels looking out over several layers of stringy fog. How wonderful to catch the encore of the night skies without the threat of Eli or anyone else. Convincing herself she was breathing in the first hint of magnolia blossoms, she hugged herself against the chill.

"Hmmm. Spring is right around the corner. And if Mr. James is right, so is war."

What if, by some miracle of miracles, the south relented and agreed to free their slaves? Not likely, but if so, then she would belong to no one but herself and God. Not even Jonathan could claim her as his own.

"But I want to be his," she whispered. "God help me, I want to belong to Jonathan Mayfield. Only not as his slave."

Try as she may these last few months, she couldn't rid her stubborn heart of the cabinetmaker who'd literally swept her off her feet the first time he met her. Dinah inhaled sharply. Tobacco mixed with the pungency of an unwashed body replaced the hint of spring.

Before her brain could dictate a scream, she was being dragged backwards down the front steps, a strong rancid overly-large hand clamped over her mouth. With every drop of strength she could muster, Dinah twisted her head just enough to discover her captor. Leering at her like a lust-filled beast was the plantation slave driver, Jethro. Something hit her with the force of a falling log. She slumped into darkness.

GAGGED AND SHACKLED, Dinah awakened to the feel of a moving wagon bed. Dawn had become a distant memory, the morning sun already beating down on her like a vengeful furnace. The wheels crunched to a stop.

"Welcome to the world of the real slave. Been waiting on you every morning and every night for three days. Knowed the sky would pull you outside sooner or later."

Dinah babbled her fury through the filthy handkerchief cutting into the corners of her swollen mouth, while Jethro shouted at her as though she were deaf.

"You can count Eli as the last slave you get to send 'cross the river. Get ready for your first day in the field, Miss Lady. Time you quit acting like some kind of house pet and learn what real slaves do." He commenced to remove the leg irons from her ankles. "Been waiting to catch Massa gone again long enough for me to put you in the place where all womens belong. Be a while before he even miss you, and by then, you'll be such a good field hand he'll be glad I brung you out here." Again she witnessed the look of abject lust she'd seen hours ago back at Riverwood. He dragged her out of the wagon and jarred her to her feet. "And you'll be my woman. Real busy, you go'n be. Field all day, mine all night."

She tried to make a run for it. But he was on top of her before she could run the length of the wagon. His knee hard against the small of her back, he pinned her arms to the warming earth.

He whispered close to Dinah's ear, his breath saturated with onions and tobacco. "Don't you ever try to run away from me again. I would'a already took you this morning if I didn't have to see to them others out there in the field. Now, I'm about to take this rag out your mouth. And you go'n behave like the lady you think you is. Or I'm go'n have to beat some manners back into you."

Fury outstripped by fear, Dinah grunted in assent. She flinched in pain as her swollen mouth, where he'd clipped her earlier, was released. She breathed in big helpings of fresh air as he removed the shackles from her wrists. For the first time she noticed how close she was to the fields already dotted with people. More women than men it seemed—their backs, some laden with infants, bent to the endless rows.

So this was it, the destiny she'd tried so hard to avoid. It would've been better to be Jonathan's house slave than this.

Struck by the maddening sameness of the lines of heaped-up earth stretching into forever, Dinah's eyes searched for some break—some redeeming feature of the landscape that got these remarkable people through the day. None. Just sun and soil and Jethro's whip. Instantly, fear was replaced by profound admiration for her fellow slaves. Jethro must have sensed this.

"Somethin', ain't it? I saved one of them *pretty* rows just for you, to get you broke in, you know." He laughed at his own joke as he dropped his whip to the ground and tied an apron of seeds around her waist. His gargantuan hands lingered past necessity. "Wouldn't want to work a beauty like you on an ugly row on your first day."

Determined she'd not be baited, Dinah choked down every

nasty retort fighting to explode in his face as he pushed her toward the expanse of workers.

"My sincere thanks," she muttered as a shrill whistle ripped past her ear. A boy no more than ten appeared seemingly from nowhere. He looked up at the slave driver, his face shining with terror and twisted admiration.

"Yes suh, Papa?"

Jethro picked up his whip. "Take her to the row and show her what to do."

"Yes suh, Papa. I'm go'n do a good job today," said the boy striking out in the direction of the field workers.

With the aggressive morning sun of a Mississippi spring at her back, Dinah made her first steps toward the cotton fields. Nobody even turned to notice. Her wrists and legs were already sore from the irons, but she assumed her full stature, set forth her determined chin, and walked into her past.

JONATHAN WAS OVERWHELMED with the need to pray, but he didn't know why. Scripture came to soothe and help him. *"Likewise the Spirit also helpeth our infirmities: for we know not what we should pray for as we ought: but the Spirit itself maketh intercession for us with groanings which cannot be uttered."*

Working alongside Benjamin, Jonathan prayed silently. "Father God, you know what's wrong. Please make it right. Please help me understand this troubling of my spirit." Jonathan's words to Dinah on their first day together revisited him like an unwanted guest. *By chance, did you happen to come from one of the houses under the Hill?* Why had he said that stupid thing? It didn't matter. He'd been already on his way to loving her, and deep down he'd known it.

Then came Dinah's own words from that night in his dependency room when she'd brought his supper. "But then, Mr.

Mayfield, perhaps I'm simply not fit for that other institution called marriage." He laid down his gouger and turned to his friend. "Benjamin?"

"Yeah?"

"I've—uh—I've a question for you."

"Yeah, what is it?"

"You spent time with Dinah when I was laid up."

"Yes?"

"Well, I was wondering if she ever said anything about . . . well . . . being a lady of the night."

Benjamin laid down his own tool and shook his head in dismay. "You don't give up, do you? It's that ownership thing isn't it? You're still trying to find a reason for not telling her the truth about why you purchased her. It's just simple ugly, joy-killing pride, you know. She hurt you by jumping to conclusions, and you won't forgive her.

"Well, the answer is no. She's never been a prostitute. She just thinks it's in her blood because her mother was forced to be one and ended up putting her hours-old infant, Dinah, on the street because of it." Benjamin's angry stare flattened Jonathan. "Satisfied?"

"No. Just terribly, terribly sorry."

"THIS IS what my mother endured, and if she did it, I can do it too."

Lifting up her skirt, Dinah stepped into the soft earth onto the row Jethro had assigned, already furrowed and ready to receive the seeds weighing down the pocket of her apron. Though back at Riverwood breakfast had barely been served, clearly the slaves out here had been laboring for a while. For all of them were far ahead of her, some headed back in her direction, and they seemed to work in twos, the leader deftly burrowing a hole as the followers, mostly children, dropped in the precious seed.

Jethro's little boy scooped out seed holes in front of Dinah with great speed. She noticed him making eye contact with a small furtive woman passing in the other direction. One eye shut tight from what looked like a recent blow, the woman tried to smile at the boy.

Dinah could barely make out the child's words over the plaintive humming that suffused the air.

"How I'm doing, Mama?"

"Doing fine, son. Just fine."

Only then did the boy seem to spot the bruised eye. "How *you* doing, Mama? Papa did that?"

"Doing fine, son. Mama's doing fine."

A wave of nausea tried to level Dinah with the rows. Instantly, she knew what was going on in the slave driver's cabin. She whispered into the turgid air, her own swollen lips barely moving. "Lord, must your people endure this beastly yoke from the Jethros of the world, too?"

One of her favorite psalms answered. *"Many are the afflictions of the righteous, but the Lord delivereth him out of them all."*

Wanting to throw her hands in the air in frustration, Dinah continued to drop the seeds instead. "But Lord, I've never felt less righteous in my life. Bitterness tries to overwhelm me—not just for myself but for every soul that walks these rows across this country and abroad."

"It's not how you feel, dear one. It's your faith. My son, Abraham believed on Me, and I credited it to him for righteousness."

Again the peace of God righted her. Feeling herself slipping into a painful and tedious yet distinct rhythm, she smiled as that word from a while back, spoken to her by her Savior, laid balm in the crevices of her raw spirit.

"Soon."

MAMA TAVIE BLEW into Jonathan's shop with the force of the Great Natchez Tornado of 1840, Mr. James close at her heels. The last time he'd seen that wild look in her eyes was when she'd lost little Samuel to the yellow jack.

"Saddle up, Joe-Nathan. You got to go to the plantation."

Jonathan looked at his watch. The sun would be setting soon. Praying and seeking as he'd done all day, he'd let time get away from. "What plantation and what for? Mama Tavie, it's nearly dark."

James stepped in front of her, looking even more desperate than Mama Tavie if that was possible. "One of the McMillan fields. You have to go, sir. It's Dinah, she's been missing all day, and a vendor just left from Riverwood after telling us he saw Jethro hauling her away early this morning shackled. I'd go myself, but I've taken enough of a risk leaving Riverwood as I have without a pass. And I don't want to chance writing another one this soon."

Jonathan barely heard the rest of what Mr. James said as he yanked his apron from around his neck. "I'll get my horse."

"Hurry, Joe-Nathan. I don't know how much more she'll be able to stand up under. She already think she ain't fitting for no man 'cause some lowdown rascal named Jack somethin'-or-'nother tried to have his way with her when she was just a girl. If that lowdown Jethro—"

"Wait." Jonathan froze. Still digesting what he'd heard from Benjamin, his body clutched with rage over what he might be about to hear. "Tried?"

Mama Tavie touched his arm. "Now, I know what you thinking, Joe-Nathan, but I meant just what I said. 'Tried.'"

Jack, that "friend of Master's" she'd spoken about. Scoundrel! What if he'd succeeded in hurting her? Not that it would've lessened Jonathan's love for her. He'd loved her gracefulness before he'd seen her face. No matter who'd tried to soil her, from the moment he laid eyes on Dinah Devereaux, she was as fresh as a bowl of wildflowers. And to him she would continue to be until he closed his eyes in death.

Mama Tavie wrapped him in a fierce hug. "Go on, get outta here."

He tore through the sawdust toward the stable behind his shop.

"I'll go with you," said Benjamin.

"No. It's mine to do. You were right. She'd never be in this horrible mess if it wasn't for me."

SUNLIGHT HAD DESERTED JONATHAN, leaving only the menacing specter-like trees topping the embankments alongside the sunken road he knew so well. Not only did this road lead past one of the McMillan plantations, it ended at the old Mayfield Plantation. "Spirits from the graveyard behind them trees," Mama Tavie used to say as they clutched their passes and hurried to beat sundown. "Can't you feel them warm spots along the road?"

Fond of the mare he'd owned for several years, he urged her as humanely as possible. Still, he had a ways to go. And Dinah was fighting for her life. Somehow he knew that.

"If it wasn't for me and my pride."

Though his pulse raced, he was forced to slow his horse down a bit. He'd forgotten to bring a lantern, and he didn't want the dangerous dips and holes in the road to injure his mount. Ever faithful, God opened up the heavens with moonlight, giving him a clearer path to the plantation ahead of him. He gave the mare free course as he galloped toward the silver ribbon of road ahead that led to the massive tract of farmland. Dinah was somewhere on these grounds waiting for him. Expecting him.

FULL DARK HAD SETTLED over the fields. She hurt everywhere. From the band of pain that had gradually tightened around her forehead all afternoon to the blisters forming on her feet. But that was all right. Like she imagined her mama had done many times before her, she'd made it through the day, and if God willed, she would make it through another.

"Soon," she mumbled to herself. Faith in God and herself bloomed all around the pain inside. Not knowing where she was headed, she stumbled away from the field behind the rest of the mute slaves. In the moonlight, she saw the little crumbling woman and her son standing together next to a barn. Jethro's voice pierced the quiet. It was the first time she'd heard it since this morning, and she shuddered.

"Go to the house!"

Quickly, mother and son turned and headed in the opposite direction as Jethro snatched up one of Dinah's sore wrists into his meaty hand. "You coming with me."

Knowing arguing would be futile, she looked straight ahead and stormed the gates of heaven.

Lord, have mercy on me.

JONATHAN RODE his mare down to the cabins. Cold-sweating at the thought of where Dinah was and what was being done to her, he beat on yet another badly constructed ramshackle door. "Have you seen a new slave today, tall dark-skinned? Beautiful girl—name's Dinah Devereaux."

"Naw suh."

"Lovely almond eyes? Thick braids?"

"Uh uhm."

Worn-out slaves in cabin after cabin shook their heads and slammed their creaky doors, fear of Jethro palpable in their blank stare. "Naw. Ain't heard tell o' nobody with no fancy name like that."

Just a couple more cabins left. Then what? Go to the big house and end up in the fields himself? Yes, he would if he had to. Finally, the last cabin, set a little apart.

"Ma'am? Have you seen—"

"She in the barn." Jethro's wife who looked like a tropical breeze would blow her away stared Jonathan in the face. How could she know what he was about to say?

"But—"

"Hurry, or it won't be nothin' left of her to look for."

"Thank you. Thank you, ma'am. One day I'll repay you for this." Jonathan was in the saddle moving before the mare knew she'd been mounted.

PINNED down in a corner full of musty hay, Dinah willed herself to think of happier times. What would Mama Tavie and Emerald and even Violette be doing right now? And Mr. James, would he have finished serving supper yet? And Jonathan. Dear and wonderful Jonathan. She sensed his nearness, though whether in spirit or naturally she couldn't say.

Soothing words from her father's earlier exhortation came to her. "Nobody can enslave my spirit but me." She knew her newfound family was praying for her—felt it viscerally—and somehow she knew Jonathan was thinking of her this very moment.

Blessed Savior, don't let them worry too much.

"JON-A-THANNNN, NO-OOOOO!"

Dinah's voice echoed through Jonathan's head as he pounded the man. She was trying to get him to stop. But why? What would Dinah know or care about what happened to Ethan

Mayfield? Or the Irishmen on the ship? Or the Franklin and Armfield thugs? Or Eli?

Or Jethro.

Oh, God. It was Jethro. He was beating a man to death. Jethro. Other voices lifted around him, cheering him on. He pulled back and stood to his feet.

No. Jonathan was not a killer. But he was a man, a man who'd almost allowed fear and bitterness to destroy him. He picked up his hat, and turning to find her, he opened his arms, and with no hesitation, Dinah Devereaux flew into them.

JUST AS DINAH HAD IMAGINED, he rode tall in the saddle. After what she'd been through today, she'd relished the time leaning back into Jonathan's chest beneath the moonlight, his chin resting on her head as they traveled the sunken road back to town. After helping her down from the horse, he carried her along the side of his house toward the shop.

"Where are we going?"

"You'll see soon enough."

He cuddled her close as she wrapped her arms tighter around his neck. Balancing her on his knee, he opened the door to the smells of sawdust and manual labor. He eased her to the floor long enough to light several lanterns.

Then she saw it. The portable gazebo, there in the back of the shop, glowing just as it had months earlier.

"What on earth—"

"I'm afraid I have Benjamin to thank for carrying out this request." He reached for her hand. "Come."

As she'd done on Christmas Eve, Dinah knelt to the chest now covered with sawdust. Savoring the ornaments again, she finally reached the star-shaped wooden box with the parchments. She looked up at him wondering why he insisted on showing her what she already knew.

"I don't understand you, Jonathan. By now you should know, much as I'm grateful, I'll never be your willing slave."

"Please, Dinah. Read the parchments, this time all the way through."

Dinah scanned the first paragraph that had so upset her months ago. Then—*In accordance with said agreement, upon receipt of this document, she is immediately and irrevocably free, not to be considered property of the buyer, no longer enslaved but free under the Constitution of the United States of America to order her life as the Almighty God directs.*

Signed, this twenty-fourth day of December of the year eighteen hundred and sixty.

Jonathan Mayfield
Natchez, Mississippi

The air thinned as Dinah dropped the paper back into the smaller box and pressed her palm against her bosom.

Free? Had the paper said free?

Hands trembling, heart out of rhythm, she reached again for the thing that had driven her desire for so long. *Freedom.* The very word itself wrapped her heart in hope, putting on the run the threat of worthlessness that had growled at her since the day she was born. And in its place the sweet possibilities of love and learning, children and family set her soul to dancing. Oh she knew the wonderful gift from Jonathan could very well turn out to be moot since the men who ruled the very ground she knelt on had months ago seceded from a country whose very cornerstone was freedom. But this rare love of Jonathan's and the boundless love of God had moved her to a place that no misguided and misaligned declaration could ever destroy. Dinah Devereaux was—how had Jonathan's document worded it?— immediately and irrevocably free.

Father God, thank you.

Not quite ready to face this marvelous man who had so

unselfishly set her on the road to true liberty, Dinah continued to kneel before the beautifully crafted chest. Tears stained the paper as she quietly sobbed.

"Oh, Jonathan, how can you bear to even look at me? I've been so awful to you. Can you ever forgive me?"

"There's another document you haven't looked at, dear lady." He knelt next to her and smiled. "And if you don't stop crying, you're going to destroy your freedom with your own tears."

Sniffs and chuckles permeated the air as she slid the second sheet from beneath the freedom paper. The words of a marriage proposal swam beneath the soft lantern light.

"Oh, Jonathan, do you really mean it? Y-you'd actually marry somebody like me?"

He helped her from the floor and led her to a swing near the Christmas tree then sat down beside her.

"Dinah, your beauty would rock the most stubborn of hearts, but your loving spirit has become like the air I breathe. I've been the worst kind of fool, trying to preserve myself from the pain of ever losing you when my heart became a part of yours from the first day I saw you."

"But—"

"Shh." He placed his fingertips to her lips. "Let me explain. I need to explain why I've been such a boor."

Dinah thought her own heart would burst from love for this man. Here she'd thought he was a big conceited oaf when all along inside he'd still been a frightened little boy who'd been forced to painfully look on while his last parent, his protector, gave up on life because he couldn't bear to live without the love of his wife.

He reached for her hand. Warmth flooded her as he repeated, to a word, the written proposal she'd just read.

"With all the love I have, I offer you my heart, and with all the heart I have, I offer you my love. Dinah Devereaux, will you make me the happiest man alive by consenting to be my wife?"

He stood and helped her from the swing. Dinah answered

him on her tip-toes as he covered her mouth with his, and together they tasted the wine of freedom. The freedom God always meant for them to have.

ABOUT THE AUTHOR

Jacqueline is a multi-published author whose works range from short stories to a memoir of growing up during and after integration. Wheelock has been a member of several writers and critique groups and is currently a member of the American Christian Fiction Writers, an organization which has afforded her valuable instruction and opportunity toward publication.

An avid reader and former high school and college English teacher, her first novel, *A Most Precious Gift*, debuted in 2014 via Mantle Rock Publishers. The sequel, *In Pursuit of an Emerald*, was published in August of 2017. Jacqueline and her husband Donald reside in Madison, Mississippi and have two adult children and one beloved granddaughter.

ALSO BY JACQUELINE FREEMAN WHEELOCK

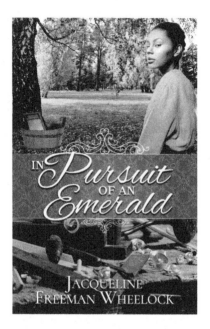

In Pursuit of an Emerald

All ex-slave Violette McMillan ever wanted is to see her troubled daughter Emerald grow up to be a better person than she has been, so when Benjamin Catlett, an old acquaintance, asks her to become his bookkeeper in 1869, in a business that is sinking due to southern backlash during the Reconstruction era, she agrees. But when his arrogance surfaces, their goals collide, and Violette wonders if she might be forced to renege at the expense of her daughter's future education.

Benjamin Catlett is plagued by his past as a free man of color whose African American father was a slaveholder. Renouncing his father's way of life, he moves to Natchez hoping to quietly atone. But his new hire, Violette McMillan, and her flirtatious teenage daughter, Emerald, test the limits of his good intentions one time too many, offending his straight-laced upbringing and tempting him to fire her.

Will the Lord who tugs at the heart of both Benjamin and Violette prevail in their efforts to tolerate each other and finally affirm the love already blossoming in their hearts?

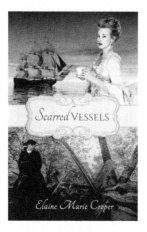

Scarred Vessels

by Elaine Marie Cooper

In a time when America battles for freedom, a man and
woman seek to fight the injustice of slavery while
discovering love in the midst of tragedy.

In 1778 Rhode Island, the American Revolution rallies the Patriots to
fight for freedom. But the slavery of black men and women from
Africa, bartered for rum, is a travesty that many in America cannot
ignore. The seeds of abolition are planted even as the laws allowing
slavery in the north still exist.

Lydia Saunders, the daughter of a slave ship owner, grew up with the
horror of slavery. It became more of a nightmare when, at a young age,
she is confronted with the truth about her father's occupation.
Burdened with the guilt of her family's sin, she struggles to make a
difference in whatever way she can. When she loses her husband in the
battle for freedom from England, she makes a difficult decision that
will change her life forever.

Sergeant Micah Hughes is too dedicated to serving the fledgling country of America to consider falling in love. When he carries the tragic news to Lydia Saunders about her husband's death, he is appalled by his attraction to the young widow. Micah wrestles with his feelings for Lydia while he tries to focus on helping the cause of freedom. He trains a group of former slaves to become capable soldiers on the battlefield.

Tensions both on the battlefield and on the home front bring hardship and turmoil that threaten to endanger them all. When Lydia and Micah are faced with saving the life of a black infant in danger, can they survive this turning point in their lives?

A groundbreaking book, honest and inspiring, showcasing black soldiers in the American Revolution. *Scarred Vessels* is peopled with flesh and blood characters and true events that not only inspire and entertain but educate. Well done!

- Laura Frantz, Christy Award-winning author

of *An Uncommon Woman*

Under This Same Sky
by Cynthia Roemer

She thought she'd lost everything –

Instead she found what she needed most.

Illinois prairie – 1854

When a deadly tornado destroys Becky Hollister's farm, she must leave the only home she's ever known, and the man she's begun to love to accompany her injured father to St. Louis. Catapulted into a world of unknowns, Becky finds solace in corresponding with the handsome pastor back home. But when word comes that he is all but engaged to someone else, she must call upon her faith to decipher her future.

Matthew Brody didn't intend on falling for Becky, but the unexpected relationship, along with the Lord's gentle nudging, incite him to give up his circuit riding and seek full-time ministry in the town of Miller Creek, with the hope of one day making Becky his bride. But when his old sweetheart comes to town, intent on winning him back—with the entire town pulling for her—Matthew must choose between doing what's expected and what his heart tells him is right.

Scrivenings
PRESS
Quench your thirst for story.
www.ScriveningsPress.com

Stay up-to-date on your favorite books and authors with our free e-newsletters.

ScriveningsPress.com

Made in the USA
Las Vegas, NV
10 May 2023

71850241R00168